HEART
QUEST.

More to Love

PRAISE FOR
CATHERINE PALMER'S BOOKS

"Each of the *Treasures of the Heart* books is a delightful read. The
adventure, and romance kept me intrigued to the end. I will defi
recommend this series to my friends."

· FRANCINE RIVERS ·
BEST-SELLING AUTHOR

A Dangerous Silence
"Palmer's contemporary thriller reads plausibly and sweeps readers i
story, pairing deep emotions with numerous suspenseful scenes
Palmer certainly doesn't preach, yet spiritual truths come part and p
with the story. Balancing her characters' flood of negative emotions w
spiritual reawakening is difficult, but Palmer succeeds admirably. .

Riveting."
· PUBLISHERS WEEKLY ·

A Kiss of Adventure
"This entertaining book is hard to put down."

· CBA MARKETPLACE ·

"Elements of *The African Queen* and *Romancing the Stone* blend
in this action-filled romance. Light, romantic fun."

· LIBRARY JOURNAL ·

Prairie Rose
"In Rosie, Palmer has created an entertaining and humorous character

Highly recommended."
· LIBRARY JOURNAL ·

HeartQuest brings you romantic fiction
with a foundation of biblical truth.
Adventure, mystery, intrigue, and suspense
mingle in these heartwarming stories of
men and women of faith striving to build
a love that will last a lifetime.

May HeartQuest books sweep you
into the arms of God, who longs for you
and pursues you always.

COWBOY
Christmas

CATHERINE PALMER
LISA HARRIS
LINDA GOODNIGHT

HEART QUEST.

Romance fiction from
Tyndale House Publishers, Inc., Wheaton, Illinois

TABLE OF CONTENTS

A Rancher's Heart by Catherine Palmer 1

Undercover Cowboy by Lisa Harris 115

The Outlaw's Gift by Linda Goodnight 223

A Rancher's Heart

CATHERINE PALMER

And he said unto him, "Son, thou art ever with

me, and all that I have is thine.

It was meet that we should make merry,

and be glad:

for this thy brother was dead, and is alive again;

and was lost, and is found."

LUKE 15:31-32

Santa Fe, New Mexico Territory
November 1885

*V*ictoria Jennings fell to her knees behind the iron potbellied stove and tore open the envelope. With trembling fingers, she spread the letter across her lap and read the words inscribed in a neat black hand:

> *Dear Miss Jennings,*
>
> *I take great pleasure in informing you that on this day, October 24, 1885, the Lazy J ranch of Lincoln County, New Mexico Territory, has been sold to the Mesquite Land & Cattle Company of London, England. This transaction discharges all debts incurred by your father, Emil Karl Jennings, during his lifetime. Enclosed, please find the record of liens against Mr. Jennings's estate and the satisfaction thereof. Also, I enclose the balance of his estate, due to you, his daughter and only heir: a cheque for the sum of two dollars.*
>
> *Sincerely yours,*

"Miss Jennings, where have ye got to now?" The shrill voice jangled Victoria's nerves as she leapt to her feet.

"Here, Mrs. O'Neal!"

"Aha!" The red-cheeked Irishwoman set her hands on her

ample hips and glared at her employee. "Hidin' behind the stove, are ye?"

"Please, ma'am, I'll be sweeping ashes just now." As Victoria drew a horsehair brush from behind her back, the letter and its envelope tumbled to the scrubbed wooden floor of the meat market. "Oh, I—"

"Just as I thought. Worthless girl!" Mrs. O'Neal bent and swiped up the letter. She scanned it; then she opened the envelope and took out a check imprinted with the address of the First National Bank of Santa Fe and signed by George T. Beall, attorney for the estate of Emil Jennings.

"Aha, two dollars!" the woman crowed, waving the check. "Well, I'll just be takin' this in exchange for the rent ye owe me. Sign it on the back now before I change my mind and give ye the sack for yer laziness."

"But those funds are all that is left from my father's ranch. And all I have." Victoria blinked back tears as her employer dipped a pen into the inkwell that sat near the ledger on the meat counter. "Please, Mrs. O'Neal, you told me room and board came with the job. I beg you—"

"Beggars can't be choosers now, can they?" She put the pen in Victoria's hand and gave the younger woman a push. "Sign yer name."

Victoria pressed the pen to the back of the check and wrote her signature with the elegant loops and flourishes of the Spencerian script she had practiced under the supervision of Mr. William Graves. She could almost hear her tutor now, praising the perfect slant of the V and the neat triple swirl with which she ended the S.

As she set the pen back in its stand, Victoria brushed away the tears that clung to her eyelashes. "My father would have wanted me to have the money," she said softly as she handed over the check. "I cannot believe he intended me to live in such a condition."

"Yer father was a gambler, and ye be the wastrel he left behind him." Mrs. O'Neal folded the slip of paper and tucked it into her skirt pocket. "And to atone for yer idle ways, ye can just sweep up those ashes and slop the pigs, too. And when yer finished, see that ye pluck those chickens in the back room. The Baptists, God love 'em, are havin' a dinner at the church this Sunday, and we've twenty-three chickens to prepare."

As Mrs. O'Neal waddled away to tend to a customer, her husband emerged from behind the carcass of a sheep that hung from a hook in a ceiling beam. He waggled his eyebrows in sympathy. "Too bad about the check," he said as Victoria swept up the ashes. "Ye'll be needin' a coat soon, Miss Jennings. Santa Fe can be cold in the winter."

Victoria reflected on the coats that once had graced her armoire. Velvet, fur, and wool in brilliant greens and luscious reds, her winter wardrobe now hung in the homes of Santa Fe's wealthy—the donas whose husbands' families had held Spanish land grants there for a century, the wives of bankers and railroad barons, and the debutantes who would wear their former schoolmate's bright coats as they hurried through the snow to their social engagements.

"I'll be all right, Mr. O'Neal," she murmured, setting aside any wistfulness for the past. She picked up the two slop buckets and stepped toward the back door. "I thank you for your concern, sir."

"Let me help ye with those," he offered, reaching out. "People are so wasteful at the restaurant next door. 'Tis a wonder to me that Jack doesn't reduce his portions."

"Please, Mr. O'Neal. I can carry them myself."

Without waiting for his response, she hurried out the door

and down the rickety steps. The last thing she needed was help from the kindly butcher. Loaded with scrapings from diners' plates, the leavings were intended for the pigs that Mr. O'Neal one day would turn into bacon and pork chops. But Victoria lifted a prayer of gratitude as she eyed the crusts of soggy bread and chunks of meat rimmed with fat.

Setting the buckets on the frozen ground near the sty's fence, she knelt and reached into one with a bare hand. Barely able to contain herself, she shoved a palmful of mashed potatoes into her mouth. How good the food felt as it slid into her empty stomach! Next she tore the skin from a chicken leg, swallowed it, and then broke open the bone to suck out the tender marrow.

By now the pigs had spotted her, and they ran squealing toward the fence, their ears bouncing and their tails stuck straight up into the air. "Wait your turn!" she growled at them as she stuffed the crusty skin of a baked potato into her mouth.

Her stomach filled at last, Victoria staggered to her feet and heaved the rest of the pail's contents over the fence and into the trough. As the swine fell on the leavings, she sorted through the second bucket, finding five more chicken bones and a chunk of bread. After hiding them in her apron pocket for later, she upended the pail.

She was no better off than those pigs, Victoria realized as she wiped the hem of her apron across her wet chin. Worse, in fact. They could always count on their slop, for Mr. O'Neal paid the restaurant owner to deliver it every day. But some evenings Victoria had to watch as the butcher himself carried the pails to the sty, and she went hungry. The pigs had shelter from the wind and storms, they had food to eat, and they had companionship.

Victoria gazed out across the smoking chimneys on the

flat-roofed adobes that made up the town of Santa Fe and fixed her eyes on the purple mountains that rose above it— the Jemez range to the west and the Sangre de Cristos to the east. She had nothing. No home. No family. Not even the two dollars her father had left her at his death.

One of the many Scriptures that Mr. Graves had bade Victoria memorize came to her now. As she surveyed the glowing golden sunset and vivid pink clouds, she whispered the words of King David from the second book of Samuel. "'The beauty of Israel is slain upon the high places: how are the mighty fallen!'"

Fallen, indeed. At this time last year, Victoria Jennings was the belle of Santa Fe high society's holiday balls—as she had been during the previous three years of her education at Mrs. Redfern's school. With such ardor the gentlemen had courted her, the daughter of a wealthy rancher from Lincoln town! And oh, she had looked lovely in her gowns of pink silk, purple velvet, red brocade. Such a beauty, everyone murmured, with her golden hair piled on her head in braids and ringlets, looped with silk ribbons and pearls. The jewels that dripped from her earlobes and neck might have belonged to a princess. And Victoria, in all her glory, easily could have borne such a title.

News of Emil Jennings's death had stunned his daughter. She had admired her father, but she saw so little of him during her childhood that even now the man was a mystery to her. Not long after the funeral, George Beall, Esq., a lawyer from Lincoln, came to call on her.

Remembering the moment with humiliating clarity, Victoria picked up the buckets and started back to the shop. Mr. Beall had brought bad news, he told her as they sat in the parlor of Mrs. Redfern's Finishing School. It seemed Victoria's father had been quite a gambler, and he had fallen deeply into debt. His eight hundred head of cattle, the vast acreage of his ranch, and his rambling stone house had all been mortgaged to the bank in Santa Fe.

No further fees could be sent to Mrs. Redfern's school, Mr. Beall had informed Victoria. The Lazy J and all its cattle must go on the auction block in order to satisfy the liens against it. If any money remained, she would receive it in the form of a check. With no living relatives—for her mother had died in childbirth—Victoria was left completely alone.

By the following morning, Mrs. Redfern had instructed Victoria to pack her trunks. Although sympathetic to the girl's plight, Mrs. Redfern asserted that she certainly could not continue housing a student unable to pay the fees. Devastated, Victoria took a room at Herlow's, a second-class hotel on San Francisco Street, and began to peddle her possessions.

Hope mingled with sorrow at the prospect of the sale of the Lazy J. The ranch was all Victoria had ever known until her father sent her to school in Santa Fe. She had expected to return there, marry a wealthy area cattleman or miner, and live at the Lazy J for the rest of her life.

As spring had turned to summer, Victoria waited on the edge of despair. Her wardrobe and jewelry gradually vanished, and she was forced to find employment. Fall arrived with its crisp air smelling of piñon smoke, but still no word from Mr. Beall. Finally, today, the letter had come, dashing her hopes.

Now, Victoria set the two empty buckets inside the door of the meat market and walked to the back room to begin plucking the chickens. The hours wore on, and at last, the O'Neals locked up the shop, leaving Victoria to sweep and mop, shake flies out of the gauze fabric that covered the windows, polish glass counters, scour meat boards, and wash and sharpen knives. Each time she considered doing anything less than her best work, she recalled Mrs. O'Neal's favorite refrain: *"I'll sack ye, Miss Victoria Jennings, and I'll send ye out to sell yerself to the railway men like the other soiled doves in this miserable town."*

As Victoria lifted the trapdoor to the root cellar, the very thought of such a future sent shudders down her spine. Though she feared the dark, cold hole in the dirt beneath the meat market, she had learned that if Mrs. O'Neal discovered her sleeping anywhere else, a harsh beating followed. She shivered as she crept onto her pile of moth-eaten blankets, dug the leftover food from her apron pocket, and ate it. Then she took out the letter Mr. Beall had sent from Lincoln.

Though she could see nothing in the darkness that surrounded her, Victoria ran her palm over the page. The Mesquite Land & Cattle Company now owned the Lazy J. She had never heard of the outfit, but she knew that several British-owned ranches dotted Lincoln County. The Carrizozo Land and Cattle Co., the El Capitan Land and Cattle Co., and the Angus V. V. Ranch, all of which abutted the Lazy J, were among them.

How Victoria had loved riding her horse across the miles of endless gray-green grassland dotted with dark mesquite brush, waving to the cowboys working their herds, and at day's end, brushing the dust from her chaps as she walked into the big ranch house. What had become of the Baca family? she wondered, as she had so many times since learning of her father's death. Though she had written them several letters, she had received no response.

Rosa Baca, who had nursed the pale newborn along with her own baby daughter, had been the only mother Victoria ever knew. Rosa's husband, Abe, had managed the ranch employees, and he kept things running smoothly each time Emil Jennings was away. Victoria grew up with the seven little Bacas and had not even been aware of her true heritage until she was almost five years old.

Where were they now, Rosa and Abe? Did they still live in the tidy adobe home a short walk from the big ranch house? What had become of the children? And did they ever think of her?

As had become her custom, Victoria bent over with her forehead to the dirt floor and began to pray. Throughout the twenty-one years of her life, she had gone to church every Sunday morning, read the Bible beside the fire each night, and memorized Scripture at her tutor's bidding. She had considered herself the model of a fine young Christian lady, and she had been prone to congratulate herself—sometimes aloud—on her own purity, virtue, and sinlessness.

At the memory of her pride, Victoria covered her head with her hands in remorse. Her life had been so empty of anything that mattered! For far too many years, all she had cared about was fashion. And boys. And balls. She recalled too well the young men she had flirted with and then cast off. Most painful of all was the memory of Jesse Conroy, the handsome young cowboy, so smart and bold and so deeply in love with her. He had pursued her relentlessly, even though he had nothing but himself to offer. That should have been enough.

And Victoria had loved Jesse Conroy with all the pent-up passion a seventeen-year-old could possess. Everything about him was special and beloved. Almost . . . almost . . . she had given him her hand.

Then Emil Jennings stepped in. He assured his daughter she was meant for a better man—and by that he meant richer. Flattered by her father's unexpected attentions, Victoria denied her love for Jesse and promised herself to William Worthing, a gold-mine owner from White Oaks. But at the opportunity to go to Santa Fe—to attend Mrs. Redfern's Finishing School, to feed her insatiable hunger for prettier clothes and finer hats, and to flirt with young men who might have even more money than William Worthing—Victoria had callously shed him, too.

Never once during all those years had she thought herself precariously balanced on the edge of a precipice. No indeed, for her father was wealthy, and he owned the Lazy J, which one day would belong to her. And everything would continue on as it always had.

How vain! How futile! But she could not blame her father for her misery, for she understood too well that the flaws in her character were of her own making. *Oh, God, You have brought me to these depths to show me my sin,* she wept. *And I see it. I see my insufferable greed. I see my petty selfishness. I see my vanity. Dear Jesus, how well I recall the hours I spent in gossip! Idleness filled my hours. Now You have shown me my sin, and I repent. Oh, God, I beg You to forgive me!*

Still weeping, she rocked back and forth in the frigid darkness of the tiny cellar. What was to become of her? She was good for nothing but embroidering fire screens and painting still lifes. And slopping pigs. She could do that. She could sweep and mop, too. And polish glass, build a fire, scrub cutlery, empty ashes, pluck chickens . . .

A light flickered on inside Victoria's heart. A small, wavering flame so tiny she almost extinguished it the moment it appeared.

No, she thought. Impossible. Surely not.

But the light grew, and she recognized it as hope. The kindling began to crackle, and then it burst into flame. Surely the new owner of the Mesquite Land & Cattle Company needed servants. Someone had to clean the ranch house, and who would know its nooks and crannies better than Victoria Jennings? She knew exactly where the silverware was kept and how many candelabras were stored in the big cupboard at the end of the hall. She knew how to plan elegant dinners, and where to plant beans in the kitchen garden, and how to make the fire in the parlor smell of mesquite, piñon, and juniper.

Can I go home, dear God? She clenched her fists tight and squeezed back the tears that threatened. It was too much to hope! She had lost everything—and deserved it. Was it possible that God might give her back a gift she had never once thanked Him for?

Unable to sleep, Victoria lay awake most of the night, praying and planning. When Mrs. O'Neal thumped the broom handle on the trapdoor at dawn, she nearly flew up the rickety ladder into the butchery.

"Ye did a fine job with the chickens, Miss Jennings," Mr. O'Neal murmured as he passed by her on his way to gather his knives. "I believe even the missus must be pleased."

"Thank you, sir." Victoria drew in a deep breath. "Mr. O'Neal, I was wondering if I might have a word with you—"

"The coffee's hot, husband!" Mrs. O'Neal bellowed from the front room. "Customers will be startin' to come in soon. Don't dawdle all day."

At the sound, Mr. O'Neal moved to obey, but Victoria spoke up quickly. "Sir, I should like to be paid my wages now."

The butcher glanced through the doorway into the store. "Have ye not been paid, miss? Not once in the two months?"

"No, sir, and I'm . . ." She squared her shoulders. "Mr.

O'Neal, I have decided to go home. I need to buy a place on the mail coach."

Without a flicker of surprise, he beckoned her to follow him behind the carcass of a large steer that hung from the ceiling. Holding one finger over his lips, he reached into his pocket and drew out a leather wallet.

"She don't know about this," he whispered. He peeled off six dollars, folded them in half, and tucked them into Victoria's apron pocket. "I take a little from the till now and again to keep me in whiskey."

"Coffee's gone!" Mrs. O'Neal sang out from the other room. "Bad luck for ye, husband."

"Nay," he called back. "For I'll send Miss Jennings next door to the restaurant to fetch me a cup."

"I should think not! She'll be steppin' in here and layin' out the meat in the counter, so she will."

"Ye think that, Mrs. O'Neal, do ye?" the man said, giving Victoria a wink and a nudge toward the back door. "Speak to Bill Sims at the drovers store down the street. Tell him I sent ye. He'll get ye a place on a jerky. 'Twill be twice as fast as a goods wagon and more comfortable than the mail coach. Off ye go, then."

Hardly able to believe it, Victoria gave him a quick hug. "Thank you, Mr. O'Neal. God bless you!"

"I could use a dose of His blessin', so I could," he said, rolling his eyes in the direction of the front room.

As Victoria hurried out the back door of the butchery, she heard him calling out. "I've sent Miss Jennings off now, Mrs. O'Neal. And next time ye drink up all the coffee before I have my first cup, I'll be givin' ye what fer!"

CHAPTER
One

"This cannot be!" Rosa Baca clapped her hands to her cheeks and stared at Victoria. "No! I cannot believe it."

"Surely this is not her." Her husband, Abe, shook his head as his dark bushy eyebrows narrowed. "Not *our* Vic."

"Such a bad beginning!" Victoria cried. "Yes, I have come home. It is I, Victoria Jennings, and I am here at the Lazy J."

Rosa and Abe gawked at her in silence.

"Have I changed so much?" Victoria asked, her heart aching. She had jolted from Santa Fe to Fort Stanton on the aptly named jerky, a red-bodied wagon with a springless undercarriage. A goods wagon had taken her down the Rio Bonito Valley, along a trail lined with giant cottonwood trees. Arriving in Lincoln at last, she had used her last twenty cents to hire old Mr. Clenny to take her out to the ranch. On foot, she had marched past the stately house that once had been her home and had made her way to the adobe residence of the Baca family. And now this.

"But . . . but the hair." Rosa held out her arms, her hands cupping an imaginary froth around Victoria's head. "No curls. No ribbons. No feathers. And this gown . . . these rags . . ."

Victoria bit her lip. "I was left with nothing when Father died, *Mamá* Rosa. Mrs. Redfern dismissed me from the school, and I lived at a hotel for a short time. Then I worked at a meat market—"

"It is her!" Rosa exclaimed. "Abe, look at the eyes! Hear how she calls me *Mamá* Rosa. It is our Victoria! *Ai, pobrecita!* My poor little one!"

Folding Victoria into an embrace, the woman rocked her back and forth. Smelling of woodsmoke and tortillas and red-hot chile peppers and everything that had ever meant home, Rosa patted the girl's back and cooed and clucked until Victoria could no longer prevent her tears.

"Oh, *Mamá* Rosa, I missed you!" she whispered. "Didn't you get my letters? I wrote every week after my father died, but you never answered!"

"Letters, what is that?" Abe scoffed. "You should have come home to us. Why you stayed away so much, Vic? We saw you only two times in three years!"

"It's true," she said, wrapping her arms around the man she had always called *Papá*. "I thought my life in Santa Fe was so important. I was too busy with shopping for hats and making social calls and practicing my stitchery to realize what really mattered. I was such a fool!"

"No, no," Rosa purred, brushing tear-streaked dust from Victoria's cheeks. "Your father sent you to the city to become an elegant lady."

"To finish you," Abe added with a snort of disgust. He crossed his arms over his broad chest. "Nobody's finished until we put them into the ground, is what I say. And from the look of you, Vic, old Emil Jennings nearly succeeded."

Victoria lowered her head. "I have been traveling, and the roads are dusty. But . . . *Papá*, what you say is true. My life has been difficult in the past months. I feared I would never see my home again."

Abe gave his wife a look of dismay. Rosa shook her head and pulled Victoria into the warmth of the small adobe house. Built three generations before by the first family of Bacas who traveled up from Mexico to begin a new life in the territory, the home had changed little over the years. The rounded fireplace in the corner crackled with burning mesquite logs that gave off a fragrant aroma. Handmade wooden chairs piled with soft pillows were gathered around the fire. Thick wool curtains hung over the small windows, and a single lamp flickered on a table.

Abe and Rosa Baca had raised their own seven children in this two-room house, and they willingly added the baby Victoria to the mix when her mother died. The home rang with laughter and the slap of bare feet on the hard dirt floor. Delicious meals made their way from the stove to the long wooden table, and each morning the aroma of baking tortillas drifted from the *horno* that had been built against an outside wall.

"Now sit down here," Rosa said, plumping a pillow on one of the chairs. "Let me make you a cup of hot chocolate. You look so thin!"

"First we must talk," Victoria told her. "I can't accept your charity, *Mamá*. I spent too many years expecting to be treated like a queen, and I won't do that now—or ever again. I've come to the Lazy J to work. If you'll hire me, *Papá*, I'll pay you for room and board. But if you can't find a place for me, then I must return to Lincoln and look for a job there."

Rosa made to protest, but Abe held up a calloused hand.

"Where do you think you are now, Vic? This is no longer the Lazy J. You have not come home. This spread is called the Mesquite Land & Cattle Company, and the owners live far away across the ocean."

"He speaks the truth, *mija*." Rosa sank down into a chair beside her husband, her hands folded in her lap. "This is not a good place for you now. Things are different. Before, your father stayed away so much that nothing was in good condition. But now we have a lot of cowboys, and Abe is busy night and day. The owners expect to turn a good profit. The new manager, he knows how to run a ranch, and he makes the hands work hard, even in winter. It's good, because we see the cattle growing fat, and we know we will all benefit from this. But what kind of job can you do here?"

"The house," she replied firmly. "I can help you, *Mamá* Rosa. I know where everything is and exactly how it should look. I've learned to sweep and mop and polish windows. I know how to set a fine table and plan an elegant meal. I brought a book of recipes with me, and I can learn to cook meals that will please the British owners."

"But those men don't live here, Vic." Abe again gave his wife a wary glance. "The owners stay in England, and they came here only one time to see the ranch. It was just two of them, so fat and smoking big cigars and complaining about the flies. They don't like our land, but they want the money from our cattle. And so they buy the Lazy J and then go away. The new manager is part owner with the British. But he's American, and he lives in the big house, and he will not want you to clean it."

"Why not?" Victoria cried. "I'm good at cleaning. I can help with other things, too. I can work the cattle, *Papá*; you know I can! I know everything about this spread, and any owner should be happy to have me in his employment."

"*Verdad*, I could use her help in the house," Rosa spoke up. "My bones hurt a lot in the winter, Abe."

"No, Rosa! Think what you say to her." He glowered. "This cannot be. And you know it."

"Why not, *Papá?*" Victoria asked, her eyes misting at his harshness. "Why would you turn me away?"

"It is not I who would turn you away, Vic," Abe said. "It is the new manager of the Mesquite Land & Cattle Company." He knitted his fingers and rubbed his palms together for a moment. Then he nodded and looked into her eyes. "That man, Victoria, is the one whose heart you broke. The one who despises you more than any other woman. That man's name is Jesse Conroy."

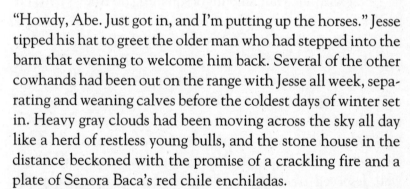

"Howdy, Abe. Just got in, and I'm putting up the horses." Jesse tipped his hat to greet the older man who had stepped into the barn that evening to welcome him back. Several of the other cowhands had been out on the range with Jesse all week, separating and weaning calves before the coldest days of winter set in. Heavy gray clouds had been moving across the sky all day like a herd of restless young bulls, and the stone house in the distance beckoned with the promise of a crackling fire and a plate of Senora Baca's red chile enchiladas.

"Things okay on the home front while I was gone?" Jesse asked his foreman.

Holding up a lantern, Abe scratched his grizzled chin. "Not too bad, boss. Yesterday, a fox got into the chickens, but he didn't get away with none of them. Rudy scared him off too quick."

"Rudy?" Surprised to learn the old cow dog was back on

his feet, Jesse chuckled as he hung a halter on its nail. "He's feeling better?"

"Rosa took him over to our place, and pretty soon Vic—" Abe sucked down a breath of air and began to cough.

Jesse frowned. Winter in the New Mexico Territory could be harsh, and Abe had been battling lung troubles off and on for several months. "You feeling all right?"

"*Si, si*. . . what I'm saying is that . . . well, it was a piece of porcupine quill that got stuck down in the dog's jaw. That's what put him off his feed. Remember when Rudy and the other cow dogs found that half-rotted porcupine carcass and was dragging it around the yard? I guess Rudy got a piece of quill stuck inside his mouth. It was working its way out, poking through the skin like a little black thorn. So I took the pliers and grabbed hold of it, and out it came."

"Not without a fair amount of squalling on Rudy's part, I'd bet."

Abe laughed. "You got that right. Ol' dog started howling and yipping like the world was gonna end. But once the quill was out and Rosa put some medicine on the wound, he perked right up. Good thing, because he saved those chickens' hides from that fox."

"We need to rig a better fence around the coop." Jesse gave his horses a last look. The tired animals were enjoying a well-deserved treat of oats. "I guess the chickens are going through their molt."

"*Si*, we're lucky to get any eggs. Rosa's complaining about it all the time."

Jesse slung an arm over his old friend's shoulder as they started for the house. "I'd just about ride into Lincoln town right now to fetch that wife of yours some eggs. I believe I'd do anything for a plate of her beans and some enchiladas."

"You don't have to go nowhere. Rosa was expecting you, boss, and she's got everything ready. You're gonna be happy tonight—she made blue-corn enchiladas."

His mouth watering at the thought, Jesse spotted a familiar tail-wagging silhouette in the distance. Letting out a whoop, he clapped his hands. "Well, if ain't ol' Rudy himself! Come here, you scroungy mutt."

Rudy, one of several mixed-breed dogs who worked the cattle on the ranch, lumbered off the porch and galloped across the yard to greet the two men. Leaping up, he set his paws at Jesse's waist to slobber wet kisses on his master's cheek as Jesse rubbed his fingers through the dog's thick neck ruff. The other cow dogs, trailing behind Jesse as always, appeared just as happy to see their companion back on his feet. They met Rudy with barks and smiles, their tails swishing back and forth in the starlight.

"Abe?" Apron around her waist, Rosa Baca stepped out onto the wide porch. "Is the boss back?"

"I'm home, Rosa," Jesse called. "We weaned the last batch of calves, and we moved their *mamás* two miles down to Cottonwood Creek. I guess we're set for the winter."

Having grown up on a Wyoming ranch, Jesse felt his heart fill with good memories at the sight of the smiling woman, the smell of piñon smoke drifting from the stone chimney, and the glow of oil lamps in the glass windows of the big house. On an impulse, he caught Rosa in a bear hug and gave her a peck on the cheek.

"*Ai*, not after that dog's been licking you!" she cried, swatting him away with her apron. "*Mi corazón!* Get in there and wash up before you give me a heart attack."

Though his childhood had been a happy one, Jesse now felt a contentment he had never known. He stepped into the large room and stood for a moment, drinking in the welcome sight. Even after living on the ranch for seven months, he could hardly believe how God had blessed him. Jesse owned these strong walls paneled in knotty pine, along with the heavy vigas and corbels supporting a ceiling of narrow wooden *latillos*. The huge fireplace with its blazing logs was his, as was the long table set with a plate, a cup, and heavy silverware.

Only this last sight gave him pause. He would have welcomed Abe and Rosa at his table, but he knew they would never join him. He was the boss now. As co-owner of the ranch and representative of the company's British partners, Jesse would be forever separated from the Bacas and from all the cowhands who once had been his compadres on the trail. He would sit at the table alone. Would he ever get used to it?

"Come on, *mijo!*" Rosa urged. "I got the water nice and hot for you."

Jesse stepped to the washbasin near the door and tugged off his boots before scrubbing his face and hands with a thick bar of lye soap. The smell of onions and chiles drifting in from the kitchen made his stomach clench in hunger, and he could almost taste the nutty flavor of blue-corn tortillas.

"Sit down; sit down," Rosa commanded as he dried his hands on a cotton towel. "You gonna take all day?"

"Bring it on," he said, scraping back the chair and taking the lone place at the table. "Why don't you join me, Abe? Another helping of frijoles can't hurt you."

Abe rubbed his stomach and shook his head. "She's gonna make me fat like those crazy barn cats she feeds all the time," he grumbled. But to Jesse's surprise, he pulled out a chair and sat down. "You go ahead and eat. Me, I'll just fill you in on what's been happening around here."

Jesse didn't like the sound of that—or the way Abe and Rosa had glanced at each other across the room. Still, he would give his foreman time to share whatever news had to be told. After Rosa set the steaming plate before him, Jesse bowed his head and gave thanks. Then he eyed the plate and shook his head in amazement.

"And an egg on top," he said, lifting a bite of enchilada covered in melted cheese and thick red chile sauce.

"The only one we got today." Rosa gave a snort as she, too, sat down. "The other night, a fox nearly scared the chickens eggless. And the milk? Susie's only giving a gallon a day. And Millie is almost that bad."

"You planning to dry out the old girls and let them rest this winter?"

"Rest? What's a rest on a ranch? We gotta have milk and butter." She sighed deeply. "I tell you, boss, trying to keep up with the ranch house and all the cowboys is wearing me out."

Jesse looked at her in surprise. "Rosa? You spry little filly?"

"She's no filly; let me tell you that," Abe piped up. "In fact, I been thinking maybe we ought to hire some more help. Like you were talking about fixing the chicken coop, boss? Who has time for that? And chopping firewood? It's been a long time since we had so many hands to feed and keep warm. The bunkhouse is full, and even though it's winter, those boys are gonna be busy breaking ice in the troughs and putting out salt and moving the cattle around."

As he chewed, Jesse studied his foreman. Abe was not himself tonight, and this suggestion to hire a new employee seemed to be at the root of his unease. But why? Jesse couldn't figure it out, even though he had worked under Abe for several years on the spread that once had been known as the Lazy J.

After a stint in Texas building up his own small herd, Jesse had returned to New Mexico determined to buy a small ranch. Instead, he had met two Englishmen in the process of purchasing the Lazy J, and they welcomed his interest in becoming a partner. Now he ran the operation for his British colleagues, gladly taking the position he believed God had been preparing him for all along.

Nothing had pleased Jesse more than finding Abe and Rosa Baca still living on the old place. Though it felt a little strange to have reversed roles, Jesse worked well with Abe. They'd never had a moment's disagreement, and each could read the other like a book. Something didn't ring right about this request for a helper.

"You're wanting to hire someone to help with chores around the main house and the outbuildings?" he asked.

"And inside, too," Rosa said. "This is a big place, and it takes a lot of dusting. I have to polish the silver and keep oil in the lamps and clean the stove. All that and more. It's too much work for one person."

"But I'm the only one here, Rosa," Jesse argued. "You don't have to polish or dust for me. I've been living in a bunkhouse most of my life."

"*Si*, but not anymore. You need to keep things nice in the big house. People talk, you know. They see how it is. Most of them in Lincoln, they remember Mr. Jennings and they know—"

"Look, I'm not Emil Jennings, and I don't intend to live any part of my life like that man." Suddenly hot, Jesse pushed back from the table and stood. Abandoning his dinner, he strode to the door and opened it to the cool night air. "If you want help, Rosa, that's fine. We can justify the cost of another hired man, and I can see the advantages to it. But don't get the idea that I'm going to turn this house into a whiskey-and-card saloon, the way it was before I left."

"No, boss," Abe said. "Nobody wants that. After Miss Victoria went to Santa Fe—"

"And don't mention that name around here either!" He glared at his friend. "I know Jennings and his daughter lived on this place a long time and folks remember them, but things are different now. I'm in charge."

"Sure, boss. That's how it ought to be."

"Everyone likes working for you," Rosa put in. She scooted the plate across the table toward him. "You treat people good, and the cattle look better than ever before. Come, *mijo*, finish your enchiladas."

Jesse's shoulders relaxed as he took in the worried expressions on their faces. The memory of Emil Jennings and his proud daughter was not the Bacas' problem. Jesse would have to manage that on his own, and he couldn't take out his hurt and anger on these two good people.

He closed the door, returned to his chair, and took another bite to assure Rosa of his goodwill toward her. "Never tasted better enchiladas in my life," he commented as he scraped up the last of the refried beans. "And these frijoles could make a man cry, they're so good."

She beamed. "I'm glad you liked them." Folding her hands on the table, she regarded him. "So, what we were thinking about, Abe and me, was that maybe it should be a girl. You know, the new hire? Like someone who knows about things."

"What kind of things? You already know all there is about cooking and cleaning."

"But you need to have parties sometimes. Or like a Thanksgiving dinner for all the honchos in town? It's the right thing, inviting everyone to come out here and have a meal or a celebration. Even the cowboys will expect some-times to enjoy a little party, like after a roundup or when the branding is done. And for Christmas, you better have a big lunch with tamales and posole. That's what the boss of a ranch is supposed to do."

Jesse had not considered this aspect of his new position in the community. Until it affected him personally, he had never given Emil Jennings's lifestyle much heed. Rarely spending time around the big house or the bunkhouse, he slept out on the range even on the coldest of nights. Victoria Jennings never would have met Jesse Conroy had she not taken a regular hankering to tie her hair back, put on a big sombrero and a pair of leather chaps, and go riding out with the cattle just like some skinny little cowboy. In fact, that's exactly what Jesse had thought she was. Until the afternoon her horse got spooked by a tumbleweed.

The sight of that skinny cowboy sprawled on the hard ground—all long blonde hair and big blue eyes filled with tears—had torn Jesse's heart out right then and there. He had helped her up, his arms sliding around her narrow waist and her cheek pressing against his shoulder, and he hadn't been the same since.

After that day, Vic chose to head her horse in his direc-tion each time she went riding. Pretty soon, Jesse was making a practice of bedding down in the bunkhouse just to spend time with her in the evenings. They talked for hours. And laughed. He played his guitar for her, and she sang to him. Everything appeared just about perfect, including his dream of building up a herd and buying his own spread on which to raise a family. At the center of his plan stood Victoria Jennings, his darling Vic, the passion of his young life.

As the annual Christmas party approached, Jesse had

made plans to slip out onto the porch with Vic and ask her to marry him. But that night, Emil Jennings had discovered his daughter in the arms of a cowboy. It was the first time Jesse had kissed Victoria. And the last. Emil saw to that.

Within days, Vic stopped riding her horse out on the range. When Jesse asked about it, she told him she had other things to do. Like ordering a new hat at the milliner's shop in Lincoln. And buying slippers for the New Year's Eve dance at the Chisum ranch, to which William Worthing would escort her. Yes, *that* William Worthing, she informed Jesse, the man who owned a gold mine over at White Oaks.

Desperate and angry, Jesse had retreated to the comfort of the open range. Though it was the dead of winter, the other cowhands couldn't talk him into joining them in the bunkhouse. During those bleak days, the cattle had been his companions, and God had been his strength.

One February afternoon, as a blizzard approached, Abe Baca had pleaded with him to return to warmth and safety. There was no use pining over Miss Victoria, he told Jesse, because she had promised her hand in marriage to William Worthing. That news only firmed up Jesse's determination to ride out the blizzard alone. Nearly frozen and half delirious that night in the blinding snow, he had seen a sort of vision of himself riding across the grassland alone, his dogs trailing behind as he rounded up a herd of his own. The vision had led Jesse to Texas and then back to New Mexico, determined to live out the life he believed God had set before him.

"I reckon a ranch boss ought to throw a party every now and then," he conceded. "Maybe I should put on a dinner this Christmas."

"That's it!" Rosa cried, giving her husband a victorious smile. "What did I tell you, Abe? He's too smart not to do the right thing." She focused on Jesse again. "You need to hire someone who can cook gringo food—like roast turkey and baked ham. That's what you need, *mijo*. You better get the house fixed up, too, with piñon branches hanging everywhere and a Christmas tree in the corner. And the table? You got to have silverware put the right way, you know? All those forks and knives and spoons? That's a job for a housekeeper who knows how to do things properly."

"A housekeeper?" Jesse said. "Now, hold on—"

"A girl is what I mean. She could live with us, no problem."

"I believe you two already have someone in mind for this job."

Rosa's eyes darted to Abe.

Her husband cleared his throat. "*Si*, we got an idea of someone. She knows a lot about things."

"She knows many things," Rosa confirmed.

Jesse had a sneaking suspicion this girl who knew a lot about things might be related to the Bacas. A needy niece perhaps, or a daughter whose marriage had gone bad.

"It's fine with me," he told them. "You can hire whoever you want."

"Anyone?" Rosa and Abe asked in unison.

Jesse laughed as he stood. "Anyone. It doesn't matter much to me what happens around the place so long as my hands and I get fed. Go ahead and hire the girl. Tell her we'll have a Christmas dinner and invite the whole town of Lincoln. But she'd better make sure to set the spoons in the right place."

As Rosa leapt to clear the table and Abe headed out to feed the dogs, Jesse climbed the stairs to the bedroom. Though he loved the snap of a chilly breeze and the first flakes of snow on his face, tonight he was looking forward to taking a hot bath and then climbing into his warm bed.

Things had changed since the days when he was just a tenderfoot. And he had a feeling if Rosa and Abe had their way, a few more changes were about to blow in with the winter wind.

~

Victoria placed the last log atop the pile she had stacked on the grate inside the large stone fireplace. Then she sat back on her heels and admired her handiwork. Any old cowboy could build a good fire, but it took a woman to make it smell nice. To the kindling, she had added a large pile of mesquite chips and handfuls of dried pine needles. The spark of the first little blaze would send a fragrant aroma into the living room of the big ranch house. Next, she had set several cottonwood limbs to get the blaze roaring. Topping those lay the *piéce de résistance*, as Mrs. Redfern would have said—though certainly not about wood—piñon. Nothing gave off better heat and a spicier scent than the scrubby piñon tree, and Victoria had welcomed the load that Abe chopped and hauled in especially at her request.

Standing, she brushed her hands on her apron and eyed the stack of wood beside the fireplace. Yes, that would be enough. Mr. Conroy, as she had decided to call the ranch owner when she had to think about him—which, unfortunately, was all the time—would walk through the door just after sunset. Rosa would be waiting for him. A few minutes earlier, Victoria would have hurried down the road to the Bacas' house.

As Jesse washed up, Rosa would light the fire Victoria had built in the living room. Then Rosa would serve him the dinner Victoria had cooked, a hearty beef stew loaded with carrots, potatoes, and onions. Next he would sample the apple pie Victoria had baked, a confection laden with sugar, cinnamon, and a hint of nutmeg. Later, as he relaxed in the brown leather chair into which Victoria had rubbed a fine paste polish this very morning, he would gaze at the roaring fire on his grate. And if it began to burn low, he would add the logs until they were all gone and the room was toasty warm.

"Abe says the *cabrito* is cooking good down in the pit!" Rosa sang out to Victoria as she hurried into the house with a basket full of clean laundry from the clothesline. "I'm telling you, *mija*, nothing tastes better on a cold November evening than roasted goat. The cowboys are already setting up to play *canuto*."

Victoria looked up in surprise at the mention of the ranch hands' favorite game. Played with hollow reeds, blankets, and piles of sand, *canuto* involved competitors racing back and forth while observers sang a Spanish song and shouted bets. *Canuto* was a raucous event, usually accompanied by far too much liquor and at least one fistfight.

Dismayed, Victoria followed Rosa to the laundry room. "Not *canuto*! Mr. Conroy will hear the racket and come to see what's going on. And the drinking and gambling—oh, Mamá Rosa! We can't have *canuto*!"

"You better accept it, *mija*." The older woman set the basket on the floor and lifted an iron to test the heat from the fire. As she wiped down the ironing table and laid a blanket across it, she tried to reassure Victoria. "Today is Thanksgiving, and all the gringos in Lincoln are eating their big dinners. But here? Nothing. The hands are not happy about it, and that's why Abe chose this night for the barbecue. If we put on a feast, we must have fun and games. Someone will bring a guitar, and there's gonna be dancing. And cards, too. You know they'll play cards."

"No cards!" Victoria cried. "My life was changed forever thanks to cards. How can you expect me to accept gambling on the Lazy J?"

Rosa looked up from the shirt she had laid out to iron. "This is not the Lazy J, Vic, and you cannot stop the boys from gambling. *Cunquián*, monte, fuzzy-guzzy—someone will start a game, and no one can keep them from betting on it. Please try not to worry so much. This barbecue is what Abe is making just for you, to say how happy we are to have you home again. I cooked tamales yesterday, and he chose our fattest goat for the roasting pit. It's gonna be a good time, you'll see."

Sighing, Victoria drew another of Mr. Conroy's shirts from the basket and examined it for holes. The man could wear out his elbows faster than anyone she knew. Finding this one intact, she set it on the ironing table for Rosa.

"I appreciate the work you put into preparing the celebration," Victoria said. "But I'm afraid. It's been almost two weeks since you and *Papá* talked Mr. Conroy into hiring me—and so far he hasn't set eyes on me. But twice, he's arrived at the barn before we realized it, and I barely got out of the house in time. *Mamá* Rosa, I'm frightened! One of these days, he's bound to see me. And then what?"

"*Si*, he will find out. If not tonight, sometime. One of the cowboys will spill the beans sooner or later. We know that, Vic. And when the boss finds out you're here, Abe is gonna tell him what a good job you do. Then Abe will say that if the boss turns you out, you're gonna be left hungry and freezing on the streets of Santa Fe."

"Jesse Conroy won't care if I starve to death! He despises me. You've said so yourself."

Rosa's warm brown eyes softened. "But he doesn't know you. You're a different girl now."

"It won't matter. Oh, *Mamá*, if he sees me at the barbe-cue—"

"If he sees you at the barbecue, Abe will hand him a plate of *cabrito* and tamales. He'll sit down by the fire and listen to the singing. He'll watch the boys play *canuto*. Everything will be okay. You'll see."

Victoria had no such confidence. The joy these last two weeks had brought made her fear its loss all the more. And with each passing day, she knew the chances that the boss might spot his new hire increased.

"*Mija*, I really don't need you to pull out all the boss's shirts before I'm ready for them," Rosa said gently. "If we plan to entertain in this house at Christmas, someone better start cleaning the bedrooms."

"But *Mamá* Rosa, you know I can't go up there yet. It was hard enough to see the living room looking just the same, and I'm afraid—"

"Do you know how often you say that? You talk all the time about how you're afraid and scared. Why you're this way? Where is my old Vic, not scared of nothing—not even a rattlesnake or a bull on the loose?"

Victoria hung her head. "If I go upstairs, I'll have to see my room, and the memories of all my mistakes will come back."

Rosa placed the iron near the fire and set her hands on her hips. "So? Are you gonna hide from the past forever? You made mistakes, but so do we all. You did good things, too. Enough good that Abe and me loved you. You were our Vic, riding the range in your chaps and sombrero. Swinging on the porch swing. Climbing in the hay barn. *Si*, you got taken up with dresses and flirting with the *novios* who courted you.

What pretty girl doesn't? Let it go, *mija*. Look ahead, not back."

"I'm trying. I want a new life. A better one."

"You have it. Now go upstairs and dust out the demons of the past. Look at that bedroom and remember the good things. Go on."

Victoria gave Rosa a quick hug. "I love you, *Mamá*."

"*Lo mismo*. It's the same for Abe and me both. We love you, too."

Squaring her shoulders, Victoria lifted her skirts, climbed the stairs, and stood for a moment in the hallway. She could do this. It was simply a part of her work now, cleaning the upstairs. She pushed open the door to her old bedroom—and it was all there, just as she had left it. The wooden bed with its layers of quilts. The armoire her grandparents had brought from England. The roses on the wallpaper, the hooked rugs and downy pillows. Even her boots. The day she went off to Santa Fe for the last time, she had set them at the foot of the bed. Worn and in need of polish, the boots would not journey into her new life, she had decided. She wouldn't need spurs, chaps, flannel shirts, or faded dungarees either.

Emil Jennings had convinced her that she was too beautiful, too educated, too wealthy for the undignified cowboys. Not even William Worthing and his gold mine were good enough for Victoria. No, she would be the belle of the ball. A fairy-tale princess. The queen of hearts!

Sickened by the memory of such selfish pride and ambition, Victoria took her broom to the old wood floor. In this bedroom she had listened to her father's card-playing friends in the living room below—men who smoked cigars and drank away the night while plotting to get rich off New Mexico's land. But the nights of scheming had come to nothing, and what had Emil Jennings left behind to show that he had been on this earth? Only a daughter who hadn't even managed to get herself "finished."

The memory of Abe's wry comment lifted Victoria's heart a little. With a smile at her own foolishness, she knelt one knee on the old bed and swung back the curtain that covered the window. This was the place to finish a young lady—a big stone house, a yard filled with pecking chickens and several cow dogs, and a barn that promised—

Jesse Conroy. Tall and lean, the man himself strode from the barn toward the house. He wore a wide-brimmed Stetson that shadowed his face, but Victoria knew him immediately. Jesse walked with the gait of a man who knew the range, his stride long and his shoulders thrown back in confidence. He wore a blue shirt, dark wool trousers, and tall leather boots into which he had tucked his pants legs. The long, heavy coat that covered his shoulders hung unbuttoned and drifting behind him. Beneath the duster he wore a black vest, a wide bandana tied at his neck, and a Colt .45 in the holster at his waist.

Her heart hammering, Victoria dropped the curtain and sank down onto the bed. Emil Jennings's house had only one door. In two minutes, Jesse Conroy would walk through it. And Victoria would be trapped.

CHAPTER
Two

*W*hat's going on down at your place, Rosa?" Jesse asked as he stepped through the front door and took off his hat. "Smells like someone's cooking *cabrito*."

Rosa stood from the kitchen fireplace where she'd been lighting the tinder she had placed there earlier in the day. "*Si*, it's just a little celebration, boss. That's all."

She scooted past him, her head down. Jesse tugged off his boots and shucked his coat. "What are you celebrating?" he called as he washed up in the bowl of warm water by the door. "Must be something big."

Carrying a plate of steaming tamales, Rosa bustled back to the table. "Thanksgiving. It's today, you know, and the hands were talking about it. Saying they wished they could have a dinner."

"You're celebrating Thanksgiving with *cabrito*?" He stared at the plate of tamales she had set in its lonely spot on the long table. There was nothing in the world he liked better than goat roasted for hours deep inside a pit. Smoky and tender, *cabrito* could send a hungry man into paroxysms of ecstasy.

"We didn't get any turkeys this year," Rosa said, giving him a guilty glance. "I don't know where they went. Anyhow, I made you tamales."

Jesse studied the plate. Under normal circumstances, this would be a welcome meal. He knew it took a woman many hours of labor to season and cook the pork, fold it into blankets of white cornmeal, then wrap those in fresh cornhusks, and boil them until they were tender. Jesse had always felt privileged to be the recipient of a plate of tamales. But this batch tonight appeared downright lonesome.

"They sure look tasty," he said. He pushed back the chair and took a seat. "I guess . . . uh . . . maybe I'll wander down to the pit and try that *cabrito* later on, too."

Rosa wrung her hands. "Well, Abe could bring you a plate up here. There'll be plenty. It was our fattest goat—that big gray one, you know? With white spots?"

Sitting down, Jesse faced his dinner. He could hear Rosa fiddling around with pots and pans behind him. And one of the dogs must have gotten into the house and wandered upstairs, too, because he could hear an occasional *thump* from the bedroom overhead.

"I think you'd better check upstairs, Rosa," he said, still eyeing the tamales. "Ol' Rudy must have come inside when I opened the door. He's probably up there on my bed. After all the pampering you did when he had that snout full of porcupine quills, he thinks he's a human."

"Sure, boss. I'll go see."

Jesse turned to find her standing at the bottom of the staircase, her hands still knotted in nervousness. "Aren't you going to say your prayer? You always say a prayer. So devout. It's a good thing, boss."

"Listen, Rosa, how come you're always calling me boss?" He frowned at her. "And why aren't you inviting me to eat *cabrito* with everyone else?"

Looking as stiff as a mannequin in a shopwindow, she took a step backward up the staircase. "Well, you are the boss. That's why I call you boss, and that's why you should not come to the celebration. Because you're the boss. You live in the big house now . . . and that's the reason."

"I'm in charge, but I'm out with the men all day."

"*Si*, but you would not want to eat *cabrito* with them."

"Well, yes, I sure would."

"But . . ." She glanced up the staircase. Swallowing, she faced him again. "I think it's a bad idea if you should come, though. You better just pray now, and then eat your tamales."

Though aggravated, Jesse propped his elbows on the table and bowed his head. As he prayed, the sound of the dog racing down the stairs and out the door put up such a racket he could hardly hear himself. Not that it mattered. Considering the mood he was in now, his prayer wasn't likely to give the tamales more than a sprinkle of blessing.

He unwrapped the cornhusk from the nearest tamale and cut off the end. Near the door, Rosa was draping her mantilla around her head. Despite the chill, she insisted on wearing the lacy, fringed square of fabric that Abe had ordered all the way from Spain for her wedding day. Jesse could feel the little woman eyeing him as he swallowed the first bite.

"Good night, boss," she said. Then she added, "So, I'll send Abe up with the *cabrito*."

"Don't bother," he replied. "These tamales are good. I'll be full when I'm done."

"Okay, then. *Hasta mañana.*"

"See you tomorrow," he answered the customary farewell.

As she pulled the door shut, Jesse set down his fork and watched her through the window as she scurried off down the road to her own house. Rosa couldn't have made her feelings more clear. Jesse would not be welcome at the celebration. She and Abe hadn't invited him, and the other cowboys must not want him around either.

Feeling like the abandoned runt in a litter of greedy little piglets, he picked up his plate, carried it to the next room, and stepped to the comfortable chair beside the fire. Let them wolf down all the *cabrito*, he thought. He didn't need to join in their fun. He had what he'd always wanted—and it was more than enough.

Rosa had been right in her assessment. Jesse was the boss. Thanks to hard work, determination, and the blessing of God, he had landed right square in old Emil Jennings's living room. Jesse set his stockinged feet on the hearth to warm his toes and drew in a deep breath of the fragrance that emanated from the crackling timbers. Only a woman would care enough to build a fire that smelled so good. He shouldn't have been so short with Rosa.

His cup was full to the brim and overflowing. Emil Jennings had been gone almost a year, and now Jesse and his British colleagues owned this house and the grass-covered range that went with it. Mesquite Land & Cattle Company— the name had a good ring to it. Jesse was more than satisfied with the long hours and backbreaking labor he'd put into making the operation a success. Next year would be even better. One of these days, he would buy out his partners. Then he would be able to stand tall and proud as the cattle king of the whole New Mexico Territory.

Jesse scraped the plate of the last remnants of tamale as he considered his future. Everything appeared perfect—except for the loud, lonely silence in the big house. He knew what he ought to do. Many a cowboy found himself a wife from a matrimony agency in about the same way he ordered his underriggin's. But a mail-order bride was not for Jesse Conroy. Other men who spent their days and nights on the range chose never to wed, and Jesse considered that a fair option. But he wouldn't object to the notion of a pretty wife and a house full of children. In the church at Lincoln, he had met several attractive young ladies. And there were more to be found in Roswell or Albuquerque. He could even go as far as Santa Fe, if he wanted a good wife.

The uppity mountain town with its politicians, businessmen, and social climbers immediately put Victoria Jennings into Jesse's thoughts. *Bah!* He jumped up from his chair and stalked to the kitchen. That woman was the last thing he needed on his mind, he fumed as he dropped his plate into the dish bucket. Ornery little gal. Self-centered and proud, she was as false as Granny's chompers.

The day she had turned him away, Jesse just couldn't make himself believe it. All he'd done was kiss her on the porch! True, he had failed to get her father's permission to court her, but the way Vic had fallen into his arms so soft and sweet that night had left him with no doubt of her desires.

One kiss. One rebuke from Emil Jennings. And suddenly Vic was tossing William Worthing and his gold mine in Jesse's face. Oh, the agonies he had suffered in the following weeks and months.

Jesse walked to the window to draw the curtains shut—wishing he could somehow close away the memories, too. The last time he had seen Victoria Jennings was on the boardwalk in front of the mercantile in Lincoln town. But her familiar flannel shirt, dungarees, chaps, and spurred boots were gone. Barely casting him a glance, she had strutted by in a purple silk gown covered with flounces from head to toe. Her hat brim stretched a good two feet across and was trimmed in enough feathers and jewels to please the queen of England.

That floozy getup had changed Jesse's remorse into a roaring rage, and he hadn't let go of it since. Choking on his anger now, he clutched the thick, cut-velvet curtains and stared out the window at the bonfire down the way. No doubt the cowboys were playing *canuto*. Probably drinking whiskey, too. Before long, someone was bound to punch someone else. Jesse knew he might as well plan for a ride into Lincoln tonight, because he had no doubt that J. C. Lea, the town jailer, would have to be called out of bed.

Jesse thought of John Chisum, owner of the South Spring spread near Roswell, who never tolerated gambling or drinking on his place. The stalwart cattleman was the finest example of a rancher that Jesse had ever met. The previous November, Chisum had passed away of cancer, and Lincoln County was the worse for his loss. He was one of those old-timers who had chosen never to marry, and he flatly forbade the presence of loose women on South Spring Ranch. Such nefarious activities led to trouble among the men, he believed. Property could be damaged. Lives might be lost.

But tonight, Jesse realized that rather than emulate John Chisum, he was following in Emil Jennings's footsteps. At the Bacas' house, the hands played *canuto*, and snatches of their song "*Paloma Lucida*" drifted along the road to the big house.

" 'Beautiful dove,' my foot," Jesse muttered, snapping the curtains shut. He'd be a fool to manage this ranch with any less vigor than his conscience dictated.

"'Beautiful dove from beautiful dove house.'" He ground out the words as he snatched his coat and hat and stepped out into the night. "'Come ready to win; come ready to lose.'"

Lose is what those boys were about to do. And that was that. If they wanted a boss, they would have one. So much for not being invited to join them in their *cabrito* barbecue. The Mesquite Land & Cattle Company didn't need a celebration on Thanksgiving Day.

Drinking and gambling were bad enough, Jesse groused as he strode down the road toward the Bacas' house. But if he caught so much as a glimpse of a woman—well, he'd just dock the whole bunch of those boys a week's pay.

"I won! I won!"

The cry from a group huddled around the bonfire confirmed Jesse's suspicions. They were playing cards—probably *cunquián.*

"*Dalas y dalas!*" someone shouted at the game's loser. The familiar taunt came from the old legend of a young boy who had hurried to tell his mother, "*Mamá, Mamá! Papá está dalas y dalas y en calzoncillos blancos!*"—the message that his father was dealing and dealing, clad only in his white underdrawers. In *cunquián*, the loser had to deal again and again, until finally he stood to lose even the shirt off his back.

As he neared the house, Jesse distinguished his men—silhouetted by firelight—engaged in every activity he deplored. The *canuto* players raced back and forth between their blankets. The card sharps were gathered in clusters near the smoking blaze. One group had a four-sided top and was spinning it in a game of fuzzy-guzzy.

"*Se durm'o!*" the men exclaimed as the top spun—motionless to the naked eye—in the dirt. The top did look as though it had fallen asleep, Jesse thought. He walked up to the men, set his hands on his hips, and stared down over their bent heads.

But they were so intent on the game that they failed to notice their boss looming over them. As they played, each man held his bowl of steaming shredded goat meat, fragrant and tender after hours of roasting buried in a pit. Tamales and beans mingled with the meat. Between spins, the men spooned down their dinner, laughing and calling out taunts to each other using favored nicknames as their hard-earned wages changed hands.

Irked at the foolish waste of time and money, Jesse lifted his head and looked around for Abe Baca. The older man sat on his front porch and strummed his guitar while a couple of the other fellows played fiddles. An accordion wheezed out the tune as the favored singer of the bunch—a red-haired youth who went by the name of Freck—belted the words in a melodious tenor.

> "O pity the cowboy,
> All bloody and red,
> For a bronco fell on him,
> And mashed in his head."

Jesse fought a grin as the familiar refrain drifted out into the night with all the mournfulness young Freck could muster. Just then the Bacas' front door opened and out trotted Rosa bearing a large, white-frosted cake on a platter. And right behind her came another woman with a—

Staring, Jesse held his breath. Blonde hair pinned high on her head in a big golden knot. Bright blue eyes and a pretty pink mouth. Narrow shoulders and womanly curves all buttoned into a soft cotton dress with a long white apron tied around a slender waist. She set a stack of plates beside the cake, picked up the knife, and cut a slice. Then she smiled at Rosa.

And it was her.

His Vic.

Jesse gaped. Took a step backward and jerked off his hat. Gawked. Put his hat back on. And gawked some more.

Every emotion he had felt when she turned her back on him three years before raced through his chest all over again. Shock. Disbelief. Sorrow. Hopelessness. And then anger. Fury. Rage.

"Hey, what's going on here!" Jesse shouted loudly enough for everyone to hear. "Abraham Baca, get over here and tell me what in the devil that . . . that *female* is doing on my land!"

The music squeaked to a halt. Freck choked out, "'And a great, big puddle of blood on the ground'" and then began to cough. The cowboys looked up from their games. The top stopped spinning and fell on its side. Rosa dropped the cake knife. And Victoria Jennings clapped her hand over her mouth with a loud gasp.

"I see you," Jesse called out. "I see all of you. What do you think you're doing? You boys better put away your cards. There'll be no gambling on the property of the Mesquite Land & Cattle Company. You reckon you can bring *her* out here and then things will be just the way they were when Emil Jennings was boss? Well, you're wrong."

Fists at his hips, he stared into the shocked faces of his men. "I'm the boss now. No cards, no tops, no *canuto* are permitted on my ranch. I won't tolerate gambling or drinking. Or women." He jabbed a finger at Victoria. "Now get on back to the bunkhouse! All of you."

No one moved as Abe Baca stepped down from the porch. "Can't we just eat a little *cabrito*, boss?" he asked.

Jesse eyed the man. Hadn't he made himself clear enough?

"Can't we eat *cabrito* and sing songs and play music?" Abe walked toward him. "We don't mind to give up the cards, boss. We can put away the *canuto* blankets. And you see no one is drinking whisky out here tonight. Only hot cider is all. But surely you won't prevent us from having a little celebration."

"This is supposed to be a Thanksgiving dinner?" Jesse asked.

"*Si.*" Abe shrugged. "Well, we don't got any turkeys, but we do have a nice fat goat. We just wanted to welcome our friend back to the ranch. Our ol' Vic. You remember?"

Jesse focused on the young woman who had paled to the color of the icing on Rosa's cake. She moistened her lips as she took a step toward him. Then she bowed her head and gave him a little curtsy.

"Hello, Mr. Conroy." Her voice was soft and demure, and her cheeks suddenly flushed a bright pink as her blue gaze focused on his face. "How nice to see you again."

Nostrils flaring, he turned on Abe. "What is the meaning of this? Is she staying with you? Is this the so-called house-keeper you bamboozled me into hiring?"

"Now, boss—"

"I see what's going on. All you men thought you had a fine thing here. Bring Emil Jennings's daughter back and—"

"No, that's not it!" Rosa scampered down the steps. "Victoria was starving in Santa Fe. Her father died, and she had no money, and so she was working at a butchery and eating nothing but pig slop. She came back here to find work, and how could we turn her out? Not our Vic!"

"In fact, we were happy to see her," Abe declared. "Everybody was glad to have her home. The boys said it was a good thing to see Vic back here."

"And she wanted to work," Rosa continued. "She was willing to do anything. So Abe and me, we asked you. We asked right up front, boss. You said, 'anyone.' That's what you told us. You said we could hire anyone to help with the house-keeping. Vic does a good job, too. She builds your fire, and she makes the stew and biscuits you like so much. She washes and chops wood and polishes the stove and all that."

"So, we wanted to make a little celebration." Abe held out his hands to indicate the others at the gathering. "A fat *cabrito* to say welcome home to our Vic. It's a feast of thanksgiving, because she came home to us from Santa Fe. And Rosa and me, we would like nothing more than to give you—our boss— a nice plate of meat. Come on, Rosa, get the boss some *cabrito*."

"*Si, si!*" The woman whirled around and picked up her skirts as she headed for the roasting pit.

But Jesse was in no humor to be further manipulated by those he once thought he could trust. Abe and Rosa had tricked him into hiring and paying his own good money to the one person he hoped never to see again as long as he lived. How long had the cowhands known she was here? How long had they snickered about their boss behind his back? Sure, they thought they could bring back Victoria Jennings and recapture the old days.

Well, this was no longer the Lazy J. There would be no more gambling. No cards. No tops. And no Victoria Jennings.

"Never mind the *cabrito*, Rosa," Jesse called out. "I believe all of you have been celebrating without cause. That woman is not welcome on any property owned by the Mesquite Land & Cattle Company. And if you men intend to get your pay at the end of the week, you'll head on over to the bunkhouse where you belong."

Turning his back on the gathering, Jesse stalked down the road in the direction of the big house. He couldn't believe it. Could not believe it. After all these years, ol' Vic had come home.

～

Victoria pushed the last hairpin into her bun and faced Rosa. The dawning sun lit the smaller woman's cheeks with a pink glow as she buttoned her coat.

"I've made up my mind," Victoria said. "Thank you for all you've done for me, *Mamá*. And now it's time for me to leave."

"*Ai, mija!* Don't say that." Rosa reached for her mantilla. "Come on over to the big house, and we'll talk to the boss. Look, I can see Abe waiting for us near the barn. Let's all go in together."

"No." Victoria was adamant. "I cannot allow you to risk your positions here. You saw how angry Mr. Conroy was last night. Just the sight of me made his blood boil. If I go anywhere near the man again, he'll run you both off, and then where will we be? No, I'll go into Lincoln and find work. Maybe the tailor will hire me. I'm good with a needle—especially beadwork. Mrs. Ellis keeps the hotel, and maybe she'll give me a room in exchange for cleaning. Mr. Dolan has the dry-goods store—"

"But you belong here, *mija!* This is your home. That young hothead is not gonna fire Abe. Jesse Conroy is a good boss, but how would he manage everything by himself? Things will look different to him this morning. He'll let you stay; you'll see."

"*Mamá* Rosa, you are too kind." Victoria hugged the dear

woman who had cared for her so tenderly as a baby. "And yet my mind is settled. I prayed about this all night, and I know God is with me. He'll watch over me, no matter what lies ahead."

"Ai-yi-yi." Rosa shook her head in dismay.

"Do you suppose *Papá* will have my pay? I'll need something to start out with."

Rosa sighed. "Come on. We'll talk to Abe."

The two women set off down the road toward the barn, the bright November sky arching over them like a great blue bowl. The gray-green knuckles of the Capitan Mountains rose to the northwest, while the Rio Bonito trickled along the valley below them. The last of the golden aspen and cottonwood leaves had blown away, and the naked tree limbs reached upward as if already begging for spring's return. Wispy clouds scudded eastward overhead, while a flock of honking geese crossed by in their journey south.

Victoria lifted her chin and forced her thoughts away from the coming hours. She had never expected to find welcome at the Lazy J, after all. The Bacas' open arms had been a gift of God's grace. Basking in their care, she was returning to health after the long months of suffering at the hands of Mrs. O'Neal. Now she would set out again, following the path God unfolded before her. New difficulties lay ahead, she felt sure. Yet she would face them with His strength.

As the women neared the barn, Victoria saw Abe roll back one of the doors. Rudy, the old cow dog, trotted out, and right behind him Jesse Conroy drove a wagon into the open yard. Spotting the two women, he clenched his jaw and tugged on the reins. Despite the chill breeze that whipped down from the Capitans, Victoria grew instantly hot and uncomfortable. He set the brake, and she braced herself for another tongue-lashing. And well deserved. Unable to bear his eyes on her, she focused on a cluster of juniper brush in the distance.

"Good morning, boss," Rosa said. "*Hola*, Abe."

"Morning, Rosa." Jesse took off his hat. "Miss Jennings."

Victoria managed a brief glance in his direction. "Mr. Conroy," she said, dipping a curtsy.

Rosa spoke up. "Victoria was just going—"

"I'm heading—," Jesse began.

"To Lincoln," they finished in unison.

Abe grinned. "Well, what do you know about this? The boss is picking up salt for the cattle. And Vic?"

"I'm . . . I was leaving," she said.

"She's going to look for work in Lincoln," Rosa explained. "Maybe at J. J. Dolan's store."

The two men stiffened at the name of the powerful rancher who had played such an important role in the Lincoln County War seven years before. James Dolan, it was believed, had ordered the murder of his rival—an Englishman by the name of John Tunstall. A weeklong gun battle involving Billy "the Kid" Antrim and his companions had erupted. The citizens of the town and county took sides, and the whole region was torn apart. The conflict lasted nearly two years, and by the time peace finally reigned again, many men had lost their lives. Politicians had risen and fallen. Monopolies had toppled, and ranches had gone belly-up. Even the United States government had participated by sending troops from nearby Fort Stanton. Dolan now owned Tunstall's store, and the Lincoln populace patronized it, some out of fear and some out of loyalty. But the very idea that Victoria would ever work for such a man . . .

Seeing the reaction, Victoria spoke up. "I'll speak to Mrs. Ben Ellis at the Lincoln Hotel first, of course."

"Well, then, I guess I'll head out," Jesse said. His green eyes grazed her face. "I suppose you were . . . uh . . . planning to take one of the horses."

"No, sir. I intend to walk."

"Walk?" Abe exclaimed. "That's nine miles, Vic."

"I'll be there before dark." She had little desire for Jesse to hear her plans or to glory in her predicament. But he showed no inclination to start the wagon down the road, so she continued. "If you have my pay for the two weeks past, *Papá*, I'll take a room at the hotel and look for work in the morning."

"I don't have money today, and if you think I'm gonna let you—"

"I'll drive Miss Jennings into Lincoln," Jesse cut in. "I intended to pick up the payroll anyhow. I'll see that she gets her wages."

Mortified, Victoria gave Rosa a panic-stricken grimace. Surely they did not expect her to climb up there on that wagon with *him!* Not with Jesse Conroy, who hated her and couldn't bear the merest sight of her!

"I'll help you up," Abe said, taking her arm.

"On Sunday, we will visit you after church," Rosa told her. "I'll bring burritos."

"Oh my, but I—"

Before she could protest further, Abe had lifted her onto the wagon. The narrow bucket seat permitted not an inch of space between Victoria and Jesse. Wishing she could just drop over in a dead faint, she clamped her knees shut and knotted her fingers into a ball as Jesse flicked the reins. This was terrible. How could it have happened?

Oblivious to their passengers' discomfort, the two horses

clippity-clopped down the dirt road. In humiliated silence, Victoria studiously examined every juniper, mesquite, and cedar bush they passed along the way. She mentally measured the length of the grass and calculated how long it would be before the cattle would need hay. The wagon passed two jackrabbits, a roadrunner, a herd of cattle. Seventeen cows, she guessed, a habit from childhood. One, two, three, four—

"Nice morning."

The unexpected words jolted through Victoria like a bolt of lightning. "Yes," she managed.

She unknotted her fingers to let the blood back into them. Despite every intention to ignore the man, she had become palpably aware of Jesse's big shoulder pressed up against her own. How magnificent that hard muscle of his had seemed to her once. What could the man not do? She had watched him rope, brand, and earmark cattle. She had seen him chop trees and build a shed. Dig fence posts. Put up hay. Anything a cowboy had to do, Jesse Conroy could do best.

But she absolutely could not think about the man at all. No, indeed. After all she had done to him, he'd been kind enough to offer her a ride into Lincoln. And he had even spoken a word of hospitality. Mrs. Redfern would be stricken with mortification that Victoria had barely answered him. She must think of something to say. Something nice—but insignificant. Something to show her gratitude perhaps, but nothing that might raise his hackles. Something warm, but—

"So, you worked in a butchery?" he asked.

She gripped the edge of the seat. "Yes, sir. More than half the year."

What could she say next? What was the right and proper

way to continue the conversation? What on earth would Mrs. Redfern—

"How come you ate pig slop?" he asked.

"It was all I had." She tried to breathe in and out. "Mrs. O'Neal—my employer at the butcher shop—she gave me bacon and bread once a day. But I was always hungry."

"You look awful skinny."

"Do I?"

Their eyes met. Instantly, she turned away again, focusing on the large cottonwood along the distant stream.

"I didn't mean that in a bad way," he said.

"No, sir. Of course not."

"Last time I saw you was in Lincoln. You had on a purple getup."

"I don't remember what I was wearing." She swallowed hard. "But, Mr. Conroy, I do recall how abominably I treated you, and I apologize with all my heart. If I could do anything to make up for it, I would. And as for my return to the Lazy J, please don't think the Bacas had any ill intent—"

"This spread is not called the Lazy J any longer," he said. "It's the Mesquite Land & Cattle Company now."

"Yes, of course." She lowered her head. "I'm aware of that. It was all I knew when I came home. If I'd had any idea you were here . . . if I had heard you were the boss—"

"You don't have to say more." Teeth clenched and jaw muscles working hard, he gave the horses a flick of the reins. "I know what you think of me."

"I doubt that," she said.

His green eyes narrowed as he leaned toward her. "And just what is that supposed to mean?"

"Only that I'm a very different person than the girl who went away three years ago. Almost every thought in my head has been altered. The things I cherished, I now no longer desire. And the things I thought unworthy, I see as most important. You cannot possibly know what I think of you."

He shifted a little on the seat. "Well, you don't know what I think of you either."

"I'm sure I do. You voiced your opinion of me quite loudly last night, sir." She pulled her shawl more closely around her shoulders as they neared the Capitans. "You were correct, of course. I don't belong on property owned by the Mesquite Land & Cattle Company. And that's why I'm leaving."

"I'm glad to hear it." He tugged down his hat brim. "Real glad."

Victoria nodded, pinched her lips tight against the urge to lash out at him for being so hard-hearted and cruel. But it was not her place. She deserved every harsh word and every rebuke he cared to offer. In her vanity and pride, she had sinned against God and against man. This man, in particular. And now she must pay the price.

CHAPTER
Three

"I feel like a bull at sorting time," Jesse muttered as he strode down the boardwalk toward J. J. Dolan's store. After he told Victoria how glad he was she'd be leaving the ranch, they hadn't spoken another word. And he had meant what he said—so much so that the rest of the way into Lincoln he kept reminding himself of it. Glad. He was real glad to be shed of her. Troublesome gal.

Outside the Lincoln Hotel where Victoria intended to seek work, he had helped her down from the wagon and turned away without a fare-thee-well. But even now, he could feel the curve of the woman's trim waist against his hands. His palms tingled so he could almost swear he'd been burned. She had set her own hands on his shoulders, one on each side, and her slight weight as he lifted her to the street had sent a shiver straight down his spine. The sweet-soap scent of her skin and the glint of gold from her hair had swirled through him like a tornado—and he was still reeling.

Fretful as a bull in a roping chute, Jesse recalled their conversation. Victoria had told him on their journey: *"The things I cherished, I now no longer desire. And the things I thought unworthy, I see as most important."* So, which herd was he in?

What do you think of me, Vic? The question had hung so long on the tip of his tongue he could almost taste it.

Blast it all! He took off his hat as he stepped into Dolan's store. Slapping it down on the counter, he barked out, "Jesse Conroy here! I've come for my salt."

Jimmy Dolan himself emerged from the back room, a large ledger in his hands. Jesse had never much liked the slight, dark-haired man. Dolan started out as a clerk and was rumored to have had his fingers in all kinds of underhanded dealings on his rise to riches—rustling cattle from John Chisum's ranch, defrauding the United States government, threatening the life of a Fort Stanton captain, operating a monopoly, and conspiring to kill a rival. After the Lincoln County War, Dolan had taken over the murdered John Tunstall's store and built it into a thriving business. Jesse would rather not patronize the place, but he couldn't count on the other mercantiles in town, which came and went. If a man put in an order, he had to be sure it would be there when he needed it.

"Here for your salt, are you?" Dolan asked. His dark brown eyes and heavily waxed mustache gave him the look of a villain in one of the traveling dramas that sometimes passed through town. Behind Dolan, another figure emerged. William Worthing of White Oaks stepped into the light that streamed in through the store's long windows.

"I was just conversing with Mr. Worthing," Dolan said. "I believe you two gentlemen know each other."

Jesse tipped his head in acknowledgment. His opinion of

the gold-mine owner was even lower than his view of Dolan. Worthing was well-known in Lincoln County as a cutthroat businessman who had few friends and many enemies. His alliances usually left his comrades holding the short end of the stick. He had cheated his three original business partners out of their shares in the mine, and one had been found with a knife in his back. The crime was never solved.

"We've met," Jesse said. He had a bad feeling the sneaky twosome were up to some kind of mischief. "Worthing, I believe I saw you at church this past Easter."

"Indeed, you did. I had recently completed the construction of my new home, and I was taking a short vacation at the Lincoln Hotel. As I recall, you had just signed partnership papers with a coalition of Englishmen, and you had taken up residence at Emil Jennings's former spread. Some years ago, I called out there a few times. Nice place. Listen, Conroy, you must come up to White Oaks one of these days. The Jicarilla Mountains are lovely in winter."

Worthing smiled, a set of big white chompers shining out from under his heavy brown mustache. Ever the dandy, the mine owner wore a fine wool suit with matching jacket and trousers, a glossy red vest, and a big silky black scarf tied into a bow at his neck. He took a cigar case from his pocket, opened it, and offered Jesse a smoke.

"No thanks," Jesse said, holding up a hand. "A few years of that when I was a boy, and I found I could hardly smell the mountain air in the morning."

"Why, certainly." Worthing snapped the box shut and put it away. "A young up-and-comer like you is undoubtedly too busy to take time for the finer things of life anyhow."

"I believe we're near the same age, Bill." Jesse couldn't resist tossing out the nickname he'd heard the man despised.

He turned to Dolan. "I reckon my salt ought to be in, sir. I'll load that up and be on my way."

"Of course. It's in the storage room. I'll have one of my clerks drive your wagon around back and load it for you." Dolan clapped a hand on Jesse's shoulder. "Stay inside and keep yourself warm, my friend. Take a look around. We've added a lot of new merchandise this past month."

Jesse would have preferred to load the salt himself, just to make sure he was getting what he paid for. But in an effort toward goodwill, he stepped aside as Dolan headed out the door to fetch his clerk. Finding himself in front of the bolts of colorful fabric that lined one wall, he eyed them up and down in the hope that Worthing would skedaddle back to the hole he and Jimmy had slithered out of.

No such luck. The man approached and studied the fabrics himself for a moment. "I suppose you're looking to spruce up your place for the big Christmas dinner," Worthing commented. "New curtains?"

Jesse stared at the cloth, assessing. Such a thing as new curtains had never occurred to him. In fact, he never thought much about how the big house looked. And how had Worthing heard about the Christmas dinner? Jesse barely recalled telling Rosa to go ahead with her notion.

"Maybe I will hang some new curtains," he said. "Word sure gets around, doesn't it?"

"Indeed it does. I'm certain your new housekeeper will have her hand in planning the festivities."

"If you're referring to Emil Jennings's daughter, she no longer works for me."

"No?" Worthing smoothed down his mustache. "Well, I'm not surprised. I didn't imagine the arrangement would turn out well. She's not exactly the sort of woman who would enjoy that kind of work, is she?"

Jesse tugged a bolt of bright crimson satin down from the shelf and set it on the counter. He knew exactly what Worthing was insinuating. The mine owner considered him to be nothing more than a no-account cowboy who had stumbled onto a patch of good luck. To Worthing, he was far beneath the dignity of a refined lady like Victoria Jennings. Well, what did the man know about her? The uppity fellow might change his tune if he found out that less than a month ago she'd been eating pig slop.

"For what my opinion is worth," Worthing continued, "I admire you, Conroy. You certainly avenged your honor. After the way Miss Jennings spurned you, I wouldn't have been surprised to hear that you had slinked away never to be seen again. But no sir, you came back and jerked the rug right out from under her, didn't you? Took her father's land and cattle." He chuckled as he slapped Jesse on the back. "You're even living in her house now!"

"I'll take six yards of this red, Jimmy," Jesse spoke up as Dolan entered the store again. "And the same amount in green." He slid the bolts across the counter toward the shopkeeper. Turning to the other man, he spoke in a low voice. "Revenge is not my ambition, Worthing. I'm an honest fellow making my way the best I know how. As for Miss Jennings, I believe she spurned the two of us exactly the same."

"Indeed she did," Worthing replied. "But now that she finds herself in more humble circumstances, perhaps she'll see me in a different light."

"Maybe she will." Jesse met the man's steady gaze. "And maybe she won't."

"Your salt's all loaded," Dolan said. "And here's your fabric. Red and green. I suppose these will become decorations for the big Christmas dinner you're putting on. We're all looking forward to it."

"Well, sure," Jesse said, grabbing the packet of cloth goods wrapped in brown paper and tied with twine. He suddenly felt like a noose had been dropped around his neck. Christmas dinner? How on earth was he going to put on a feast for the whole town?"

"Yes, sir, this is going to be a holiday to remember," Dolan continued. "Lee Rudisille tells me he's getting the children ready to present their exercises at the schoolhouse on Christmas Eve. The next day, we'll come out to your place for the noonday meal. And that night everyone will go to the Saises' house for the traditional ball. I hear Pat Garrett and his wife are driving in for the festivities, and I know for a fact that Smith Lea has bought himself a bombazine cashmere suit—all of a kind. I ordered it for him from Santa Fe myself."

"How about that?" Jesse murmured, feeling the noose tighten. He ran a finger around his collar. The cool air outside would do him good. Dolan always stoked up his stove too hot.

"I suppose you'll be wanting your payroll, too," the merchant said. "I've got the money right here in the safe."

"That'll be fine." Jesse waited as Dolan headed into the back room where he kept the heavy iron safe. Most of the citizens of Lincoln County either kept their meager savings with Dolan, or they had rung up so much debt at his store that they owed him their earnings till kingdom come. Once, John Chisum had been president of the Lincoln County Bank, with his colleagues Alexander McSween and John Tunstall acting as vice president and cashier. But McSween and Tunstall had lost their lives in the war, and now Chisum was dead, too. Dolan, it appeared, was exactly where he'd always wanted to be.

"Here you go," he said, setting the large leather wallet on the counter. "I've added the salt to your account."

"Thank you, sir. Good day to you both." Jesse took the wallet and gave Worthing a tip of his hat as he left the store.

He could not have been happier to set foot on the boardwalk again. A certain heaviness oppressed him when he was forced to spend time with men like Dolan and Worthing. He had felt it in the presence of Emil Jennings as well. It was their sin, Jesse had decided. Brought up to be a churchgoing man, he had stepped forward to proclaim his faith in Christ and to be baptized in a cold Wyoming creek when he was just a little sprout. His mother had taught him that sin was a black and heavy weight on the heart, and Jesse could always sense its presence. He believed a man ought to do everything he could to keep Satan at bay—and that meant forbidding liquor, cards, and loose women on his property. It meant cultivating a generous spirit and goodwill to all men of like mind. It meant working hard and caring for the land and the creatures God put in one's trust. It meant doing exactly what Jesse Conroy was doing.

Feeling his spirits lift, he was startled to see Victoria Jennings hurrying down the boardwalk toward him. In her gray skirt and old brown coat, she was hardly the picture of purple-ruffled glory he once had passed on this very street. She waved her hand, as if eager to stop him.

"Mr. Conroy," she called. "Please, I must speak to you for a moment before you go!"

Her cheeks had blossomed a bright pink from her exercise, but her face remained pale and stark. Seeing her this way—in the full light of day—Jesse realized how much Victoria had changed. The hem of her skirt was peppered with burn holes from tending an open fire. Dark smudges marred the porcelain skin beneath her blue eyes. And she was thin. Too thin.

"Please, sir," she began as she stood before him. Breathing hard, she wove her gloved fingers into a gesture of prayer. "I beg you, Mr. Conroy, may I please have my pay for the two weeks I worked at the Lazy J—I mean the . . . the . . ."

Her eyes filled with tears.

"The Mesquite Land & Cattle Company," he filled in, for some reason suddenly feeling like a low-down skunk. "Sure you can have it. I'd forgotten what Abe told me this morning."

"I forgot, too, because you were so angry with me it was all I could think of. But now . . . now I can see that I'll . . ." She brushed a tear from under her eye. "Mrs. Ellis already employs two girls to clean and wash at the hotel, and the tailor has no need of a seamstress or beader. So I'll apply with Mr. Dolan. If he can't use me, then I—"

"Now, hold on there, Vic. Where's your handkerchief?"

She sniffled deeply, her head hanging so low it looked like it might fall right off her scrawny shoulders. "I don't have one."

"Well, I'll be jiggered." Jesse dug in his back pocket and tugged out the square of white cloth that Rosa had washed and ironed for him. Or had Victoria been the one to do that task? Handing it to her, he clenched his jaw and glanced through the windows of Dolan's store.

"You don't really want to go to work for Jimmy Dolan, do you?" he asked.

"Thank you, sir," she said, dabbing the hankie across her cheeks. "At this moment, I'd be happy just to have my pay, please."

Jesse opened the wallet and peeled off what he thought was fair. Then he added a dollar more, just because he was a Christian. As she folded the money and tucked it into the pocket of her coat, he suddenly thrust the packet of fabrics at her.

"You might as well stay at the ranch till Christmas," he blurted out. "Rosa talked me into hosting a dinner for the whole town, and she could use an extra cook, I guess. Here's some cloth I bought—red and green. You could sew up some curtains."

"Curtains?" She looked up at him, her blue eyes shining through the tears.

"Well, or tablecloths. Whatever you want." Disgusted with the whole confounded situation, Jesse took off his hat and raked his fingers through his hair. "I'm going over to Doc Wood's house to check on one of my men. Horse stepped on him the other day. Here—" he took out several more dollars—"go buy whatever you'll need to make the house look right. I think I saw some popcorn in there."

"Popcorn?"

"To make strings for the tree. Or . . . well . . ."

Unable to think of another thing to say to Victoria, Jesse stalked off down the boardwalk.

~

"Miss Victoria Jennings!" The gentleman who stepped through the door to the back room of J. J. Dolan's store gave her an expansive smile. "Welcome back to Lincoln County."

"Why, Mr. Worthing. This is a surprise. What brings you from White Oaks?"

Her heart hammering at the sight of the man, Victoria paused at the rack of ribbon spools she had been inspecting. Before leaving for Santa Fe, she had broken off their engagement. The planned marriage had been encouraged and abetted by her father. Victoria herself had not admired the mine owner, and she had heard rumors of his underhanded dealings. But he had turned her head with his flattery, and she had been easily wooed by his promises of a future filled with luxury and the social gatherings she craved. Of course, Worthing promised they would make their home at the Lazy J, and he would visit his gold mine only when necessary.

Then Victoria had spurned the gentleman with hardly an explanation. Yet the few words she did speak had enraged him. She was off to finishing school, she informed him, and their wedding plans must be canceled. Besides, if she were to marry anyone, she added heedlessly, she would much prefer Jesse Conroy, who at least knew how to kiss a girl.

"Mr. Dolan and I have been conducting a meeting today," Worthing now explained to Victoria in a genteel voice, as though her cruel words were completely forgotten. Stepping around the counter, he lifted her gloved hand and pecked it lightly. "We have been considering a business partnership. But I do indeed reside in White Oaks. I have a new home there—just completed, in fact. Wood construction, of course. None of this adobe for me. You must come up for a visit."

"Thank you, sir, but I'm busy at present." Ducking her head, she resumed comparing ribbons. Worthing would not be deterred. He stood beside her, one hand lightly resting on her back.

"I understand you seek employment, Miss Jennings," he offered in a low voice. "Perhaps I could assist you in finding a position."

"You're mistaken, sir," she replied. "I'm to continue in my place at the Mesquite ranch."

"But Mr. Conroy just said—"

"He reconsidered." She favored the man with a quick smile. "In fact, I'm purchasing ribbons to decorate the house for Christmas."

"Ah." Worthing glanced at Dolan, who was arranging stock inside one of his counters. "That is good news. Then you'll be staying in the area. Perhaps we shall see one another on occasion, Miss Jennings. I often drive down to Lincoln for church."

"Perhaps so." Victoria selected three ribbons—gold, red, and green—and lifted the spools from their rack. Her heart hammered with the dread of what she knew she must do. She had not endured the root cellar of Mrs. O'Neal's butcher shop in vain. God had spoken to her there, and Victoria was determined to obey Him no matter the cost to her own pride.

"Mr. Worthing," she said, turning to him and touching his sleeve with her fingertips. "On the occasion of our last encounter, I was more than rude to you. I was boorish, unladylike, and the most deplorable example of a Christian. I beg you, sir. Forgive my thoughtlessness."

"Why, Miss Jennings." His face suffused with pink as he clasped her hand in his own. "Of course I forgive you. You were hardly more than a child at the time, and I realized at once that you could not know your own mind on such matters. I see now how changed you are." Holding her hand to his lips, he kissed it again. "In manner and training, you are every bit the woman you were intended to be. Yet in circumstance, you are sadly fallen, and my own suffering on your behalf is great indeed."

"How kind you are, Mr. Worthing," she said, seeing a softer light in his gray eyes. "I hardly expected such gentility."

"Then you hardly know me." He pressed his lips to her hand again. "I am, madam, most alert to your predicament.

And I must assure you that I stand at the ready to do all in my power—"

With a loud bang, the wind blew the front door open as Jesse Conroy stepped into the store. "Miss Jennings, I'm—"

Catching sight of the two figures near the ribbon rack, he halted. His face darkened. Victoria jerked her hand from Mr. Worthing's grasp and stepped to the counter where Jimmy Dolan was taking inventory of the collars he had set up for sale.

"Six yards of each ribbon, please," she said quickly, laying the money out for him. "Five pounds of popcorn. Two buns and a half pound of cheese. One ream of writing paper. And a bottle of India ink."

In the uncomfortable silence of the store, Dolan counted out the change and wrapped Victoria's purchases. Unwilling even to look at William Worthing again, she fastened her attention on Jesse as she arranged her shawl over her head. "The bread and cheese are for lunch," she told him. "I imagine you're hungry, Mr. Conroy."

Without answering, he took the packets from her and turned to the door. But Worthing was determined to have the last word, and Victoria winced as he called her name.

"Miss Jennings, I shall write to you," he said. "And remember, if you have any need of my assistance—"

Victoria nodded to him and hurried through the door Jesse was holding open for her. Though she felt awkward in barely acknowledging Mr. Worthing's offer of help, she had no desire to encourage the man. He had been polite, but from their previous acquaintance, she knew better than to believe him free of ulterior motive. Practically forced to run to keep up with Jesse's long stride, she lifted her skirts and followed him around the side of the store to the wagon.

"Stinkin' polecat," he growled as he took Victoria's arm and helped her up. "That skunk is up to no good."

"If you mean Mr. Worthing, I must tell you he was most gracious to me. He accepted my apology immediately."

"Apology?" Jesse's green eyes narrowed on her as he walked around the wagon and climbed in. "Sorry you turned down his marriage offer, huh? Well, that figures."

He flicked the reins, and the wagon started with a jolt. Victoria had to grab the seat and hold on tightly as Jesse urged the horses at a clip far too fast for a wagon bearing a heavy load of salt.

"I apologized to him for my callous disregard for his feelings, same as I did you," she told him. "Only Mr. Worthing forgave me."

Jesse glanced at her out of the corner of his eye; then he pulled his hat low on his brow. "Hand me one of those buns, would you? I'm hungry."

Victoria pursed her lips to hold back a tart response. Instead, she took out one of the fluffy white rolls, broke off a chunk of cheese, and gave them to him. Then she pulled off a bite of cheese for herself. As she chewed, she pondered the character of the man who sat beside her. Jesse Conroy was handsome; no doubt about that. With his deep-set olive eyes, sandy brown hair, and broad shoulders, he cut as fine a figure as any cowboy on the range. He could play the guitar and sing, too. He understood how to work cattle better than anyone she'd ever known, and he hadn't met a horse he couldn't gentle. On top of all that, he had been smart enough to work his way into the position of co-owner and boss of one of the largest spreads in Lincoln County.

But spiteful? Oh my, the man could cut steel with his words. And one look from those eyes sent a stab of icy pain into Victoria's chest. Though his decision to hire her back had kept her off the streets, she had no doubt he hadn't done it out of kindness. He just didn't want Dolan to have anything that Jesse himself might find useful. And as for William Worthing, well—

"I reckon you better tell me your ideas about this Christmas shindig," Jesse spoke up. "If I'm going to do it, I want it done right. How many folks you think might come?"

Caught off guard by his softened tone, Victoria relaxed her shoulders. If they must make this long ride together, the least they could do was behave in a civil manner. Clearly Jesse had decided to focus on the business of planning the dinner.

"Last week's edition of the *Golden Era* reported a hundred and eighty families living in the Lincoln area," she told him. "That's about seven hundred people in all."

"Seven hundred!" he exclaimed. "Good gravy, gal, that's more than an army regiment."

"Don't worry." Without thinking, she reached over and laid her hand on his arm. "The survey counted all the children, you know."

"I guess we won't invite young'uns, though I'd prefer them to some of the adults I know. Seems like Christmas is more fun with children around. That's how I remember it, anyhow. When I was a boy, my mama always made a big celebration out of it. On Christmas Day, she was up before dawn cooking the turkey."

"You told me she made sugarplums, too. And before you went to sleep on Christmas Eve, you and your brothers and sisters hung socks by the fire."

He smiled. "When we got up in the morning, we'd find nuts and beef jerky in our stockings."

"Oranges, too, if I recall."

"Yep, and peppermint sticks."

"You could make yours last the whole day, but your brother always gobbled his down first thing."

"Then he'd come begging for some of mine," he continued with a chuckle. "But I wouldn't share. Nope. I'd go hide in the barn—cold and miserable, shivering like a plucked chicken—but at least I had my peppermint stick all to myself. I sure was a fool-headed little cuss in those days."

"Good thing you grew out of it," Victoria said, trying to suppress a grin.

He glanced at her, then shrugged. "And you? It was just you and your father every Christmas, right? You told me he was always too bushed from his party the night before to spend time with you."

"I ran to the Bacas' house," Victoria said, recalling those lonely Christmas mornings and the loving family who always welcomed her. "They took me with them to church, and then we ate posole for lunch. *Mamá* Rosa made a piñata every year, and we had a lot of fun whacking it with a stick until it broke open and the candy fell out." She sighed, basking in the happy memories. "Yesterday, *Papá* told me their sons and daughters are coming home for Christmas this year, along with all the grandchildren. Many of the families around here will want to spend the day together. They'll have their own celebrations planned, so they won't expect a dinner invitation from you."

Jesse shook his head. "Even so, Vic, that still leaves a passel of folks."

At the sound of the name he had always called her, Victoria realized he had slouched comfortably down in the seat, and she was leaning against his big shoulder. Her hand on his sleeve felt just right, as though her knitted wool glove belonged there atop the worn leather of his coat. In the waning sunlight, his hat formed a shadowy silhouette on the fabric of her skirt. How often they had sat together under the leafy limbs of a cottonwood tree, his head on her lap and her fingers stroking through his soft hair.

Beyond Rosa and Abe Baca, no one knew Victoria better than this man. She had told Jesse Conroy everything—her joys, her fears, her pain, her dreams. And he had done the same. Then came the Christmas night her father had discovered his daughter in a cowboy's arms. As if suddenly aware of Victoria for the first time, Emil Jennings had showered her with clothing, jewels, flattery, and all the attention she had craved from him for so many years. Succumbing to empty promises, she had tossed aside Jesse's love.

But the loss of love, home, family, and wealth had been God's gift, Victoria reminded herself. That loss had brought her to her knees in surrender. It had taken her into the arms of Christ Himself, with whom she had all she could ever truly need in this life. Recalling the vain sin that had led her down a reckless path, she drew away from Jesse and forced herself to remember her lowly position.

"The Christmas dinner will be manageable," she told him. "I bought paper and ink today, and I plan to write out invitations. We'll ask the two biggest ranchers, of course, Charles Fritz and Antonio Torres. All the shop owners in Lincoln must be made welcome, too. That would be the families of Ben Ellis, Judge Tomlinson, George Peppin, Jimmy Dolan—"

"Whoa, there. You sure we need to invite Dolan?"

"What a thing to ask!" she exclaimed. Crossing her arms, she faced him. "Mr. Conroy, aren't you a Christian?"

"Well, of course I am. You know that as well as anybody."

"I knew you once, but maybe I don't anymore. As Christians, we're not to be at enmity with men like Jimmy Dolan.

Or William Worthing, for that matter. We're to be examples of Christlike love and charity. 'Charity suffereth long, and is kind,' the apostle Paul told the Corinthians. Charity 'seeketh not her own, is not easily provoked, thinketh no evil.'"

"Yeah, well Charity never met J. J. Dolan and Bill Worthing. Everyone knows Worthing is a cheat. And I hold Dolan responsible for the war that tore this county apart. How am I supposed to feel anything good about those two?"

"Forgiveness," she said, "is not really a feeling so much as a choice."

"Forgive a couple of lying, cheating, land-and-money-grubbing scalawags—when they don't intend to change their ways? No, ma'am." He gave the reins another sharp flick, and Victoria had to grab the seat again. "Besides, who're you to be preaching me a sermon, Miss Victoria Jennings? Seems I recall Paul telling that same bunch of Corinthians that charity doesn't go around vaunting itself and getting all puffed up."

Again, the icy knife of Jesse's words plunged into Victoria's heart. Unable to hide from truth, she shrank into herself. "You're correct, of course," she admitted in a low voice. "I have no right to tell you anything. I showed you little Christian charity. My love for you was real and true, but it grew only as deep as my own shallow vanity and pride would allow. I did vaunt myself. I was puffed up. Truly, I was the worst . . ."

Unable to continue speaking as the realities of her own past assailed her, Victoria tugged her shawl across her mouth and looked away. *Oh, Lord, forgive me,* she prayed once again. *I know I deserve every harsh word from Jesse's mouth. His contempt for me is justified. You know I would make it up to him if I could. Please forgive my many failings and—*

"All right, you can invite Dolan," Jesse said. "And Worthing, too. Trouble is, the whole thing puts me in mind of that last Christmas I spent at the Lazy J. Not that the place didn't look fine. In fact, I don't recall much about how anything looked except . . . well, except you. You had on a blue dress."

Victoria searched her memory. "Oh, yes. I had ordered it from New York. It didn't fit right."

"No? I thought it looked mighty good on you."

"But the bustle, remember? It kept . . . well, it just—"

"Are you talking about that wire contraption under your dress? The thing that kept on swinging out to one side every time I do-si-doed you around the dance floor?" A deep chuckle emanated from his chest. "What's it called?"

"A bustle."

"Sounds about right. It sure was bustling all over the place that night."

Victoria muffled a giggle with her glove. "That afternoon, Rosa and I spent more than an hour trying to figure out how to put it on. I don't think we ever did get it right."

"Didn't matter. You looked sweet as molasses—" He bit off his words and nudged his hat back up on his brow. "Anyhow, the food tasted good, and the games were fine. Charades and horseshoes. But something wasn't right."

"Father was gambling."

"And drinking."

"He caught us on the porch." She blurted the words and then stiffened with shock at her indiscretion. Clearing her throat, she babbled on. "But I think it was the cards. We won't have cards this Christmas. Nor liquor. I'll do my best to make it go off without a hitch. I promise."

The wagon was rattling down the road toward the big house now, and Victoria drank in the purple and blue shadows that fell across the old porch where the dogs lay basking in the last of the sun's rays. How could she thank Jesse enough for allowing her to return to the only home she had ever known? She could endure all his bitterness and hurt and anger if he would only let her live here.

Christmas was less than four weeks away, and Victoria knew she must do all in her power to convince him that she was the meekest, mildest, most perfect housekeeper he could ever want. If not, he would toss her aside, just as she had done to him. And she would deserve every agony that came her way.

"You once made me a lot of promises you didn't keep," he said to her in a low voice as they approached the house. "I guess we'll see if eating pig slop did you any good."

Stricken at his harsh words, Victoria swung around, ready to retort that he was the cruelest man she had ever met! But at that moment Rosa Baca hurried out onto the porch with Abe right behind her.

"You came back!" the woman exclaimed, her arms spread in happiness. "Look at them, Abe! See, he brought her home. What did I tell you? I knew he would bring her. I knew he loved her too much to turn her out. Oh, *mija!* You have come back to us!"

Swallowing her tears and anger, Victoria jumped down from the wagon though it was still rolling. *Love her?* she thought as she dashed across the yard. Jesse hated her. The only true love she would ever know on this earth stood waiting for her on the porch. Hitching up her skirts, she took the steps two at a time and threw herself into Rosa's embrace.

CHAPTER
four

Jesse settled his hat on his head as he studied the snow-flakes drifting onto white mounds outside the window. He could hear Victoria in the kitchen singing a hymn. As she worked around the house all day, she hummed, sang little songs, chattered to the dogs—and it was about to drive him loco. Since agreeing to let her stay on at the ranch three weeks before, he had done his level best to keep the woman at a distance. Until today, it was clear she had decided to do the same thing.

By the time he descended the stairs each morning just after dawn, Victoria had lit a fire in the hearth, stoked the stove and cooked him a plate of eggs, biscuits, gravy, and ham, and then vanished again. He took his breakfast out of the warming oven and ate it alone at the table. Then he stopped by the door to pick up his satchel—already stocked with a sup-ply of bread, cheese, boiled eggs, baked potatoes, cookies, and other goodies that pleased him more than he cared to admit. He spent his day finding things to do to stay away from the house—mending fences, setting out salt, checking the herds, fetching supplies from Lincoln.

Returning home at dusk, Jesse sometimes saw Victoria hurrying along the road toward the Bacas' little adobe, her shawl wrapped tightly over her head to keep out the cold. Inside the big house, he always found the fire blazing, his supper hot, and his wash water warm. He never wanted for a thick bar of lye soap, a well-honed razor, clean shirts, mended britches, and polished boots.

Though it would have comforted him to believe most of the labor had been done by Rosa, he knew Victoria's hands had been at work. Two weeks ago, Abe's troubling cough had progressed into pneumonia, and Rosa stayed by his side night and day. Doc Woods had looked in on the man twice and believed he was recovering, but Jesse wouldn't hear of Abe coming out into the biting wind until he was healthy again.

So it was Victoria who swept and mopped, wiped away layers of dust that accumulated on shelves and bookcases, cleaned the stove, and scrubbed the saltillo tiles on the kitchen floor. She changed Jesse's sheets, fluffed his pillows, and made sure his lamp wicks were trimmed and their bowls filled with oil. Anything a man could want in a tidy and comfortable home, Jesse had. Even the dogs seemed happy.

Until this morning, when blinding snow made outdoor work difficult, Jesse and Victoria had steered clear of each other. Even on Sundays, when he took her and the Bacas into town to church, she sat on a back pew and averted her eyes each time he glanced in her direction.

Truth be told, he wasn't even sure the same ol' Vic had returned to the ranch. She seemed too meek. Too ready to dig into hard, unpleasant labor. Certainly too poorly dressed. And never out gallivanting across the ranch on a horse. But today—with her singing, talking to the dogs, sweet-talking the cats, and flitting from room to room—Jesse knew she hadn't changed a whit. Not the kind, honest, tender heart of the woman. In the way he had loved her the most, she was exactly the same.

He almost shouted hallelujah when one of the few cowhands still around on a late Saturday afternoon arrived at the house. Freck brought the bad news that two bulls had gotten into a skirmish, and it appeared one had broken a leg. The younger man dashed away again to see if he could round up help at the bunkhouse. Eager to escape the turbulent tide of emotion that had been raging through his chest all day, Jesse pulled on his boots and settled his hat on his head.

Drinking down a breath of courage, he strode into the kitchen to inform his housekeeper he'd be late for supper. At the sound of his boots, Victoria glanced up from a bowl of soft white dough into which she was about to plunge her fingers. Spotting Jesse inside the doorway, her blue eyes went wide, and her pink lips molded into a perfect O.

"Am I disturbing you, Mr. Conroy?" she asked. Brushing back a golden tendril, she dusted a smudge of flour across her temple. "I'll stop singing if you'd rather—"

"No, no, it's fine. I've always liked your singing . . . so, anyhow . . ."

Blast it all! Now why had he gone and said that? Shifting from one foot to the other, he berated himself for letting her know he had even heard her. If she had any idea that the sound of her voice took him back to those nights when they had sat together on the bunkhouse porch—

"I'm afraid I was a little loud," she spoke up. "Bread does that to me."

"Bread?"

"When I knead it. I suppose it's the smell and the way the dough oozes through my fingers. I just can't help singing."

Unable to contain a grin, he nodded. "You can sing all you want, Miss Jennings. Maybe that's how come your bread always tastes so good."

Beaming, she glanced over his shoulder. "Did Rosa come in? I thought I heard the door."

"It was Freck. There's a bull down with a broken leg over at the draw."

"Oh dear."

"Looks like we've got our Christmas dinner."

"I suppose so." She worked the dough as she spoke, her hands lifting and pushing as she kneaded. "God does that, doesn't He? Turns sorrows into blessings, I mean. I had hoped to serve turkey for the main course, but the boys only managed to shoot two. I guess the birds aren't around much this year. Rosa suggested roasting another *cabrito*, and Abe has been pressing for smoked ham. But it seems God had beef in mind. And that's a good thing, because I was beginning to get into a panic."

"Panic? You?"

She glanced over at him, eyes sparkling like water on a summer lake. "Christmas is only three days away, and the latest count for dinner is fifty-four. That's how many folks answered the invitations. It'll be people like the sheriff and the judge and the schoolmaster—so we want things to be just right. I've polished all the silver and set up the epergnes and sewed new tablecloths."

Wiping the dough off her fingers, she swung around and drew apart the double doors of the pantry. Jesse's mouth fell open at the sight of the gleaming utensils, heaps of ribbon tied into bows, stacks of red and green satin napkins and linens, and rows and rows of sparkling glassware.

"I put the raspberry cremes and fruited jellies in the storage room where they'll stay cool and fresh," Victoria went on, swirling away from the pantry and opening the door to yet another room Jesse had never even noticed. She turned to him, ticking off items on flour-covered fingers. "I've made mayonnaises, custards, and meringues. Those will keep. But I still have to prepare the scalloped oysters, two turkeys, six rabbit pies, roast chicken, at least one ham. And now beef!"

With a laugh, she threw up her hands and returned to her dough. "I never thought I'd be much good at cooking, you know. When I was growing up, the kitchen was always Rosa's domain. But I got a copy of Mrs. *Beeton's Book of Household Management* at the finishing school—"

Victoria stopped speaking and clamped her mouth shut. Blushing, she turned away and focused on her kneading. Jesse had to fight to keep from begging her to continue. He wanted to hear all about her raspberry cremes, rabbit pies, and even epergnes—whatever they were. He wanted Victoria to tell him everything that had happened to her at the finishing school in Santa Fe. He wanted to know all about her cooking endeavors—and he ached to tell her how much her meals pleased him. And the Christmas dinner she had been working for weeks to prepare? He would give anything to sit here in the kitchen with her and listen to what she was planning . . . just to listen to her sweet voice and watch her as she fluttered around like a golden butterfly.

"I'm keeping you from your work," she told him. "That poor bull must be suffering."

He gazed at her, longing to take her in his arms and erase all the pain between them. *Let it be good again the way it was*, he found himself praying silently. *Lord, please let us be together like we were. Nothing changed. No pain between us.*

"I guess I'll head out then," he said reluctantly. "Maybe you could tell me more of your plans when I get back."

She dipped her head in acknowledgment as he turned to go. "Oh, Mr. Conroy," she called. "One more thing I must tell you about the dinner. William Worthing has accepted the invitation."

"I figured he would. Life can't all be sugarplums."

She smiled for a moment; then her face sobered. "His letter of acceptance included a message for me. Mr. Worthing has asked me to marry him again. Not marry him again, because I never did marry . . . what I mean is, he asked me again—"

"I know what you mean," Jesse barked out, unable to contain his irritation. "He's after the best of everything, just like always. He's got his gold mine and his fancy new house. And now he wants you. Well, that's fine with me, because I'm doing good just the way I am. I don't need all that."

The blue eyes darkened. "No? But aren't you after the best of everything, too? You got your cattle, and now this land and the house. How are you any different from William Worthing, Jesse? Can you tell me that?"

His heart thumping, he took two steps forward and jabbed his forefinger at her. "Because I'm an honest man, that's how. I don't cheat my partners. I never stabbed anybody in the back. I care about my land and the people who work my cattle. What I do is for honor and respect—not for making money by stepping on people."

"I know that," she said, squaring her shoulders. "And I'm proud of you for it."

He felt like he'd been socked in the gut. "Proud? . . . You are?"

"Of course I am. I knew that's the kind of man you were

the minute I met you. You were different from my father and the scalawags who came around the Lazy J to play cards and drink whiskey till all hours. You'd been brought up right, and your life showed it." Now she stepped toward him, her own finger pointing in accusation. "But there's a hard, cold place inside you, Jesse Conroy. It's filled with a tangle of bitter vines, and one day they're going to twist around your heart and choke out every good and noble thing that makes you such a fine man."

He grimaced at the pain her words inflicted. "Don't accuse me of things you know nothing about, Vic. If there's a hardness to me, you're the one who caused it. You with your fancy curls and purple ruffles and glittering jewelry."

"That's not who I am anymore."

"Oh, really? How come you came back here, then? Was it just to work and be a servant like you claim? Or are you out to get some of your own back? You've already got the Bacas fawning all over you, roasting the fattest *cabrito* in the flock, and throwing you a big shindig. You got all the men cheering you on, so happy to have Emil Jennings's daughter home again. And what's next? Did you think you could talk me into marrying you? Put you back in your old place as head of the house?"

With a gasp, she stepped back, her eyes filling with sudden tears. "Marry you? You? The coldest, cruelest man in Lincoln County? I came here because I needed work. God allowed me to dig myself a deep hole, Jesse. Every shovelful of it was vanity and pride—yes, and purple ruffles and jewels, too. Those things led me straight down to a place where I had nothing left at all. Nothing but my faith in Jesus Christ. He's all I had when I came back—the faith and hope that He gave me."

She picked up the corner of her apron and blotted her cheek. "I didn't know you were here," she went on, the confidence in her voice a contrast to the tears that rolled from her eyes. "And when I found out how you felt about me, I tried to leave. But you asked me to stay on. You gave me work, which was all I'd asked of you or ever hoped for. Because of that, I thought perhaps you had softened some. I thought maybe you were learning to forgive me. Not because I need it—because *you* do, Jesse. Now I see I was wrong. You have cultivated your little patch of bitter vines, and they're choking every last bit of tenderness out of your heart. And I'm sorry for you, Jesse. Truly, I am."

Turning away, she lifted a shawl from its hook. "Excuse me, sir. I have to fetch some firewood. I've let the oven go cold."

Jesse stared after her as she hurried out the back door. He crossed his arms and gritted his jaw, wishing he could wipe the sight of her tears and the ring of her accusations from his mind. Tugging his hat low on his brow, he headed to the front door, whistling for the dogs to follow. Well, anyhow. He had to go see to that bull.

~

Victoria took the fragrant loaves out of the oven and set them on the kitchen worktable. As angry as she was at Jesse, she knew he would come in cold and hungry. And when he stepped through the door, she intended to hand him a cup of hot coffee. She would set to work cutting, grinding, and storing the fresh beef, knowing that a thick pork steak, a bowl of baked beans, and a loaf of warm bread waited for her employer.

And here he came now, she thought as the thud of heavy footsteps sounded on the front porch. She grabbed a towel to protect her hand as she poured out a cup of coffee. A liberal dollop of warm cream and three spoonfuls of sugar would help it settle into his empty stomach just right. Carrying the mug to the front door, she prayed mightily that her attitude would be one of kindness and humility. She had done enough preaching at the poor man for one lifetime.

"Welcome home, sir," she said, drawing open the door.

But instead of Jesse, two strangers stood outside. Both gentlemen were clad in high-topped beaver hats, thick black coats that fell to their boots, and generous wool scarves wrapped up to their walrus mustaches.

"Good evening, madam," the taller one said, doffing his hat and sending a shower of snowflakes into the mug of hot coffee in Victoria's hand. "We have come to speak to Mr. Jesse Conroy."

Before too much hard-won heat could escape the house, she stepped back and invited the men inside. "Mr. Conroy has gone to see about an injured bull, sir. I expect him back momentarily. May I take your coats and hats? And won't you please sit down?"

As they unwrapped themselves, the taller one gave her a bow. "I am James Wilson, madam, and this is Henry Richards. We have traveled from London for the express purpose of speaking with Mr. Conroy. We are his partners in the Mesquite Land & Cattle Company."

"Oh, my goodness! Mr. Conroy didn't tell me—"

"He did not expect us."

"Certainly not." Stunned and uneasy at the unannounced arrival of such important guests, Victoria gave them the best curtsy she could manage. "I am Victoria Jennings, sir. The housekeeper. May I offer you some coffee? I'll fetch another mug, and—"

"Indeed, madam, coffee is all well and good," Mr. Wilson cut in, "but really we must see Mr. Conroy. It is a matter of great import."

"Yes, can you please send someone to fetch him at once?" Mr. Richards asked. "We have come an extreme distance at the most difficult time of year, leaving our families and business—"

"Fearing the worst, as you can imagine," Mr. Wilson continued. "For the letter we received left us with only the most dire imaginings."

"Dire imaginings?" Victoria shook her head. "What can you mean?"

"Why, that the ranch is in disrepair, that the cattle brought very little on the market, that few of the bills have been paid—in fact, that Mr. Conroy has mismanaged the whole operation straight into arrears."

"But that's impossible!" she exclaimed. "Everything here is fine."

"How could you possibly have such information, madam?" Mr. Wilson asked. "I intend no insult, but you are merely a housekeeper. Your employer would hardly make you privy to the details of his business dealings. No, indeed, he would do all in his power to keep the unhappy status of the accounts a secret for as long as possible."

Mr. Richards nodded. "Madam, please see that Mr. Conroy is summoned immediately, for we have come to relieve him of his position as manager. We mean to sell the Mesquite Land & Cattle Company."

"Sell the ranch?"

Victoria stared at the two men. How could this be possible? Everything she had seen indicated just the opposite of what these men were saying. The cattle appeared healthy.

The boys talked about the trail ride to market as though all had gone well. Abe Baca had mentioned nothing about debt or failure to pay bills. The ranch was in arrears? Impossible!

"There's no one here to send for Mr. Conroy," she told the men. "I'll go after him myself. Excuse me, please."

Grabbing her skirts, she dashed up the stairs and flew into her old bedroom. Forbidding herself to grow either nostalgic or repentant over memories the room evoked, she tore open her armoire and pulled out her riding gear. Her heart thudding, she peeled off her bodice and skirt and tugged on the faded dungarees, soft flannel shirt, and heavy old leather coat that once had been her primary wardrobe. She stepped into her boots and yanked them on; then she lifted the big felt hat from its hook and stuffed it on her head.

Bounding down the stairs, she called out to the men, "Jesse's over at the draw. I'll have him back in half an hour!"

Vaguely aware that the Englishmen were gaping at her, she grabbed her scarf and wrapped it around her neck up to her nose as she dashed out of the house and across the yard. Should she run up to the little adobe and tell Abe what was happening? No, he'd insist on going out after Jesse himself, and that wouldn't be good for his health on such a cold night. Freck would have called out all the cowboys still at the bunkhouse, so the place would be abandoned. The only option was to ride to the draw by herself.

Though it had been three years since she'd sat in a saddle, the familiar smell in the barn welcomed Victoria like a breath of perfume. Several of her father's horses remained at the ranch, and she chose Apache, a steady gelding she had ridden many times before. It took her no time to saddle up 'Pach, who seemed as eager as she to be out in the crisp night air.

As she mounted and guided the horse out of the barn, Victoria noted that the snowfall was diminishing and a bright silver moon had emerged through the clouds. Setting Apache off at a canter, she rode down the long drive and then urged the horse into a gallop.

Coyotes howled in the distance, no doubt signaling one another the news of the fresh kill. They soon would be skulking around in hopes of scavenging the offal, though Jesse would hardly leave anything that might attract predators so near his valuable bulls.

The eerie yips of coyotes always unsettled Victoria, and she hunched low in the saddle as the horse followed a familiar trail. She knew the creatures worked in packs, cutting off a newborn or injured animal and sometimes taking a favorite cow dog. Tonight, their cries echoed across the snowy expanse, through the bare cottonwood limbs, and over the stunted mesquite and piñon scrub.

"This way, 'Pach," Victoria murmured, heading the gelding across a field toward the draw. "Let's fetch Jesse. C'mon, boy."

The sure-footed horse raced across the snow, hooves pounding like a muffled drumbeat. Victoria's nostrils iced up, her cheeks burned, and her eyes stung, but she hadn't felt so alive in ages.

Those men couldn't sell the ranch out from under Jesse, could they? He was a partner, fair and square. Surely he would have a say in what happened.

Could it be true that Jesse had mismanaged the place? Surely not. There must be some mistake.

The thought of Jesse losing the ranch—the goal he had worked so hard to attain—filled Victoria with sorrow. Though he had been hard-hearted to her, Jesse deserved this land. She had meant what she said about him. The man did make her proud. Everything about him was right and good, and even if he never saw fit to forgive her, she wanted him to keep the old Lazy J.

Spotting a group of men in the distance at last, she could see that they were gathered around the fallen bull. Lanterns hung from tree limbs to guide Jesse, Freck, and one other fellow as they worked. Nearby, a wagon stood half loaded with the fresh meat.

As she rode toward the draw, Victoria waved her arm and gave a whistle. "Jesse! Jesse!"

He looked up in her direction. Straightening, he took off his hat and wiped his brow with the back of his hand.

"Jesse!" she called again.

At that moment, a pack of coyotes rushed out of the brush onto the path that led to the draw. Teeth bared, they circled the old gelding. Apache planted his hooves in the snow and tossed his head.

"Get on!" she shouted at the coyotes, ripping off her hat and swishing them back. "Get out of here, you varmints!"

But they were hungry and must have realized that Jesse was leaving nothing of the bull for them to scavenge. Frenzied, one of them darted forward and snapped at Apache's hoof. The horse gave a squeal of pain and reared into the air. Victoria hung on for all she was worth, but 'Pach bolted and kicked across the ground in a panic as the coyotes circled. When a second varmint sank its teeth into a tender tendon, the gelding leaped up, arched his back, and sent his rider sailing.

Victoria landed with a thud that knocked the breath out of her lungs and flattened her in the snow. A nearby shotgun blast shattered the night, and the coyotes took off, vanishing into the brush without a trace. In pain, Victoria turned her head to see Apache trotting around in circles, shaking his head and snorting. And then three cowboys appeared in her sight, all staring down with puzzled expressions on their faces.

"Who is it?" Freck asked. "I ain't never seen him afore."

"Don't look like nobody we know," said Stump, one of the shortest of the cowhands.

"It's me," she coughed out. "Vic."

"Vic!" Jesse reached a hand out toward her. "Good gravy, gal! What're you doing out here?"

"The Englishmen," she said. "They're here."

"Wilson and Richards? Here?" He scowled, then turned to the other men. "Freck, Stump, go catch that fool horse. And don't let those coyotes get anywhere near our Christmas dinner."

"Yes, boss." Freck shook his head as he gave the fallen woman a last glance. "I'da never thought it was you, Miss Victoria."

"You look plumb different in them britches," Stump confirmed.

Victoria tried to edge up onto her elbows, but she winced as a sharp pain drove through her side. "Oh, no. I may have broken a rib."

Kneeling down beside her, Jesse scooped her up into his arms. "Don't even try to move, Vic," he said, cradling her in his lap. "Just be still a minute. Catch your breath."

She looked up at him, struggling against the tide of memory his face brought back. He had held her just so on their first encounter. She had stared into his green eyes, and he had spoken such kind words.

"Aw, Vic," he said now, his voice low. "You look just like you did the day we met."

Reaching up, she laid her hand on his cheek. "You're the same, too, Jesse."

"First time I laid eyes on you, your hair was splayed across the ground like a golden halo. From that minute on, you were my angel. And now here you are again, only sprawled out in the snow."

"Looking more like a big ol' gingerbread cookie, I reckon."

He chuckled, but in a moment his face sobered. "Vic, what happened to us? Back then, I loved you so much."

"I loved you, too, Jesse. I loved you with all my heart—but it was a small, selfish heart. A proud, silly heart. Too foolish to understand what a treasure true love can be."

His eyes deepened as he bent near her. "You're different now," he murmured, his lips moving near her cheek. "But you're still the same sweet girl."

"Oh, Jesse." She sighed as his mouth covered hers in a warm, tender kiss that sent tendrils of pleasure through her. She lifted her arms and slid them around his neck, drawing him closer. And he kissed her again, this time longer and with greater urgency, as though he could not get enough. Shivering with delight, she welcomed the kiss, drifting in the sheer joy of his presence, reveling in the pressure of his mouth against hers and the rough graze of his cheek—

"Okay, boss," Freck's voice rang out. "I guess that's— woops."

Victoria froze as Jesse faced the cowboy who was ogling the pair in the snow. Freck shrugged. "Shucks, boss, I didn't aim to cut into—"

"If you don't get back to cutting up that bull," Jesse snarled at him, "I'm going to nail your hide to the barn door."

"Yessir." Freck scuttled away as if a skunk were after him.

Jesse looked down at Victoria. "Listen, Vic, I didn't intend to—"

"Oh, my goodness, the Englishmen!" She stiffened and

rolled herself off his lap despite the stabbing pain in her left side. "You've got to get to the house, pronto! Those two fellows came all the way from England to see you. They think you've run the ranch into debt."

"Now, where'd they get a blame fool idea like that?"

"I don't know, but they told me they're planning to sell the ranch."

"Sell it?" He helped her to her feet as he stood. "Vic, I'd better go see what's going on, but—"

"But nothing, Jesse. Just go! Please!" She gave him a push. "I'll help the boys finish up the bull. I've done it a hundred times."

"Are you feeling all right?"

"Sure," she said. "Go on, now. Don't let them sell this place out from under you, Jesse. It's your dream."

"Aw, Vic." He reached out and touched her chin.

"Get out of here, Jesse. I mean it."

She watched as he tugged his hat down low and headed for his horse. As he climbed into the saddle and rode off up the trail, Victoria touched her fingertips to her lips. The kiss had been every bit as wonderful as the first. And better.

"Hey there, Miss Vic," Stump said as she approached the two cowboys. "You okay? That ol' hoss arched his back like a mule in a hailstorm."

She smiled. "The coyotes spooked him."

Freck snorted out a laugh. "You got throwed so high I was looking to see if St. Peter had whittled his initials in your boot soles."

"Seems I heard you've been bucked off once or twice yourself, Freck," she retorted.

"Yeah, but I never puckered up to the boss." He snickered.

"You're gonna have the poor fellow hog-tied afore he knows what hit him."

Victoria set her hands on her hips. "You can sing all right, Freck, but you're about as chuckleheaded as a prairie dog. Now let's get to work and finish this up. I don't know about you boys, but I'm hungry."

Both men were chortling as she picked up a knife and began to carve.

CHAPTER

five

When Victoria arrived back at the big house later that evening, Jesse and the two Englishmen were long gone. Abe Baca told her they'd headed out with no word as to where they were going or when they'd be back. "It's business," was all Jesse would say.

Rosa decided they ought to go ahead and prepare for the Christmas dinner, even if Jesse didn't get home in time to join his guests. Telegraph lines had not yet reached as far into the New Mexico Territory as Lincoln, and there was no way to let people know if the event was canceled. Besides, maybe the boss would return by noon on Christmas Day, Rosa said hopefully. Agreeing, Victoria tightened her corset against the pain in her rib—no doubt it was cracked, Abe declared—and she went to work. As the Baca children and grandchildren began to arrive, everyone joined in preparations for the big celebration.

The morning before Christmas, Victoria directed the men as they set up plank tables around the large main room. Then she and the women laid out bright red and green table linens, erected epergnes filled with pinecones, juniper branches, holly, and apples, and placed dishes and silverware. They were just tying bows on each chair when the Baca brothers hauled in a large pine tree they had chopped down in the nearby Capitan Mountains. The imposing tree all but demanded that everyone drop whatever they were doing and rush to string popcorn, clip on candles, and drape ribbons.

In the kitchen and around the large *horno* outside, the Baca women bustled about baking breads, roasting turkeys, seasoning ham, and cooking rabbit pies. With much argument and haranguing, they attempted to follow Victoria's recipe for beef á la mode—which involved bacon, vinegar, savory herbs, carrots, and any number of other items they never would have included had not *Mrs. Beeton's Book of Household Management* insisted upon it.

Though the meat smelled heavenly as it cooked, Rosa declared Christmas was just not right without posole. This sent all the women into a frenzy of soaking hominy, stewing pork, and peeling chiles in preparation for the piquant soup. And who could eat posole without tortillas? *Biscochitos* must follow, of course, which meant stirring up bowls full of dough for the small, anise-flavored cookies.

By the time Victoria dropped into bed on Christmas Eve, she was aching and so weary she could hardly hold her eyes open. And yet she discovered she could not sleep. What had become of Jesse? Were he and the Englishmen negotiating the sale of the ranch even now? Would he vanish, as he had not long after she rejected him—heading for Texas or Wyoming? Was it possible that a new owner would ride up to the house tomorrow and expect everyone to welcome him with open arms?

Near dawn on Christmas morning, Victoria fell into a fretful sleep and awoke only when Rosa shook her shoulder. Tired and disoriented, she hurried downstairs to join the Bacas on their way to church. The service passed in a blur, and only as they returned to the ranch at midmorning did Victoria realize the full impact of the monumental task that awaited her the next few hours. As the women flew into the kitchen to begin final meal preparations, she took a moment to lean against the window, lift the curtains aside, and peer at the barn to see if Jesse had returned.

"He's not home yet," Abe said, laying a hand on her shoulder. The dear man had recovered from his bout of pneumonia, for which Victoria endlessly thanked God. Though he remained weak, Abe was gaining strength by the day.

"He will come back, *mija*. You'll see."

Victoria turned and wrapped her arms around his broad chest. "*Papá*, I know the Bible teaches us to worry about nothing. But I can't help it. What if Jesse loses the ranch? What if I never see him again?"

"You love him, *si*? I knew it. He's a good man. He'll make you a fine husband."

"How can you even think such a thing, *Papá*? You know how he feels about me."

"I know he was kissing you two nights ago!" He laughed at her surprised expression. "News travels fast even without a telegraph wire, eh?"

"What are you two doing standing around like this?" Rosa flapped her apron at them. "Abe, those lazy sons of yours need to bring in more firewood. And Vic, you go upstairs right now and put on a nice dress. You can't serve the honchos of Lincoln in that old skirt!"

Unable to argue with the truth, Victoria raced up the

stairs. Peppered with burn holes and discolored by stains, the skirt deserved to be thrown in the rag pile. But what else to wear? In her old room, she opened the wardrobe and studied the gowns hanging inside. The pale yellow muslin was far too lightweight and summery. The beautiful green wool ensemble had been eaten to shreds by moths. The polka dots were too silly. The pink chiffon looked like a birthday cake. What had she been thinking when she bought such frippery?

That left only the purple ruffled gown she had been wearing when she snubbed Jesse on the street in Lincoln. Victoria took it down from the wardrobe and laid it across the bed. The bodice had a lovely shape with a modest neckline and long, slim sleeves. The skirt draped perfectly. But there were too many flounces. Ruffles by the hundred! If she removed them, though, the gown would be perfect. Everyone was busy downstairs, and the guests would not arrive for an hour.

Victoria sprang to her dresser and took out a small pair of sewing scissors. Sitting cross-legged on the bed, she began to snip. The ruffles slithered away like long purple snakes, sliding across the bed and down onto the floor as she loosened them from their hold on the skirt.

What would Jesse think if he saw her in this gown again? Would he see her as that same proud little twit who had strolled past him with her nose in the air? But why should she even worry what Jesse would think? He might never come back to the ranch again!

Oh, why had she ever spurned him in the first place? He was a fine man, so handsome and bold. What had made her such a fool? How could she have discarded Jesse's true, deep love at the mere suggestion of her father—a man who had shown her precious little affection of his own? Her eyes filling with tears, Victoria cut and tugged at the offending flounces.

She had craved Emil Jennings's approval, she realized, but she never earned it. Neither all the purple ruffles in the world nor all the gold in William Worthing's mine would have been enough to win what her father didn't have to give. But in trying to gain his love, she had lost Jesse's. Why, oh why had she let him go?

Dear God, forgive me . . . forgive me. . . . As had been her custom in the root cellar of Mrs. O'Neal's butcher shop, Victoria bent over and began to pray. Forehead pressed into the soft bedspread, she wept out her agony. *Please forgive me, Lord! I beg You—*

"Hey, Vic, where are you? Everyone is coming in, and Rosa is nearly going *loca!*" Abe Baca's voice filled the room as he stepped through the door. "Victoria? What's wrong, *mijita?*"

Sniffling, she sat up and faced the man who had truly been a father to her. "Oh, *Papá,* I'm so miserable."

"Miserable? No, you should be happy today. Look, you have friends and family downstairs. You made a beautiful Christmas dinner. Everything you touch is like . . . like perfect, Vic. Why do you sit up here and cry?"

"Oh, *Papá,* I was such a fool!"

"This again?" He stepped to the bed and sat down near her. "You listen to me, Vic. Don't think Rosa and me don't know how you cry at night. We hear you. We listen to the sound of your weeping night after night, and now it's time you listen to your *Papá. Bastante!* Enough!"

"But you don't understand—"

"Yes, I do understand. I know you were a little *boba*—too silly in the head to see the good man right in front of your eyes. You turned him away, *si?* That was *estúpido.* Big mistake, and then you skipped over to Senor Worthing and said you would marry him. Another craziness. Ah-huh, you did a lot of them. Next, you went off to Santa Fe, and you didn't come home to see Rosa and me but only three times. What was that? *Estúpido!* You got proud and thought you were so pretty, and the handsome caballeros came to court you. And then *pfft*, all of it went away. You learned you had nothing, and that pretty face could feed you only pig food. *Si? Am I right?"*

Victoria nodded miserably. "You're right, *Papá*. Everything you say is true."

"So, now here you go crying night after night about how bad you were. Didn't you ask God to forgive you for that sin of your past?"

"I did, *Papá*, but—"

"And you don't think He forgave you?"

"Yes, but—"

"*Pero* nothing! When God forgives, that's it. Finished. *No más*. He puts it away from Him as far as the east from the west. It's gone, *mija*. So why you keep asking Him to forgive you? You think He's *estúpido*, too? You think He forgot that He forgave you? God doesn't forget nothing! It's you who won't forgive yourself."

"I don't know how."

"Put it away, *mija*. God does not hold you guilty for something He forgave. You know who puts that sin back in your face every day and every night? *El diablo*. That's right. Satan cannot let you forget what a *boba* you were. He keeps you sad and crying and beating yourself like a *penitente* who thinks he has to suffer for sins already nailed to the cross with Jesus. Don't give this victory to *el diablo*, Vic. You're a strong, smart girl. You can butcher a bull and sew Christmas tablecloths. You can do those hard things, and now you can forgive yourself."

As Abe spoke, Victoria felt a peace slide through her bones like warm honey. It wasn't God who had been convicting her of sin over and over. He had forgiven her the moment she first asked Him. Satan was the enemy who threw her past at her every time she tried to rest.

"*Papá*," she sighed, hugging him tightly. "You're right. You're right, *Papá*."

"Of course I am." Setting her away, he picked up a handful of the silky purple gown. "I think there's somebody downstairs gonna like to see you in this dress. You better hurry up, Vic."

"Is Jesse home? Did he sell the ranch?"

"He's here, but I don't know what happened. He just comes in with the Englishmen and starts greeting the guests. He don't smile too much, you know, so maybe it's true. Maybe they sold the place. But he doesn't talk to me about it yet." He shrugged as he stood. "You come down, Vic. Maybe you can get him to tell you."

She nodded. "I'll be there in a moment."

Though the peace of God's undeserved grace filled her heart, Victoria snipped away the last ruffle with trembling fingers. Had Jesse been forced to sell the ranch? More important to her, could he ever find it in his own heart to forgive her for all the hurt she had caused him?

And how on earth would he react when he learned what she was planning to do?

~

Jesse nearly choked on a mouthful of hot apple cider as a vision in glowing lavender appeared on the landing and began to descend the staircase. Good gravy, what a woman! Victoria had coiled her long hair on top of her head like a shining gold crown. Rosy cheeks and bright blue eyes were all the jewels she needed to glitter like a queen. Her long, bare neck was set off by the snug purple bodice that fit all her curves exactly the way a man liked—soft and feminine, but not the least bit tawdry. And that skirt. Where had she found fabric like that in Lincoln? Jesse didn't remember seeing anything so nice in J. J. Dolan's store.

Dolan himself was staring slack-jawed as Victoria stepped into the sea of guests who were milling about looking for their assigned seats. As the men turned to gawk at the young lady and their wives smiled at her in admiration, Jesse had a mind to march right across the room, scoop Vic up in his arms, and order Justice Wilson to marry them double-quick. It was all he could do to make himself listen to Mrs. Ellis gabbing on and on about the new addition to the Lincoln Hotel.

"Soon as we get the railroad tracks laid," she was saying, "we'll have guests aplenty at the hotel."

"I'm sure you're right, ma'am." His gaze followed Victoria as she hurried toward the kitchen. "Well, if you'll excuse me—"

"I see you've spotted your lovely employee," a voice said at his shoulder. "Seems every eye in the room is on Miss Jennings today."

Jesse turned to find William Worthing blocking his path to the kitchen. "Happy Christmas to you, sir," Jesse said, determined to behave like a Christian gentleman ought. "I trust you had a good trip down from White Oaks."

"Indeed, I did." The mine owner grinned, revealing his impressive set of big white teeth. "Things couldn't have gone better, really. I considered staying home in order to continue preparing for the wedding, but I thought I'd better drive on down and make sure you're treating my little fiancée right."

Jesse went rigid. "Fiancée?"

"Why, Miss Jennings and I are to marry, of course. Surely she told you."

Jesse tried to keep breathing. For the past three days, all he'd been able to think about was that night in the snow and the way Vic had felt in his arms. How she had melted into his kiss. How her arms had slid around his neck. How her lips had pressed so warmly against his own.

"She . . . she told me that you had asked for her hand," Jesse acknowledged.

Worthing chuckled. "You seem surprised Miss Jennings might agree to such an arrangement."

"Well, I guess I am." Thinking hard, Jesse ran through the last conversation he'd had with Victoria. She had mentioned Worthing's offer. But almost in the same breath, she said how proud of Jesse she was. On the other hand, she'd quickly gone on to tell Jesse how hard and bitter she considered him. How unforgiving. And when he had accused her of plotting to take back her position at the ranch by marrying him, she had denied it at once, labeling him the coldest, cruelest man in Lincoln County.

"You placed the poor creature in a most untenable position, Conroy," Worthing said. "You said you'd keep her employed only until Christmas. You told her you needed a cook, that's all."

"How—how did you hear about that?"

"She wrote to me, of course. Told me everything. That you require her to live in the home of another poor family, that you barely speak to her, that you never even pay her."

"Well, but I . . ."

It was true. Jesse hadn't thought to add Victoria's name to the others on his payroll list, and when he doled out the cowboys' money at the end of each week, she never even crossed his mind. Vic had come to seem like she just belonged there at the house. Like part of his family.

"She's a lovely young woman," Worthing said. "I'm eager for the day she becomes my wife. And now if you'll excuse me, I notice that Mr. Dolan has formed an acquaintance with your English guests. Perhaps he'll introduce me to them."

Dumbfounded, Jesse couldn't make himself move as the former sheriff of Lincoln, Pat Garrett, and his wife descended on him. Garrett had shot down Billy "the Kid" Antrim four years earlier, his major claim to fame. A year afterward, he published a book titled *The Authentic Life of Billy the Kid, the Noted Desperado of the Southwest, Whose Deeds of Daring and Blood Made His Name a Terror in New Mexico, Arizona, & Northern Mexico, a Faithful and Interesting Narrative by Pat F. Garrett, Sheriff of Lincoln Co., N.M., by Whom He Was Finally Hunted Down & Captured by Killing Him.* To Jesse's chagrin, the sheriff and his wife regularly recounted his exploits with about as much wordiness as his book's title.

They had just begun updating Jesse on the book's sales when a ringing bell signaled that the meal was to begin. Abe Baca, already at his place at the table, motioned Jesse to join him. Departing the Garretts with a polite word, Jesse stepped to his seat. He would have prayed over the meal, but he had more urgent things to discuss with God, so he asked the pastor of Lincoln's church to offer the blessing.

As the minister prayed, Jesse clutched the back of his chair and squeezed it until he heard the wood crack. *Lord, please don't let Vic marry that snake!* he prayed. *Where have I gone wrong? What have I done to deserve this? I'll do anything You ask me, God; just please show Vic how much I love her. Please—*

"Amen," everyone said in unison.

Jesse had no choice but to sit down and listen as John Poe, the current sheriff of Lincoln, and James Brent, the man who would take Poe's place in January, regaled him with the latest news from town. If Jesse had felt glum when he walked in the door and saw the enormous crowd of people inside his house, he felt downright miserable now.

But he had no choice except to watch as Victoria joined the Baca daughters in toting one delicacy after another from the kitchen. There she went in her pretty dress—serving J. J. Dolan and her scalawag future husband, William Worthing. Look how that polecat grinned at her! Like a skunk eating cabbage.

Jesse barely tasted the dishes set before him. How could he? All he wanted was a moment alone with Vic. How could she have agreed to marry Worthing? The man was a known cheat. A liar. Possibly a murderer. Had Victoria reverted to her old ways—putting the chance for money and fine possessions above common sense and Christian decency? That must be it. *Lord, have mercy!*

Feeling like a couple of bears were rassling in his stomach, Jesse watched her move back and forth. She didn't look any different than she had the night he held her and kissed her. Fancier, maybe, but as sweet as molasses. She smiled and chatted with people. Helped old Mrs. Wilson with her napkin. Relit a candle for the Ellises. Patted the minister on his back. Once in a while she glanced at Jesse, turned red as a beet, and rushed away again. What did that mean? And what was he supposed to do about it? Should he challenge Worthing to a duel? Should he throw Vic over his shoulder and tote her off to Texas and *make* her marry him instead of Worthing? Should he—

"Excuse me, everyone!" Victoria's high, clear voice rang

CATHERINE PALMER

out over the gathered guests. Everyone turned to the young woman who stood at the foot of the long table directly opposite Jesse. "I have an announcement to make."

This was it. Jesse hunkered down in his seat and tried not to glower at her. What a time and place for an engagement announcement. Did she think he'd be glad? Sure enough, she was back to her wicked ways—proud of her victory and ready to flaunt it in his face. Come to think of it, wasn't that the same purple dress she'd been wearing the day she had snubbed him in town? It was! Why, someone ought to tan her sorry little hide.

"Because it's Christmas Day," she was saying, "we have so very much for which to thank God. Most important, we thank Him for sending His Son, Jesus Christ, who was born in a stable and grew up to die on a cross—all to save us from our sins. How grateful we ought to be for the undeserved forgiveness He has offered to each and every one of us!"

The diners clapped and a few gave hearty *amens*. Victoria picked up a glass filled with apple cider. "Not only has God given us this holy gift, but He has chosen to bless us with earthly things. As many of you have noted, we are honored to be joined by two of Mr. Conroy's partners in the Mesquite Land & Cattle Company. Mr. Wilson and Mr. Richards have come all the way from England to make merry with us today." She lifted her cup. "So I offer a toast to the Mesquite Land & Cattle Company. Long may it grace the grand Territory of New Mexico!"

Jesse gaped as everyone downed a swallow of cider. What on earth was Vic up to? What was she doing? Now she held her cup aloft again and continued to speak.

"On this glorious Christmas Day, I propose that each man and woman who has been blessed by Jesse Conroy and the

102

Mesquite Land & Cattle Company should stand and offer a toast. And I shall begin. Mr. Conroy—" she turned those sapphire eyes on him—"you have been the kindest, the most honest, and the most generous of employers. I came to this ranch with nothing, and you gave me everything. Thank you, sir. I salute you!"

"Hear, hear!" someone shouted as the gathering raised their glasses.

"I'll go next," Abe Baca said, scooting back his chair as he stood. "I've worked for many a cattleman in my days, but never have I met a man as fair as Jesse Conroy. He is good to his hands, and he treats the livestock how they ought to be treated. Here's to my friend and my boss!"

As everyone drained their glasses, the Baca women raced to refill them.

And now Stump got to his feet. The cowhand cleared his throat a couple of times; then he raised his cup of cider. "I ain't much of a speechifier, but here's what I got to say about the boss. Mr. Conroy's all heart above the waist and all guts below!" To a burst of laughter, the man flushed bright red and took his seat again as everyone toasted Jesse.

By now, Jesse was about as flustered as Stump. This wasn't what Victoria had been planning to do, was it? She was going to announce her engagement to William Worthing. And where was the blame fool woman anyhow? One minute she'd been standing at the foot of the table saying the nicest things Jesse had ever heard about himself. And the next she was gone.

Jesse started to go look for her, but he realized that Freck had stood up and pulled out his guitar. Good gravy, the buckaroo had written a song.

Freck strummed for a moment, then lifted his voice:

*"There once was a time when our cattle had no joy,
But up rode the bravest and smartest young cowboy,
He fenced up the land,
And treated us grand,
Our wonderful boss, Jesse Conroy."*

"Shucks, now," Jesse spoke up as the crowd clapped and stomped, insisting on more songs. "That's enough, folks—"

"I have something I'd like to say." It was Mrs. Ellis. "While I haven't known Mr. Conroy long, I would like to say that he eats lunch over at the hotel when he comes to town to fetch supplies. And of all the fellers round these parts, he has the best table manners I've ever seen."

The diners had barely downed her toast when Saturnino Baca stood. And then Pat Garrett. And John Poe. As the afternoon wore on, it seemed everyone in Lincoln had something nice to say about Jesse and his cattle company. Everyone but William Worthing, who slinked away about ten minutes into the proceedings.

Worried that Worthing had gone after his fiancée, Jesse tried to cut off the flow of compliments. But it seemed Victoria had started a flood that wouldn't be stopped. There was nothing to be done but sit and listen to one person after another tell how much they admired and respected Jesse. And all the while, he was worrying that he wasn't going to get to put in a word of caution before Vic up and married Worthing.

When Rosa Baca stood to give the final toast, shadows lay long across the room. She burst into tears as she told how Jesse was like a son, and everyone in town loved him, and all his employees thought he was wonderful, and even the cattle loved him and had gotten twice as fat as they'd ever been before, and she sure hoped the two Englishmen wouldn't sell the ranch out from under him—

And that was what this was all about! Vic had started the whole town talking about how great Jesse was so that Wilson and Richards wouldn't sell the ranch. That crazy gal! Where *was* she?

As Abe Baca embraced his weeping wife, here came their daughters with the desserts. Pies and puddings and custards! Jesse took one look and set off like a coyote with its tail afire. He wasn't about to stand around another minute.

Striding across the room, he grabbed his coat from the hook by the door and burst out onto the porch. Snow had begun falling again, and he stomped out into the yard to look around. Now where had that woman gone? If Worthing so much as touched her, well, Jesse would just have to give him what for.

"Victoria Jennings!" he shouted up into the evening sky. "Where are you?"

There was a moment of silence, and then a voice spoke out. "I'm right here behind you, Mr. Conroy."

He swung around, and there she sat on the old porch swing. Clad from head to toe in her riding clothes, she tapped her boot on the floorboards as she gazed at him.

"You don't have to holler your head off," she said. "It's not like I'm in China or someplace. I went for a ride to work the kinks out of my sore ribs is all. I'm not going anywhere."

Striving to calm his heart, Jesse stepped up onto the porch again. "You're not? I mean, I thought you . . . you're not leaving the ranch?"

"Well, not unless you fire me again. Personally, I think that would be a mistake. I've done you a lot of good, and Rosa needs the help. I'm better at mending than she is, which she's happy to admit, and you wear more holes in your britches than any man ought. I know how to set a table, too. And I've got *Mrs. Beeton's Book of Household*—"

"What about Worthing?" Jesse cut in. "You're marrying him, aren't you?"

"Certainly not. Like I told you, he asked me. He wrote me a passel of letters, only one of which I answered. I replied that I was happy here living with the Bacas and working for you. And even if you did forget to pay me, I had more joy than I deserved."

"You—you turned him down?"

"Just now. He found me in the kitchen while everyone was toasting you, and he repeated his proposal. I said no, of course. The very idea of it irked me so much I needed to take a ride out on the range. What would I want with a husband like William Worthing? I'm looking for a Christian man. Someone honest and kind and—"

"And forgiving." Jesse fell to his knees at her feet. "Oh, Vic, can you ever forgive me? I'm the real rascal of the two of us, not you. I held my hurt like a little seedling, feeding and growing it into that tangle of bitter vines just like you said. I forgive you a hundred times over for anything you ever did to me. Will you forgive me now?"

"Not if you don't get up and give me another one of those kisses of yours," she said, laying her hand on his shoulder.

Jesse leapt up, moved onto the swing, and wrapped his arms around her. "I love you so much, woman. I don't know what I'd ever do without you." He kissed her on the lips. And then on the cheek. And then on the lips again until she was giggling and purring at the same time.

"I sure hope nobody's looking out that window," she said, her eyes glowing as she gazed up at him. "All my hard work helping you keep the ranch will go for nothing if they see the two of us spooning on the front porch."

"You *loca* gal. I sure was honored by what everyone said, but you didn't need to go and do all that for me." He smoothed his hand down her long flowing hair. "I never was in danger of losing the ranch. My partners in England got a letter from Jimmy Dolan—written at Worthing's instigation, it turns out. Those no-good skunks were planning to buy the ranch and become the sole owners of the Mesquite Land & Cattle Company."

"Oh, those wicked men! So they lied to the Englishmen?"

"Not at all. Dolan sent a notarized record of my accounts with him. It was accurate, all right. I have less than fifty dollars in his safe. That's because I keep most of my money in the bank at Roswell. I took Wilson and Richards there to look at what I had put away. I also showed them my plans for the ranch and the letters I've received from folks I'm starting to do business with—a horse breeder who wants my extra hay, a fellow who's selling me fruit trees to start an orchard next spring, a company that makes fencing wire. My partners were more than satisfied with the way I was managing the company."

"I knew you hadn't run the ranch aground!" she exclaimed, catching his face between her hands and planting a kiss of her own right on his mouth. "Oh, Jesse, I couldn't be happier!"

"Well, I sure could." Setting her a little apart, he took her hands and knelt at her feet once again. "I won't know a moment's happiness until you agree to be my wife, Victoria Jennings. Say you will, and you'll make me the greatest gift a man could ever want."

With a laugh of delight, she pulled him to his feet. "Of course I'll marry you, Jesse!" she cried. "I love you with all my heart. Oh, God is good, isn't He?"

Jesse held her close, his Vic. How near he had come to letting those bitter vines choke out his love. But forgiveness won out in the end. And Vic had been right. Forgiving healed him even more than it did her.

"Merry Christmas, my darling girl," he murmured as he brushed his lips across hers.

She smiled. "Merry Christmas, indeed."

When our family lived in New Mexico, we always enjoyed this wonderful traditional stew made by my mother-in-law. Helene would set a beautiful table with her hand-decorated felt Christmas tablecloth, a large tray of shrimp to peel and eat, a generous bowl of shrimp dip, and a big pot of posole. What happy memories! These directions may sound a bit vague, but exact measurements aren't necessary. Just combine the ingredients until the posole tastes good to you!

HELENE PALMER'S CHRISTMAS POSOLE

1 pork loin roast
1 lb. posole corn (These hard kernels of field corn may be found in health-food stores or large groceries. Substitute 4 cups of canned hominy, if necessary. Posole corn has not been processed, so the taste is more intense, earthy, and robust than hominy.)
4–5 red chile pods (If you can find only fresh green chiles in your store, set out a few to dry and turn red.)
2–3 cloves of garlic, crushed
pinch of oregano
pinch of salt
1 tsp. chile powder

Wash pork roast and trim off fat. Cover with water and cook until tender. Cool and remove lean meat from bone. Cut into bite-sized pieces.

Wash posole corn well. Cover with water and simmer till tender.

Add cooked meat to corn. Add water and a little broth from cooked meat. Wash chile pods and remove seeds and tops. Add to stew. Add garlic, oregano, salt, and chile powder. Simmer several hours, adding more water if necessary. This can also be made in a slow cooker.

༄ A Note from the Author

Dear Friend,

Isn't forgiveness hard? As I've grown and matured in my Christian life, this area has been a big stumbling block for me. I have a favorite quote from the film version of Jane Austen's *Pride and Prejudice*. The character Mr. Darcy says, "My good opinion, once lost, is lost forever." How humbling it is to admit that this could describe me perfectly. Sometimes I fear I'm just like Jesse—nurturing, coddling, and revisiting my grudge as though it were a precious treasure! Do you ever do that? This is harmful in so many ways, not only to the person we can't forgive but also to ourselves.

Unforgiveness and resentment can easily consume us and block our relationship with Christ. If you've read J. R. R. Tolkien's *Lord of the Rings* trilogy, you'll remember Gollum. He's the pale, pathetic, obsessed little creature who is only a shadow of his former self. Gollum covets the evil Ring in the same sick way we often cling to our bitterness.

I'm sure Christ knew all about the harm of unforgiveness, because He talked about it so often. He could not have made things any clearer when He said, "If you forgive those who sin against you, your heavenly Father will forgive you. But if you refuse to forgive others, your Father will not forgive your sins" (Matthew 6:14-15, NLT).

Some of us have trouble forgiving others, and some have trouble accepting God's forgiveness. Like Victoria, we berate ourselves over and over because of something we did. What a wonderful thing to realize that if you've repented of your sin, God is not your accuser! You're free.

Thank you for walking in the boots of Jesse and Victoria as they worked their way toward forgiveness. I pray that you, too, will find the peace such grace can bring.

Blessings,
Catherine Palmer

⌒ About the Author

Catherine Palmer's first book was published in 1988, and since then she has published more than thirty books. Total sales of her books number more than one million copies.

Catherine's novels *The Happy Room* and *A Dangerous Silence* are CBA best-sellers, and her HeartQuest book *A Touch of Betrayal* won the 2001 Christy Award for Romance. Her novella "Under His Wings," which appears in the anthology *A Victorian Christmas Cottage*, was named Northern Lights Best Novella of 1999, historical category, by Midwest Fiction Writers. Her numerous other awards include Best Historical Romance, Best Contemporary Romance, and Best of Romance from the Southwest Writers Workshop; Most Exotic Historical Romance Novel from *Romantic Times* magazine; and Best Historical Romance Novel from Romance Writers of the Panhandle.

Catherine lives in Missouri with her husband, Tim, and sons, Geoffrey and Andrei. She has degrees from Baylor University and Southwest Baptist University.

Undercover Cowboy

LISA HARRIS

To my husband, the hero in my life

CHAPTER One

Colorado, 1890

Abigail Covington stared at the Wanted poster on the wall, a gnawing ache growing in the pit of her stomach. Randall Jackson was the crookedest man alive, and she'd had the gall to fall for him.

"Suckered the whole town if you ask me, Miss Covington." Sheriff Jefferson leaned back in his chair and rubbed his fingers through his short white beard. "Never met a man with such a fine disposition that turned out to be a cold-blooded killer. Even had Mrs. Simmons fooled—and she knows everything about everybody."

Not everybody. Abby winced inwardly then forced a smile. Thankfully, no one except her father knew what a shock Randall's crime and subsequent arrest had been to her.

The last time she'd seen the handsome rogue, he'd asked her to marry him—and she'd almost said yes. The fact that she had hesitated did little to take away the sting of betrayal. She'd loved him. Or at least thought she had.

"'Wanted, dead or alive, for the robbery of the Meadow Springs Bank and the murder of Deputy Miles Baker.'" Abby read the poster aloud, hoping the cold words would extinguish any feelings that remained. Anger mounted at her inability to have seen Randall for who he was. Ripping the poster off the wall, she crumpled it into a tight wad and threw it into the waste bin beside the sheriff's desk. "You won't be needing this anymore."

Randall Jackson would hang in the morning.

Taking a deep breath of renewed resolution, Abby set her shoulders back, then smoothed down the narrow pleats of her wool coat. "I need to get back to the ranch before dark, Sheriff, and I have one more stop. Thanks again for sending the carved horses for the boys at the orphans home."

"It's the least I could do. I'm looking forward to the Christmas Eve party you're planning." The sheriff stood and shoved his hands into the front pockets of his vest. "As long as the children don't mind an old codger like me showing up."

Abby laughed despite her somber mood. At least she had something productive to take her mind off Randall's hanging. "The children will love you."

"Give my regards to your father."

Abby stepped out of the sheriff's office and headed toward the mercantile along Meadow Springs's narrow boardwalk. The cold December air nipped at her face while narrow rays of sunlight glimmered across patches of white snow. She'd met Randall for the first time outside the sheriff's office. He'd made their accidental meeting into a romantic encounter. But the truth was, as the daughter of the wealthiest man in the area, she'd been nothing more than another conquest on his list.

She hadn't been the only one taken in by his subtle charm. Randall had captivated the entire town, enamoring the women and proposing business deals that had the men turning over their bank accounts faster than a bullet shot from the barrel of a Winchester.

He'd even graced the doors of the church every Sunday. Almost too late, she'd realized his songs of praise were nothing more than empty words of show. The reality of where his soul would go without a Savior haunted her.

Jolted out of the past, Abby collided into the broad chest of a stranger.

The cowboy took a booted step back and lifted his Stetson an inch, revealing a patch of blond hair. "Excuse me, ma'am. I must not have been looking where I was going."

He reached out and took her elbow to steady her. Her jaw tensed as she looked up into a pair of pale, sky blue eyes. "I *am* sorry, ma'am."

Irritation over the infraction flared. In the back of her mind, Randall's last words of apology resounded as a dissonant refrain. She eyed the clean-shaven face before her, and the anger she'd tried to suppress only minutes ago resurfaced like a bubbling pot of water on hot coals.

"Sorry?" she demanded. Her hands balled into fists against her sides. "Is that all you have to say?"

"Ma'am, I—"

"Do you know what the problem is with men like you?" He closed his mouth as the procession of words she'd been holding inside demanded escape. "You come into town with your fancy clothes and pockets full of cons, wooing the hearts of women with stories of adventure and fortune. Then, before they can count what's left of their meager savings, you're gone with nothing more than an I'm sorry—if even that."

The cowboy took off his hat and held it in front of him. "Ma'am, I don't know what to say, except I hope you're not includin' all men in your assessment. I believe there just might be one or two good ones left."

Abby looked into the face of the stranger she'd just confronted and stopped cold, realizing what a fool she'd made of herself. She watched in horror as his lips curled into a grin, revealing a dimple on his left cheek.

"I . . . " Seldom was she at a loss for words, but the blue-eyed stranger's sympathetic gaze did little to dissolve the embarrassment of the situation.

"If you'll excuse me," he said. "I was on my way to the livery."

"Of course." Abby swallowed hard, chastising herself inwardly for losing her temper. "But first, I'm the one who owes you an apology."

"No need, ma'am." He tipped his hat and stepped aside to let her pass.

~

Cole Ramsey watched the young woman with dark auburn hair turn and stride down the boardwalk. His training as a Pinkerton operative had taught him there was more than met the eye in most situations. Discovering the truth behind the secrets behind a person's façade had become not only a challenge but a way of life for him.

He headed toward the livery, recalling the set of cinnamon brown eyes that had flashed at him. Her smile, while lovely, had held of touch of sadness. Anger? Hurt? Betrayal? If he weren't here on assignment from his home office in Chicago, he would have enjoyed finding out more about this woman.

He turned for one last look, but she'd vanished into the

crowd mingling in front of the mercantile. Maybe someday, when he'd retired from the profession and bought himself a piece of land, he'd have time to pursue something other than horse rustlers and train robbers.

His work as an operative had brought a dozen years of undercover assignments, but at thirty-six years old with a leg that ached in the cold from an old gunshot wound, his days of fieldwork would soon come to an end—and a life behind the desk was not an option for him.

He missed the mountains and had done everything but beg to get this job. His former partner, Dirk, had discouraged him from taking the assignment, but he knew enough about the land and cattle from growing up in Montana to more than make up for his loss of agility.

Cole secured a horse from the livery, relishing the feel of the smooth leather saddle beneath him as he rode out of town. Scanning the horizon, he made a mental note of the layout of the land. High peaks formed majestic, craggy lines to the west. The Rocky Mountains were a sight of beauty that never ceased to amaze him. To the east, the terrain lay flat with gentle rolling hills as far as the eye could see. Tall grass blew in the breeze amongst a sparse scattering of trees.

The border of Covington Ranch began five miles past town and stretched across fifteen hundred acres of prime land. Before his arrival Cole had learned the basic facts about the ranch owner accused of sabotaging the surrounding properties. He'd picked up additional information from a waitress named Betsy at the hotel dining room between sips of black coffee and bites of apple pie.

Aaron Covington had been injured nearly thirty years ago when a gunfight left him crippled. His wife passed away last winter, and he had one daughter who helped run the ranch.

Abigail Covington, he'd been told, was not only beautiful but intelligent.

He planned to secure a position as a ranch hand and discover if there was any truth to the rumor that Aaron Covington was indeed rustling cattle and sabotaging the land. He'd been hired by two of the victims, but Cole preferred to not only work undercover, but without the knowledge of the men who hired him. He'd found anonymity his best ally and more akin to his nature.

The sun began its descent behind the mountains, leaving an explosive trail of pink, orange, and yellow. He pulled his coat around his neck to block the cold and nudged the horse to pick up its pace. If he was lucky, he'd arrive at the ranch in time for chow—and a job. If not, he'd have to find another way inside.

~

Abby flicked the reins of the buggy, urging her horse to hurry across the flat plain. The sun had already slipped behind the grandeur of the Rockies. If she didn't make it home before dark, her father would be furious. How many times, with the recent string of problems in the area, had he attempted to persuade her not to go into town by herself? And how many times had she assured him she would be fine?

As chairwoman for the Meadow Springs's Orphan Committee, she was responsible to collect not only gifts for the upcoming Christmas party but coats, blankets, clothes, and schoolbooks throughout the year. She couldn't wait for one of the ranch hands to escort her into town every time she had a function to attend. They had enough work to do riding the lines, mending the barbed fences, and taking care of the cattle.

A splintering crack of wood snapped beneath her. Abby felt a sharp jolt as the buggy plunged forward. Trying unsuccessfully to maintain her balance, she tumbled from the seat and onto the cold ground.

CHAPTER *Two*

*A*bby's eyelids fluttered open, and her gaze met a sea of sky blue. It was him—the cowboy she'd accused of being nothing more than a common swindler.

"I . . . " She closed her mouth, not knowing what to say. He'd left her tongue-tied. Again.

"Are you hurt?"

"I don't think so." She sat up slowly and took a deep breath, waiting for the ground to stop spinning. "It just knocked the wind out of me."

She let him help her to her feet, then brushed the dirt off her coat, attempting to recover her composure. *"Fancy clothes and pockets full of cons."* How could she have spoken that way to a total stranger?

"About what I said earlier in town—"

"There really is no need to apologize, ma'am." He grinned, and the corners of his eyes crinkled into a smile.

Abby held her head high and blew out a deep sigh. Why did he have to be so nice and all-to-pieces handsome?

"There's no excuse for my behavior. It's just that there is . . . was . . . someone I thought I cared about. He didn't turn out to be the man he claimed to be." She ran her tongue across her dry lips. "When I collided into you, I'd just left the sheriff's office with news he'd been sentenced to hang tomorrow."

"That must have been quite a shock, ma'am."

He did it again—smiled at her with those eyes that left her yearning to escape the confines of his mesmerizing gaze. She nodded and turned her head toward the mountains. "It's been several months since I saw him last. . . ."

She let her words trail off, shaking her head. This time, instead of assaulting him with her words, she'd confessed things that didn't need to be shared with a stranger. Here stood a man to avoid, considering the fact he'd managed to spin her emotions tighter than a bale of hay.

"Betrayal always stings."

Choosing to ignore his sympathetic words, Abby turned to the horse and buggy that stood half a dozen steps beyond them. Valentine, her palomino mare, munched on grass with the damaged buggy still hooked behind her.

"I've got to get back to the ranch. My father will send out a posse if I'm not home soon." She held the reins and rubbed her hand against the side of the horse. Valentine jerked in response. "Settle down, girl. It's all right."

"She's still a bit skittish. The accident must have scared her too," he said, unhitching the harness from the buggy and freeing the horse. "You'll need to send someone to haul the buggy out in the morning."

Abby kept a hand on the reins and surveyed the damage. The seat had splintered in two upon impact.

"It's a miracle you weren't seriously hurt."

He was right. It could have been much worse. If she'd been

trapped beneath the buggy, or broken a bone . . . a chill shot through her heart, and it had nothing to do with the brisk wind blowing against her face. While their equipment and herds remained unharmed, strange things had been happening to the surrounding ranches the past few months. Cattle were missing, fences cut, supplies damaged. She had assumed it was only a matter of time until their ranch was hit. Maybe *this* was the work of the saboteur.

She'd heard the ugly rumors that her father was involved. Sheriff Jefferson's investigation had come up with no evidence to support the accusations, but neither had he discovered who was behind the attacks. One thing she knew for sure. Her father would never resort to scaring people off their land—for any reason.

"What would cause the wheel to fly off?" she asked finally.

Cole crouched beside the axle, examining the place where the wheel had detached. "A loose bolt, perhaps? It's hard to say."

He didn't want to tell her what he'd found. Deep cuts in the wood implied that someone had tampered with the axle. So far, the numerous acts of sabotage hadn't endangered anyone's life. But if his suspicions were right and this wasn't an accident, then cattle rustling had just spiraled into attempted murder.

Cole looked around. It would be dark soon. The faint smell of smoke drifted through the air from someone's supper. A coyote howled in the distance. He needed to get her home. Soon.

"You never told me your name," she said.

He caught the hint of suspicion in her eyes. Of course

she'd be worried. He was a total stranger to her. "Name's Cole Ramsey."

"I'm Abigail Covington."

Her name took him off guard, and he blinked hard in response. "You're Aaron Covington's daughter?"

She nodded. "My father owns Covington Ranch."

His left brow rose slightly in question. This revelation changed things significantly. She wasn't simply the daughter of one of the ranchers whose land had been plagued. Abigail and her father owned the one place not yet hit by the destruction.

If this *wasn't* an accident, but an act of sabotage, it weakened the case against Aaron Covington. On the other hand, the loose wheel could be a ploy to shift suspicions away from the wealthy ranch owner. But what kind of father would endanger his daughter's life to save his own?

"I'm headed to Covington Ranch looking for work." The revelation of who she was made him all the more determined to get hired, especially if her life was in danger. "Heard one of your cowhands was laid up after a wild bronco threw him."

"What do you know about working a ranch?"

He looped his thumbs through the front pockets of his jeans. "I was born and raised on a ranch in Montana. Lived half my life in the saddle."

"And the other half?" She cocked her head, a hint of sarcasm in her voice.

He laughed, trying to ease the tension between them. "Don't worry. I've never been arrested or convicted if that's what you're worried about."

She lowered her gaze, seeming to weigh the situation. "My father does the hiring. You can sleep in the bunkhouse tonight and talk to him in the morning."

At least she hadn't sent him back to town. "I certainly appreciate it, ma'am. Anything you need to get from the buggy before we head on?"

She shook her head. "It's empty. I took a load of food from the mercantile to the orphanage earlier today."

Thunder clapped in the distance. Cole looked up at the dark clouds rolling in from the north. "We best get movin' if we're going to beat the storm."

Darkness had settled across the terrain by the time they arrived at the ranch house. The ride had been quiet, with only the sounds of the horses' hooves and distant thunder breaking through the still of the evening. Drops of rain began to splash against the hard earth as he led the horses toward the barn. Abigail continued toward the one-story structure where smoke billowed from a rock-and-mortar chimney.

Quickly bedding down the horses for the night, Cole passed the bunkhouse where he'd sleep later and knocked on the kitchen door of the main house.

A plump, gray-haired woman opened the door, and the pleasant aroma of beans and meat filled the air. "You Cole Ramsey?"

"Yes, ma'am. Miss Covington said I could come in for a bite of supper."

"Got a bowl of hot stew right here. Sit down at the table and help yourself."

Abigail entered the large kitchen as he sat at the long wooden table. She'd changed into a simple blue, long-sleeved dress sprinkled with tiny white flowers. Her eyes appeared darker in the dim light of the room, laced, he thought, with a hint of sadness.

Her hands gripped the back of one of the Windsor chairs across from him. "Mr. Ramsey. I'm sorry, but it appears that my father hired someone this morning while I was out." She met his gaze, her head held high. "I'm afraid we won't be needing you after all. You may stay in the bunkhouse tonight with the other cowboys and leave after breakfast."

Cole guarded his expression to hide his disappointment. He wondered if there was any truth to the story, or if it was simply because Abigail had convinced her father not to hire him. He'd seen the way she looked at him. Suspicion, caution, maybe even a spark of fear. What had that rogue she'd spoken of done to make her so distrustful? She'd fallen for a man condemned to hang. That alone would be enough to shake the trust and confidence of any woman, no matter how strong.

His objective, though, remained clear. Working at Covington Ranch was by far the best choice of action in discovering the truth behind the rash of mishaps—especially if her father was to blame. Now, with the possibility of Abigail's life in danger, he had another reason to stay—and he had less than twelve hours to find a way.

CHAPTER Three

$\mathcal{C}$ole finished his supper then hurried through the cold rain, hoping the wet weather wouldn't turn to snow. Inside the stale-smelling bunkhouse, four men sat around a table playing cards and smoking. A dozen bunks filled two walls of the wooden structure, one of which was occupied by a man wearing spectacles and engrossed in a book.

"I'm Cole Ramsey," he offered to no one in particular, slamming the door behind him to stop the gush of cold air. "I was told I could spend the night here before headin' out in the morning."

The men at the table raised their heads in acknowledgment. "Name's Carter." A balding man spoke up. "This is Shorty, Jim, and Tyler. Kip over there's lost in his cheap dime novel. The rest of the hands are out running the line camp."

Cole nodded at the men. "Where can I put my bag?"

"You can have the bottom bunk there." Carter pointed to a bed empty of personal belongings.

"Came lookin' for work." Cole threw his bedroll onto the

mattress with a soft thud. "Planned to talk to Mr. Covington in the morning, but his daughter told me someone else was hired today."

Carter nodded toward the lanky cowboy beside him. "Jim here's going to be fillin' in for a while."

So Abigail had told him the truth.

"Maybe if I talked to Mr. Covington tomorrow—"

Shorty cut him off with the shake of his head. "Talkin' to the old man won't make no difference."

Cole raised one brow. "Why not?"

Carter slapped down four aces and leaned back in his chair, invoking groans from his companions. "Aaron Covington might own this ranch, but his daughter's the one who runs it."

Cole woke early the next morning. He'd forgotten how cold a bunkhouse could be in the dead of winter. Still, he knew the mountains and fresh air would more than make up for the musty smell of cigars that filled the room.

He hadn't realized how much he missed this way of life, as difficult as it often proved to be. Lonely days spent in the saddle with nothing but sagebrush to talk to, cruel winters where cattle froze or were buried beneath the snow in a blizzard. It was a way of life he was familiar with.

Someday he'd buy himself a small spread and spend the winter nestled in a cozy ranch house with a wife and children. But today he had work to do. Carter's statement concerning Abigail's role had him reevaluating his next move. He'd planned to speak directly with her father but now wondered if that would make a difference. It might instead prove wiser to appeal to Abigail's sense of guilt over yesterday's encounter. A shrewd move perhaps, but one that had proven successful throughout his career.

After nodding good morning to the other cowhands, Cole dressed quickly and went outside to stretch his legs. A clear sky and bright sunshine greeted him, with no traces of yesterday's rain.

An older man sat in a wheelchair near the front door of the ranch house, his legs covered with blankets, a cup of steamy coffee in his hands.

Cole decided his next move. "Good morning." He took the stairs two at a time up to the long porch that ran the length of the house and held out his hand. "I'm Cole Ramsey."

"Ahh. The man who rescued my daughter yesterday evening." Dark eyes and broad cheekbones mirrored Abigail's. "Pleased to meet you. I'm Aaron Covington."

Cole smiled and shook his hand. If the man felt indebted to him, he would make it work to his advantage. "Nothing any decent man wouldn't have done."

The older man smoothed his long, graying mustache with a weathered hand. "I've told her over and over I don't like her traveling at night. Too dangerous with all that's been happening in these parts lately."

Cole leaned against the porch rail and examined the man sitting across from him. His black cotton shirt, fleece-lined waistcoat, and red bandana knotted around his neck gave him the distinct look of a cowboy. Here was a man with the outdoors in his blood, now forced to play the role of spectator while hired hands ran his spread.

Cole would expect the man to be resentful of the one who'd crippled him. For this ranch owner, gone were the days of roaming the land with his saddle molded beneath him as he cut through a herd or took aim at a calf with his lariat. Could years of bitterness and anger over a lost life be enough motivation to ruin another man's livelihood?

"I heard about the cattle rustling and damage done to the area ranches," Cole said.

Aaron's gaze scanned the horizon to the west. "Tell me what kind of man would destroy the lifeblood of another?"

Cole weighed his first impressions of the man. Heavy lines etched his bronzed face, his brow furrowed in concern. A man overwhelmed with life's responsibilities? or plagued by guilt?

"Thankfully, your daughter wasn't injured in the mishap last night," Cole said.

"Do you think it was an accident?"

Cole watched the man's eyes carefully. For Abigail's sake, he wanted to believe he was innocent. "I didn't tell your daughter, but there were indications the axle had been tampered with."

Aaron let out a deep sigh and set his coffee on the small table beside him. "I'm glad you were there. I've told her not to go out alone. If there's anything I can do to repay you—"

"Actually, sir, I'm looking for work. Grew up in Montana on a large spread. I know my way around a ranch."

Aaron wheeled his chair forward a few inches and leaned toward him. "What did you say your name was?"

"Ramsey. Cole Ramsey."

"From Montana?"

Cole folded his arms across his chest. Montana had been a lifetime ago—a place full of ghosts from a past he'd rather not revisit. "Yes, sir. My father owned the Circle Five Ranch."

Aaron held out a crooked finger and grinned. "Had a good

friend named Ramsey who left for Montana. Gold fever hit about that time. I chose to come here to try my luck at making it big. His name was Philip Ramsey."

Cole's stomach lurched at the name he'd struggled for twelve years to forget. "Philip Ramsey was my father."

"Your father?"

Cole nodded, cringing at the poignant memories of deception his father's name evoked. He worked to keep the emotion out of his voice. "Married my mother, Claire, back in '53. I was born a year later."

"By the horn spoons!" Aaron slapped the tops of his legs, his face lit by a crooked smile. "I knew your parents in Boston before they headed west. How are they?"

Cole looked away toward the mountains. "They were killed in a fire twelve years ago." For a moment, he was back in the parlor of his parents' ranch house. Thick smoke surrounded him and orange flames licked at his flesh. He'd tried to save his mother and Sara. Sweet Sara. How many nights had he tried to chase her haunting cries out of his dreams? He'd loved her and would have married her the following May, if only . . .

Where were You that night, God? He choked back the question he'd asked a thousand times. Finding no answers, he'd decided to forget what could have been. Running to Chicago and becoming a Pinkerton had been his way to erase the past.

"I'm sorry to hear they're gone," Aaron said. "They were wonderful people."

Cole took a labored breath but didn't answer. Let Aaron remember his father the way he had been.

"The job's yours if you want it."

Cole raised his gaze in question. "I thought—"

"We can always use another good man."

The front door squeaked open, and Abigail stepped onto

the porch. "Good morning, Father." She nodded at Cole. "Mr. Ramsey."

Aaron turned to his daughter. "Just discovered I grew up in Boston with Cole's father, Philip. Tried to get Philip to come to Colorado with me, but for some reason he and Claire had their sights set on Montana."

~

Abby lowered her brow, hating the suspicions that ensued. When would she be able to look at a man and not question his motives?

"I want you to take Cole on a tour of the property this morning so he can see what kind of spread he'll be working for."

Abby bit her lip in frustration. "You told me you'd already hired someone, Father."

Last night she'd been thankful for the excuse to send Cole Ramsey on his way. She looked at him, his presence disconcerting. The morning light added golden flecks to his eyes. Stubble gave depth to his square jawline. His black Stetson, heavy wool shirt and pants to mask the cold, and a pair of stovepipe boots had been selected with care to cope with the brutal Colorado climate. When he caught her gaze, she turned away, confused by the sudden racing of her pulse.

Her family had already been taken in by one con man, and there was no telling who this presumed cowboy really was. Her hands clenched at her sides. "Father, I need to speak with you—alone."

"Abby, go change into your riding clothes," her father said, ignoring her request. "After the three of us have had a decent breakfast, you two can head out."

An hour later, anger still simmering, Abby set off on Valentine with Cole beside her on one of her father's chestnut mares. Over a hot breakfast of biscuits, gravy, and ham her father had told story after story of his life in Boston with Cole's father. Despite the past connection of their families, her intentions this morning were to keep conversation impersonal and to a minimum.

"My father struck gold back in the sixties and put it all into this land." She lowered her Stetson to block the sun that hung above the horizon. "We run about eighteen hundred head of cattle. Stretches as far as you can see to the north and east of here."

"There's a passion in your voice when you talk about the land."

She knew he watched her, but she kept her gaze ahead, focusing on the surrounding plain dotted with cattle. "I've lived my entire life here. There's nothing like the satisfaction of knowing you've been a part of making this place what it is today."

Even in the dead of winter when cold winds blew across the flat land, broken only by the string of a barbed-wire fence, she could ride Valentine and find an indescribable peace—a peace she refused to let anyone steal from her. Not Randall Jackson. Not Cole Ramsey. Not anyone.

"Are you all right?"

This time she caught his gaze. Piercing blue eyes peered out from beneath the shadow of his hat. Why was it he seemed to see right through her? Through her wall of strength and independence, leaving the deepest places in her heart exposed. "Of course I'm all right. Why?"

"If I remember correctly, you told me your friend was to hang today."

She shook her head at the emotions Randall's image evoked. "He deserves it. His actions affected more than me. He swindled the whole town and left one young mother a widow. Fortunately, my father's a shrewd man. He was one of the few whose money Randall wasn't able to steal." *So he tried to steal my heart.*

Movement in the distance caught her eye. "There's a calf ensnared in the fence ahead."

Abby edged her horse closer, then dismounted, approaching the animal cautiously.

"Is it one of yours?"

Abby noted the brand. "Belongs to Jeremiah Ford, the ranch just north of us."

She examined the wire, careful not to get too close to the injured animal in case he decided to kick. "We're going to need to pry the wires apart."

"Let me do it," Cole said, coming to stand beside her.

She ignored the offer and began to force the bottom strands of barbed wire apart in order to free the calf's legs. The wire sliced through her glove and thumb, but she pushed aside the pain until one hoof slipped through and dropped to the ground.

The calf bawled faintly, trying desperately to free the other wounded leg.

"Abby—"

"Hold his head while I release the other side."

In a few seconds the calf was free and trying to stand on wobbly legs where pointed barbs had eaten into the flesh.

Abby stood back and drew out a sigh of relief. "His injuries could have been much worse. We've lost a number of calves—"

A crack of gunfire split the morning stillness. Abby turned to Cole and froze. He stumbled toward her, clutching his left shoulder where splatters of blood now stained his shirt.

CHAPTER
four

𝒞ole opened his eyes and squinted against the bright sunlight streaming through the window beside him. A searing pain shot through his left shoulder as he fought to sit up.

He felt a hand press gently against his arm. "Whoa, slow down, cowboy. You're not going anywhere right now."

Struggling to focus on the man looming above him, Cole took a deep breath and fought a wave of nausea. Beady eyes peered at him through a pair of narrow spectacles.

"Where am I?" Cole groaned and shifted his gaze beyond the man to the unfamiliar room where yellow-papered walls surrounded the four-poster bed he lay on.

"This is Doc Pearson." For the first time, he saw Abby in the background. Her auburn hair shimmered in the sunlight. "You were shot, and he took the bullet out."

Cole caught the expression of concern in her gaze, and slowly the details of their morning ride surfaced. "I remember the calf caught in the fence . . . and a shot. . . ."

The doctor nodded and finished washing his hands in a

flowered basin in the corner of the room. "You're fortunate whoever shot you hit you where they did. A few inches to the right and you'd be singing on the other side of glory."

Cole touched the bandaged spot and winced at the pain. "Doesn't sound like a bad place to be right now."

"You may be groggy for a while. It's important you rest the next few days."

Cole leaned against his good arm. "I can't just lie around. Mr. Covington hired me this morning."

The room spun, and his determination to get up wavered.

"The wound may not be life threatening, but you lost a lot of blood." The doctor snapped shut his cracked leather bag. "I'll be back tomorrow morning to look in on you."

Cole let his head fall back against the pillow as the doctor left the room. He didn't have time to lie in bed nursing a wound. His duties as an operative had taken a sudden twist and become personal. There had to be a connection between the problems on the surrounding ranches, the mishap with Abby's wagon, and today's shooting.

If someone was after her . . .

The thought hit him like a riding whip striking a rearing horse. Now there'd been two attempts at murder. He had to find the connection, and if Abby's life was in danger he had to find the link quickly.

He watched Abby pour water from a rose-colored pitcher into a small glass. Her left hand was bandaged, and streaks of blood covered the front of her dress.

"How's your hand?" he asked.

She offered him the glass. "It's fine. The doc put some salve on it and bandaged it."

He let the cool liquid run down his parched throat. "Do you have any idea who could have done this?"

Abby shook her head slowly. "All I could think of at the time was your safety. Shorty heard the shot and helped bring you back to the house." She glanced down at her skirt. "I need to go change, but I'll be back later with some stew for your supper."

He fought against the pain and struggled again to sit. "You wouldn't mind throwing in a steak or two, would you?"

"You better lie down and rest." She folded her arms across her chest and smiled, her cheeks reflecting the rosy hue of her dress. "I had a feeling you'd be a difficult patient, and I was right."

"Wait. Before you leave . . ." He didn't want to worry her, but if he was right, he owed her the truth.

She sat on the bed beside him. "What is it?"

"I'm worried about you."

"As I recall, you were the one shot, not me."

He measured his words carefully, uncertain what her reaction might be. "What if the bullet was meant for you?"

She shook her head, her eyes narrowing in question. "What are you talking about?"

"Last night you asked me what would cause the wheel to fall off the wagon."

"You said it was an accident."

"I didn't want to scare you, but I'm certain someone tampered with the axle."

"What?" Abby stood and faced the window. Rays of light filtered through the curtains, leaving shadows to dance across the hardwood floor. "You must be mistaken. Who would do such a thing?" She turned to face him, her eyes filled more with anger than fear. "You think this has something to do with whoever's been sabotaging the ranches?"

"I'm not sure, but after what happened today I thought you should know."

She walked back toward the bed. "I'll talk to the ranch hands and have them watch for anything unusual. Other than that, I'm not sure what we can do."

"The sheriff needs to know about this."

She nodded. "My father's already sent for him. I'm sure he'll want to talk to you. Especially after what you just told me."

Cole reached out and grasped her hand. It felt soft and smooth, and he didn't expect the course of emotions that shot through him. He had to find a way to protect her. "Promise me you'll be careful. I don't want anything to happen to you."

She drew back her hand. "Why does my safety matter so much to you?"

"I lost someone once . . ." Cole paused. He didn't need to tell her about Sara. It was something private and personal. A piece of his past he'd rather leave buried.

Abby sat on the edge of the bed again. "Tell me about her."

"How'd you know—?"

"That it was a woman you lost?" She cocked her head and regarded him intently. "I can see it in your eyes. You loved her, didn't you?"

He nodded. "I tried to save her. The house caught fire, but by the time I got there it was too late." A swirl of memories surfaced, threatening to engulf him in their wake. "According to the sheriff, someone set the fire deliberately, but they never found the perpetrator. My parents died that night as well."

How could he tell her that he suspected that his own father started the fire? He hated the guilt that ensued. Hated the anger that simmered corrosively in his heart.

"For the wrath of man worketh not the righteousness of God." The verse from James, once memorized eagerly as a child,

came to mind uninvited. Anger might not be from God, but what kind of God would allow such a horrible thing to happen to those he loved—and had tried to protect?

"I'm sorry about your family." Abby played with a loose thread on her bandage. "What was her name?"

"Sara. We were supposed to get married the following spring."

Sara had been his first love. The woman he planned to spend his life with. He could still see her working in his mother's flower garden, her long dark hair blowing in the soft breeze. Then the fire destroyed everything he'd known and loved.

"Has there been anyone since?"

"No." He shook his head and looked at her.

For a moment, he was lost in Abby's intense gaze. Her eyes flickered as if trying to hold back her own hidden emotions. He fought the impulse to reach out and brush her cheek with his hand.

Abby smoothed down her skirt and stood. "I'd better go now. Is there anything else you need?"

"I'll be fine."

Cole cleared his throat, confused at the surge of emotions that seemed to pass between them. He briefly closed his eyes and took a deep breath. He mustn't forget why he was here. Abby would have nothing to do with him if she discovered who he was and the fact that her father was his prime suspect.

Cole watched her leave the room, her long skirt swishing behind her. Turning onto his right side, he tried to forget her mesmerizing expression when she looked at him and instead analyzed the facts of the case.

Until now, Covington Ranch was the only spread not touched by the random acts of sabotage. And until yesterday, the damage had been to property only, never to any persons. The question was, had the tampering with Abby's wagon and today's attempt on his life been carried out by the same person?

One thing still didn't fit. Aaron Covington. Being the only rancher unaffected by the problems made him a suspect for many, but surely he wasn't involved in the shooting. Especially if Abby was the intended target.

But what if the bullet hadn't missed its mark? Could Aaron have somehow found out that Cole was a Pinkerton operative and hired someone to get rid of him before he discovered the truth?

Cole stifled a yawn and tried to get comfortable. The unanswered questions only added to his irritation. Closing his eyes, he wished he could pray. Once he would have turned to God in a difficult situation like this, but that was before he lost Sara.

It was then he'd realized that the only person he could trust was himself. Hadn't he relied on God once, then lost everything? Ignoring the gnawing guilt, Cole gave in to his fatigue and drifted off into a troubled sleep.

Abby leaned against the porch railing and watched the sun sink behind the distant mountains. It was her favorite time of evening, yet even the last mellow hues of the golden orb couldn't remove the uncertainty she felt. What if Cole was right, and someone had attempted to take her life? They'd missed her this time. Would they try again?

The sheriff had visited the ranch earlier. She answered his questions the best she could, but there was little to report. He searched for footprints and traces of evidence but found nothing. If it was the saboteur, they were still no closer to finding out the truth.

A coyote howled. Lightning flashed in the distance. Something moved along the side of the barn. Her heart pounded as the figure ran the length of the building, then stepped out into the light of the full moon. She sighed in relief as a bark rang out, and she realized it was only the neighbor's black mutt.

"Thou wilt keep him in perfect peace, whose mind is stayed on Thee: because he trusteth in Thee." The words, a verse spoken long ago by the prophet Isaiah and ingrained in her mind as a child by her mother, worked as a salve on her troubled spirit.

I want to trust in You, Lord. If someone does want to harm me, I pray for Your protection. And also for the protection of Father . . . and Cole . . .

"Abby?" She turned around at the familiar sound of her father's voice. "How's your hand?"

"It's fine."

Her father wheeled onto the porch and adjusted the thick wool blanket on his legs. Always the cowboy despite his disability, she smiled at the characteristic black vest and red bandana he wore.

"You could have been the one shot today, Abigail."

"But I wasn't." She leaned back against the railing and let the wind whip through her hair. " 'Thou shalt preserve me from trouble; Thou shalt compass me about with songs of deliverance.' "

"One of David's psalms?"

She nodded. "When I was younger, I often resented Mother's insistence on memory work. Today, I find it a comfort."

"She was a godly woman."

Abby rubbed her hands together, wishing she'd remembered her gloves before coming outside. "You miss her, don't you?"

He nodded slowly. "Especially on nights like this, when the stars are bright." Her father pushed on the wheels of his chair and inched forward across the porch toward her. "I need to ask something of you, Abigail."

The moon cast a narrow beam of silver light across his face and caught the frown that hid beneath his mustache.

"What is it? You know I'd do anything for you."

"I want you to stay close to the house until they find out who did this. No trips into town alone, no riding out on Valentine—"

She shook her head. "Father, I'm not going to let this incident, one that more than likely has nothing to do with me, keep me from my responsibilities. I've got the ranch to run and the Christmas party for the orphans to finish planning—"

"I know this isn't easy for you, but you have to understand why I'm concerned about your safety." He leaned against the wicker back of the wheelchair. "And I've been thinking about something else. If you were to get married—"

"I don't need a man to run this ranch." Abby turned toward the mountains that were now nothing more than a purple shadow in the darkness and fought the conflicting emotions warring inside her. She knew her father wanted only what was best for her, but after Randall, how could she ever trust a man again? "I love this land. You know that. I've helped make this ranch what it is today."

"And you've done a fine job, but you're still a—"

"A woman?" She whirled to face him. "And what does that mean, Father? That I can't run things as effectively as a man would?"

He reached out to grasp her arm. "Of course not, Abby, but you have to admit, if you had a husband—"

She pulled away, shaking her head.

"What about Cole?" he continued. "I knew his parents well, and they were fine people. He may only be a ranch hand, but he's a good man."

Her heart quickened at his name, but she ignored the unwanted reaction. "You don't know him at all. What if he's involved in all of this and working here is his plan to throw us off track?"

"Why would he do that? Abby, please be reasonable. Cole told me the wagon was tampered with. Carter brought it back to the ranch and confirmed Cole's suspicions. Then today with the shooting . . ."

Abby closed her eyes, not wanting to believe her father's assumptions.

"Cole will be up and around in a few days," he continued. "Until then, I'm asking you to please stay close to the ranch house. And I'm going to talk to him about guarding you until all this is over. I trust him."

"You trusted Randall."

His eyes seemed to plead with her. "Not all men are like Randall."

She took a step back toward the rail. "I don't know . . ."

"Abby, come here."

Out of respect, she obeyed and knelt in front of his chair.

He looked her straight in the eye. "I may have lost the use of my legs, but I can still provide for—and protect—my daughter."

Tears welled in her eyes. "I never meant for you to feel inadequate."

He ran his hand down the side of her face and wiped away

a tear. "I came to Colorado with a dream to strike it rich. The same dream thousands of other men had. I never imagined I'd be so blessed as to find gold and marry your mother as well.

"Then I lost the use of my legs and thought my life was over. Your mother was the one who taught me there was more to a person than what was on the outside." Abby could still see the love for her mother in his expression. "You've taken on so much responsibility, especially since your mother's death. I love this land, but none of that matters to me as much as you do."

He took her hand and clasped it tightly in his. "You're all I have, Abigail, and I would do anything to ensure your safety. Anything. I'd give up all of this without a second thought if I knew it would make you safe."

Abby nodded. "I know, Father."

"Promise me you won't go into town alone or off riding until the sheriff catches the man responsible?"

"I—"

"Please, Abigail."

The front door squeaked open, and Bertie, their cook, stood in the doorway. "Miss Covington? The stew's ready for Mr. Ramsey. Do you want me to take him a bowl?"

"Thank you, Bertie. I'll take care of it." Abby stood and turned to her father before following her into the house. "I don't agree with you, but I'll do what you want."

Abby's shoes clicked against the newly scrubbed wood floor as she made her way toward the kitchen behind Bertie.

"I almost forgot, Miss Covington." Bertie reached into her skirt pocket and pulled out a folded piece of paper. "Found this in Mr. Ramsey's ruined shirt pocket. Thought it might be important."

"Thank you. I'll give it to him."

Abby started to put the paper in her pocket when she noticed her name scrawled on the back.

"Miss Covington? Are you all right, ma'am?"

"I'm fine." She forced a smile. "Go on in the kitchen. I'll be there in a minute."

Unfolding the paper, Abby's hands shook as she scanned the rest of the handwritten page. On it were directions to the ranch, detailed notes about her father, herself, and the ranch hands, as well as explicit details on the layout of the ranch and surrounding area. Why did Cole need this kind of information?

Turning over the paper, Abby drew a sharp breath, gasping at the familiar face. Randall Jackson's picture stared up at her from the front of his Wanted poster.

CHAPTER

five

*C*ole Ramsey had to go, that was all there was to it. Abby ladled the thick stew into a bowl while Bertie pulled the hot bread from the oven. As soon as he was well enough to travel, Abby would watch him ride away with a smile of relief on her face.

The aroma of sourdough filled the room, causing her stomach to rumble. After setting the bowl on the tray, she added a glass of fresh milk. If this was Cole's last meal in this house, it wouldn't be soon enough for her.

It was simply too much of a coincidence. Why had Cole been carrying Randall's Wanted poster? Could there be a connection between the two men? At one time, she wondered if Randall was behind the acts of sabotage, but the problems continued after he'd been arrested for murder.

But if Randall had a partner . . .

Abby shook her head in frustration and hurried down the short hallway with the food. Was she letting her imagination get the best of her, or could Cole really be a criminal? And what about this morning's incident? None of her speculations answered the question of who shot Cole.

Balancing the tray on her hip, she opened the door to the guest room, ready to confront Cole about the paper and watch his reaction. Even if he was a con man—or worse, a cold-blooded killer—he wouldn't have the strength to hurt her with his injured shoulder in a sling.

He lay in bed, his eyes closed, and a slight smile across his lips. Reddish blond stubble etched his tanned features. Broad cheekbones, square chin, and a strong neck gave way to muscular shoulders. Stirring slightly, he peered at her, his gaze questioning at first.

She set the tray on the table beside the bed, forcing herself to remember why she was here. "Hungry?"

Cole attempted to sit up. "Starving."

"Bertie fixed you some beef stew and fresh bread."

"Smells wonderful. I'd about decided that you all were trying to starve me."

He smiled at her and Abby felt her defenses weakening, but yielding to his masculine charms was something she couldn't afford to do. "You won't ever starve around here. Bertie's about the best cook there is."

Using a pillow to prop himself up, he maneuvered into a sitting position. "If you wouldn't mind setting the bowl in my left hand I think I can manage."

The stew spilled onto the white sheet as he attempted to hold it.

Abby frowned and shook her head. "This will never work."

Taking back the bowl, she sat next to him and spooned the thick stew into his mouth, attempting to ignore his mesmerizing gaze. Good looks and charm would not be enough to capture her this time. She'd learned that lesson all too well with Randall.

"This is delicious." He shot her a smile and nodded at his wounded shoulder. "You've certainly got the advantage over me today."

The Wanted poster burned in her pocket, and she fed him another bite without responding.

"I guess you'd rather be anywhere right now than playing nursemaid," he said. "Am I right?"

"I don't mind."

"You just don't seem like the typical domestic woman."

Abby frowned at the comment. "I'm not sure if I should take that as a compliment or an insult."

"I definitely meant it as a compliment."

She set the spoon in the bowl and handed him the glass of milk. This man exasperated her. How could one look into his eyes churn her emotions faster than a wooden dasher turning cream to butter? She didn't trust him, and yet for some crazy reason she wanted to.

"I understand from Carter and Shorty that you're the one who runs the ranch," he said. "I know from experience it's not an easy task, yet I'm impressed with what I've seen so far."

"Like I told you this morning, I love this land."

Cole finished the milk before giving the glass back to her. Her fingers brushed the back of his hand, and she jolted at the brief contact. Pulling away from him, she slipped the Wanted poster out of her pocket. It was time for the truth—if he was capable of telling her the truth.

"Bertie wasn't able to salvage your shirt and vest, but she did find this paper in your pocket."

"Thank you." He took the paper, and a look of mild surprise registered on his face. "Glad it was the shirt that couldn't be salvaged and not my shoulder."

She ignored the attempt at humor and watched his expression closely, looking for a hint of guilt in his eyes. She wanted an explanation that made sense. One she could believe.

"Do you always do such thorough research on a spread before seeking a job?" she asked.

He lowered his brows in question but held her gaze. "What do you mean?"

Abby frowned at his ploy of innocence. "I couldn't help but notice my name scrawled on the paper, along with detailed information about my father and the ranch."

He shrugged his good shoulder. "I figured I had a better chance of getting hired on if I knew something about the place."

"Why Covington Ranch?"

"I talked to one of the waitresses in town. I believe her name was Betsy. She told me one of your ranch hands had been injured, and you might need someone."

A plausible explanation, but could she believe him? "And what connection do you have with Randall Jackson?"

He shook his head. "Who's Randall Jackson?"

"The man on the Wanted poster in your lap."

"Randall Jackson?" Cole picked up the paper and opened it. Understanding registered on his face. "He's the con man who was hanged today, isn't he?"

Abby dropped her gaze and stared at the multicolored quilt covering the bed.

"I needed a piece of paper and found this on the ground at the train station." He placed his thumb against her chin and gently turned it toward him. "You believe me, don't you?"

She pulled back at his touch and closed her eyes for a moment, wanting to trust him. Wanting to believe he was simply the son of her father's old friend. Not a man with a hidden agenda.

"I don't know who to believe anymore." She shook her head. "What do you do when half the town thinks your father's the saboteur?"

"Why would they assume that?"

"They think he's hired someone to scare people off their ranches so he can buy up the land, though no one has a good explanation why. Even the sheriff, my father's longtime friend, suspects he might be guilty. He hasn't said so, but I've seen it in his eyes." She stood and moved to sit in the spindle-backed Boston rocker across the room, needing to put distance between them. "My father would never harm anyone. He's a God-fearing man who takes his faith seriously."

"I'm sure he is."

"Do you believe in Jesus?"

He didn't answer for a moment, and when he did, his voice was barely above a whisper. "I did once."

She watched a shadow cross his face and wondered if losing Sara had caused his faith to waver. *Lord, show me what to do. I want to trust him. Want to believe he's the man my father thinks he is, and yet how can I?*

"What changed?" she asked.

"Everything. My mother raised me in a Christian home, and while my father didn't take much to religion, he never discouraged her. When my parents and Sara were killed, things started to spin out of control."

"Just because things don't happen the way we want them to doesn't mean He's not in control," she said. "'For I know the thoughts that I think toward you, saith the Lord, thoughts of peace, and not of evil, to give you an expected end.'" She gave him an apologetic smile. "When I was young, my mother made me memorize Scriptures."

"So did mine." Cole chuckled, but his smile quickly turned into a frown. "They haven't seemed to have done any good."

"I'm not sure about that. Do you ever have times when a verse comes to mind?"

Cole swallowed hard and closed his eyes for a moment.

"God's working on you," Abby said. "He wants you to trust Him."

"You make it sound simple."

She shook her head. "Faith is a conscious belief. Either God's in control of everything or He's not."

"Are you telling me you can continue to trust God in a world full of criminals and con men?" He held up the Wanted poster, and the yellowed paper crackled between his fingers. "Look what this Jackson fellow did to you. And now someone might be after your life."

"God's the only hope I have. People let you down. God never will."

"I wish I had a faith like yours." Cole stifled a yawn. "Sorry. I don't think the medicine the doc gave me has worn off yet."

"Why don't you sleep awhile?" Abby stood and picked up the tray, puzzled over their conversation. Randall had loathed vulnerability, while Cole made no attempts to hide his. "I'll come check on you later."

He nodded and lay against the pillow. Abby slipped out of the room, wondering for the first time if there was a reason God put Cole Ramsey in her life.

~

Cole stood at the rail of the front porch and watched the large flakes of snow drift to the ground. Newly fallen powder, the milky white color of a palomino's mane, glimmered in the late-afternoon sun that peeked through the clouds.

It had been four days since the accident, and it felt good to be back on his feet again. The doctor cautioned him to take it easy, but Cole had never been one to slow down for long.

Despite the welcome freedom from having to rest, one thing still held him captive. Abigail Covington. He knew she didn't totally trust him, and if it hadn't been for her father and the accident, more than likely he'd be long gone. Whatever doubts she had, though, hadn't stopped the riveting conversations they'd shared about faith, politics, and John Bunyan's *The Pilgrim's Progress*. Their conversations on faith challenged him the most. Her resolute belief in God stretched him to the point where he realized he'd relied on his own strength for too long—and not on God.

Would he ever be able to again fully put his trust in God? Was there forgiveness for one who'd left behind his faith to lean solely on his own abilities?

"*Come unto Me, . . . and I will give you rest.*"

He remembered the quiet, simple words from Scripture and shook his head. *It can't be that easy, Lord.*

"*Take My yoke upon you, and learn of Me.*"

I don't know if I have the strength to let go.

"*I am meek and lowly in heart.*"

I'm unrefined and self-centered.

"*And ye shall find rest unto your souls.*"

Rest. Isn't that what he longed for? How much time had

passed since he'd given up relying on God, and in turn, relied only on himself? And what had it done for him?

The door to the house swung open, and Abby bustled onto the porch, armed with a tray of tea and cookies. "I know you were expecting to play chess with my father tonight, but he's not feeling well and asked me to take his place."

She smiled, and a slight blush rose to her cheeks. Her woolen dress and white shawl were simple, but perfectly complemented her womanly figure. Cole let out a slow sigh. He was finding it more and more difficult not to become emotionally involved in his job.

She put the tray next to a wooden chessboard and sank into one of the chairs beside the table. "Would you still like to play? It's a bit chilly out, but I love watching it snow. It's so beautiful and peaceful."

Peace. He'd failed to see it for so many years, but wasn't God the creator of the beauty that surrounded him now? From the gentle snowfall to the brilliant setting sun, His presence emanated through the world He created. Not through the evil paths man chose to follow.

Cole sat beside the board and followed her lead by moving an ebony pawn forward, then leaned back in his chair. "Is there anything I can do for your father?"

"He'll be fine. He has good days and bad days. This just happens to be one of his bad ones."

"I've enjoyed spending time with him the past few days. Hearing stories about my parents, my mother especially, has meant a lot."

"He's enjoyed his time with you as well."

He longed to ask if she'd enjoyed their time spent together as much as he had. He didn't remember the last time he'd met a woman who captivated him as she did.

"I see you've been reading the Bible," she said, pulling him away from a place where he was tempted to lose himself.

The book still lay where he'd left it beside the chess set. "I found a copy in the guest room. I hope you don't mind me borrowing it."

"Of course not."

Cole took a sip of the tea, enjoying the comfortable silence that settled between them as they focused on each move.

"I've been thinking about what we talked about," he said midway through the game. He rotated one of the smooth, wooden pieces between his fingers. "The fact that we have to make a choice as to whether or not we're going to serve God."

"'Choose you this day whom ye will serve.'"

"Joshua's plea to the Israelites?"

Abby laughed and stirred another spoonful of sugar into her tea. "So you haven't forgotten everything your mother taught you."

"She was the kind of woman who never let you forget anything important."

"Tell me about her."

He watched her concentrate on the chess pieces, amused at how seriously she took the game. "I remember one year—I must have been seven or eight—she decided to cancel Christmas."

"You're kidding." Abby reached across the board and grasped his rook in triumph.

Cole frowned and moved his knight. "You didn't know my mother, but ask your father. She could be extremely stubborn and opinionated at times. I must have taken after her, for I was a very strong-willed child."

"Really? I can't imagine that being the case." She widened

her eyes in mock disbelief and made her next play. "What did you do?"

"I tried to steal one of our neighbor's prized watermelons." Cole gripped one of his wooden pieces and took Abby's bishop. "Problem was, he saw me. I stuffed that melon down my overalls and ran for my life. He chased me across the field until I fell facedown on top of the melon."

Abby let out a soft chuckle. "I wish I could have seen that watermelon explode all over your overalls."

"My mother was furious with me for months. Her whipping stung, but promising to take away Christmas was the worst."

"You deserved it." Abby sat back in her chair and folded her arms across her chest. "Did she keep her promise?"

"Even my mother couldn't deny me my favorite holiday of the year."

Abby smiled and moved her queen closer to his king. "I think I would have liked her."

"She would have liked you. And you would have had plenty in common."

"For instance . . ."

"Are you prodding for a compliment?"

"What woman wouldn't enjoy being complimented by a handsome man?"

She was distracting him. In keeping the conversation focused around him, she'd managed to maneuver her queen into a prime position. The game of wits became a game of survival on his part, and he struggled to keep up the defensive. He rested his fingers on his king and paused before making his move.

Her hand covered his as she caught his gaze. "I'd be careful."

He drew his hand back slowly, enjoying the easy banter. Was this a means of flirtation on her part, or was his imagination getting the best of him? It had been so long since he'd been interested in a woman that he'd almost failed to notice the subtle changes in her response toward him. He moved his king to the left.

"Checkmate."

Cole stared at the board, astounded he'd miscalculated his last move. Her queen had cornered his king. He sat back in the chair and gazed at her in disbelief. He'd lost the game, yet couldn't help but wonder if he might be losing his heart as well.

CHAPTER

Six

C ole walked into the sitting room of the ranch house and paused. Abby stood holding a framed daguerreotype in her hands. He took a moment to watch her as she traced the lines of the photograph with her finger. Her burgundy velvet dress gave her an elegant presence, but the shadows of the room couldn't hide the mark of sadness on her face.

She pushed a loose wisp of hair behind her ear, and a soft sigh escaped her lips. In the past two weeks he'd found himself attracted to her beauty, but it was her heart that drew him to her. For the first time since losing Sara, Cole began to wonder if he could take another chance at love.

But what was the likelihood of her loving him once she discovered his undercover agenda? He wasn't simply a grub-line cowboy or the son of her father's old friend, and he hated the fact that their relationship was based on false pretenses. Despite the harsh reality of their situation, he found himself fighting the urge to gather her into his arms and kiss her—and he had no doubt that kissing Abby would change his life forever.

When Cole cleared his throat to announce his presence, she turned to face him. Her lips curved into a smile, and he hoped she was glad to see him.

"I know my father has appointed you as my personal guardian, but I really am fine," she said.

"I'm sure you are." He grinned at her insistence on independence. Playing the role of her protector had been the best part of this case. "Carter's going into town, and I wanted to see if you needed anything."

She shook her head. "I appreciate the offer, but Bertie went yesterday and picked up what we needed."

His gaze drifted to the photograph she held in her hands. "Is that your mother?"

She nodded. "How did you know?"

"You have her wide, dark eyes and determined chin. She's very beautiful."

"My father used to always say it was a good thing I look like my mother instead of taking after his side of the family." Abby set the photograph back on the curio cabinet that stood in the corner of the room. "This was taken about a year before she died. At the time, we didn't even know she was sick."

"Her death must have been difficult for you."

"Yes, but I have many good memories. She loved trifles and curios." She rearranged several small wooden carvings that lay on display beside the frame. "I think her favorite time of year was Christmas because it gave her an excuse to fill the room with holiday bric-a-brac."

He looked around the tastefully decorated parlor filled with mahogany furniture and marble-topped tables, but void of any traces of the coming holiday. "Christmas is a week away. Don't you plan to decorate? Maybe put up a tree?"

"Not this year." Abby moved to an intricately carved chest that sat in front of the sofa and opened the lid. The smell of inlaid cedar permeated the room as she singled out a medium-sized box.

"My mother collected Christmas decorations." She sat beside the chest and picked up an angel with an embossed shiny paper face and golden paper wings.

The box was filled with ornaments—wax replicas of angels and children, handmade wooden figurines, elaborately painted eggshells, and other finely crafted pieces.

He sat cross-legged beside her on the floor. "Your mother had quite a collection."

"My father gave her most of the store-bought ornaments, but I think she preferred the handmade ones. Every year, we spent hours baking cookies, fancy cakes, and candies. Then we would hang the sweets on the tree with paper chains and ribbons."

Cole warmed at the memory of sitting around the kitchen fireplace with his mother. "I remember making long chains of popcorn and raisins."

"There's nothing like the smell of popcorn simmering over the fire, mingling with the smell of cinnamon and a fresh pine tree."

He leaned back against the palms of his hands on the ornate rug and regarded her. "So why not this year?"

She shrugged a shoulder and frowned. "This is the first Christmas since my mother died, and the holiday brings back so many memories. I can't imagine spending it without her."

Cole picked up a glass-blown ornament, its rich, cobalt blue color glistening in the light. "Tell me about your mother."

He noted the unconscious smile that graced her lips at his request. She was close enough that he could smell the scent of rose petals adorning her skin, and his heart quickened.

"It's hard to know where to begin. She loved parties and holidays. Christmas especially." Unwrapping several layers of white tissue paper, Abby held up a wooden horse. "This was her favorite ornament, not because it was the most elaborate one she owned but because her uncle carved it. It's a replica of her horse, Beauty. He gave it to her the Christmas she married my father."

Cole took the horse and studied it. The dark wood had been carved in great detail. "Your uncle was quite talented."

"He owned a lumber mill, but his passion was carving. He crafted numerous figures and sold them right up until he died. I have several more of his pieces set on the shelves of the curio in the corner."

"I noticed the carved doll by your mother's picture."

"That was another favorite piece of hers." She rewrapped the wooden horse and set it in the box.

"Did your mother meet your father back East?"

"No." She lifted out a small handmade woolen angel with tiny buttons and gold wings.

"They met after my father came to Colorado looking for gold. My mother was living in Denver with the uncle who carved these, helping to care for his sick wife. According to my father, he fell in love the first time he laid eyes on her."

"And what about your mother?"

Abby leaned her arm against the chest and laughed. "I believe it took her a bit longer to be convinced that she should marry this gold-hungry outrider instead of the city man who'd been courting her. But as my father tells the story, he'd never been one to hang up his fiddle once he got a hankering for something, so he invited my mother to every church social in the county and finally stole her heart."

Cole chuckled at the vivid description. "Sounds just like your father. I don't think anything could stop his determination when he gets his mind set on something."

She searched through the chest again and pulled out another photograph. "This is of my parents on their wedding day."

Cole let out another soft chuckle. "Your father's lost a bit of hair since then."

"And gained a pound or two." Abby smiled. "They were good together."

Cole glanced around the room, an idea forming in his mind. Near the front window would be the perfect spot for a tree. He could picture it laden with her mother's ornaments and lit with dozens of small candles. He couldn't bring back her mother, but he could ensure that this year Abby had a Christmas she'd never forget.

And that's exactly what he planned to do.

Abby finished pouring the yellow yolks into the frothy egg whites, then added a generous portion of sugar. If she couldn't be out on the ranch, at least she could do something useful.

She'd promised to bring an assortment of cakes and cookies to the orphans for the upcoming Christmas party. Hank Wethersfield, owner of one of the two restaurants in Meadow Springs, agreed to supply the meal for the festivities, but extra sweets were always welcomed by the children.

Her thoughts of the impending celebration were interrupted by a sharp pounding on the front door. "Who could that be?"

Abby dried her hands on a towel and told Bertie she'd be back. Maybe it was Cole. He'd left after their talk in the parlor this morning, and she hadn't seen him since. Why was she questioning where he'd gone? Wasn't she the one who'd insisted that she would be perfectly safe without his constant protection? Still, she'd come to look forward to their daily conversations, games of chess, and short rides around the property together.

A mass of green limbs greeted her at the door. The tree shifted to the left, and Cole's face peered through the boughs. "Merry Christmas!"

Abby set her hands on her hips. "What in the world have you done?"

"I went out and found you a Christmas tree."

She shook her head in astonishment, smiling at the picture he made. Standing at her doorstep—red cheeks, frosted hair, and a white wonderland behind him—he could be a character straight from a Currier & Ives winter scene.

"I told you, I don't want a Christmas tree." She stifled a laugh.

"Yes you do."

"No I don't."

His expression begged for a truce. "Can we please discuss this inside? It's freezing out here."

Cole dragged the tree through the doorway and set it in the entryway. His hand moved to his hurt shoulder.

Abby cringed at what he might have done to the wound. "How'd you get this tree down from the mountains? The doctor will have your hide."

"One of the ranch hands helped me."

"Let me help you set this up in the parlor, and then I'll get you some hot chocolate." She bustled to the other side of the tree, trying to avoid being poked by one of the branches.

They lugged the towering Douglas fir into the parlor and managed to secure it in a large tub filled with dirt and rocks.

Abby stood back and cocked her head. "It's crooked."

Cole stood beside her and matched her stance. "You're right, but does it matter? It's only an inch or two."

"It matters."

Cole crouched under the tree and attempted to adjust the base.

"Now it's leaning too far to the right," she said.

"What about this?"

She eyed his progress. "A little bit more to the left . . . a little bit more . . . perfect."

He stood and took a few steps back. There was a crackling noise, and the tree began to tip.

"Cole!"

In a matter of seconds, it toppled to the floor.

Abby didn't remember ever laughing so hard as they made a second attempt to secure the tree in the base. "Are you sure it won't fall over this time?"

He looked at her and snickered. "Not at all."

Three hours later, the room had been transformed into a Christmas scene straight out of *Harper's Bazaar*. Boughs of Rocky Mountain juniper graced the top of a large mirror and several pictures. The tree shimmered in the soft light of a kerosene lamp and flickering candles. A fire blazed in the hearth, warming the decorated room and bringing back happy memories of Christmases past. Gratitude welled within Abby's heart. Cole had given her much more than a tree covered with decorations. He'd given her a renewed hope for the future.

He stood beside her, tall and handsome, and she wondered why she'd ever doubted him. Reaching up on tiptoe, she
kissed his cheek, then stepped back in dismay. A warm flush
flooded her cheeks as she watched his eyes widen in apparent
surprise over her untamed boldness. The same horror she'd
felt after the impulsive words she'd spoken at their first
encounter washed over her.

Cole smiled. "I don't have any mistletoe, but I've been
wanting to sneak a kiss all evening." His eyes held her gaze,
and she felt him put an arm around her waist and draw her
toward him. "May I?"

She nodded, unable to speak or think of anything beyond
the fact that she wanted Cole Ramsey to kiss her.

He tilted her chin, and she lost herself in the now familiar
sea of sky blue eyes gazing into hers. Tightening his grip
around her waist, he drew her closer and let his lips brush
against hers. The soft caress grew with a gentle intensity until
he finally pulled away. A smile rested on his lips.

Abby struggled to catch her breath—struggled to find
reality in the dreamlike world she'd stepped into.

Someone cleared a throat from the doorway of the parlor,
suspending the magic of the moment. "Miss Covington? Dinner's ready."

~

Abby set her copy of The Pilgrim's Progress on the flowered
sofa beside her and watched her father and Cole converse
over a game of chess. Dinner, dessert, and now reading
couldn't erase the feel of Cole's lips against hers.

Looking for a distraction, she strode to the Swiss music
box her father had bought her mother for their twenty-fifth

wedding anniversary. Hand-painted flowers adorned the front of the walnut case, adding to the detailed inlay on top. She turned the crank and closed her eyes as the music began.

"May I please have this dance?" Cole stood before her.

She looked to her father, who leaned back in his wheelchair and grinned. "Of course." Her heart pounded as the melodic strains of a waltz played in the background.

The open space in the room was far from adequate, but nothing mattered to Abby except that she was in Cole's arms. He held her tightly, his gaze never leaving hers.

"I had a wonderful day," he said.

"So did I."

She floated in his arms and felt lighter than an autumn leaf soaring gently in the breeze. His bay rum aftershave and the subtle wisp of his breath against her cheek left her senseless. Long before she was ready, the song ended.

"Thank you," he said.

"You're welcome." She stepped out of the warmth of his embrace, longing to return.

Someone knocked on the front door, and Abby heard Bertie shuffle from the kitchen to answer it. A moment later, Sheriff Jefferson entered the room, his hands stuffed into the back pockets of his denim trousers.

"Evenin', Sheriff." Aaron pushed his wheelchair away from the marble-topped table and edged toward his longtime acquaintance. "What can we do for you?"

"Evenin', Aaron," he said, then nodded toward Cole and Abby. "Wish this was a pleasure call, but it's not."

Abby watched as her father's expression turned grave. "What is it, Sam?"

"Aaron, as a friend I'm here to tell you that I'm taking Shorty into town for questioning. Claude Simpson's barn burned down tonight. Witnesses placed Shorty at the scene."

Sam cleared his throat, and an eerie silence followed as they waited for him to continue. "But as the sheriff, I have to warn you, Aaron. If you have anything to do with the destruction that's been taking place these past six months, I'll personally see that you hang."

CHAPTER
Seven

$\mathcal{C}$ole straddled a chair in the sheriff's office two days before Christmas and listened to Sam Jefferson's assessment of the case. A lantern sat on the table beside him, leaving enough light to cast smoky shadows on the bare walls. Tomorrow was Christmas Eve, a time of celebration for most people, but Cole had little time to think about the holiday tonight.

"Do you really think Aaron's involved in this?" Cole asked.

Jefferson eyed him steadily and poured a second steaming cup of coffee. "He's been a friend for twenty years, and I never would have thought him truly capable until last week."

Cole leaned forward in his chair. "What happened?"

"Jeremiah Ford, who owns the land north of the Covington Ranch, decided to move back East after all the trouble that's been going on. I checked with the land office and discovered that Aaron bought his ranch."

Cole sat back and whistled through his teeth. "There's nothing illegal about buying land, but the implications are there."

"Exactly." Jefferson offered Cole one of the tin mugs, then moved to sit across from him.

"Thanks." Cole took a sip of the drink, relishing the warmth of the strong brew.

"Considering that Ford's ranch was one of the hardest hit," Jefferson said, "it certainly doesn't look good for Aaron at this point."

Cole set the mug on the table beside him. "What about Shorty? Did you find a connection between the two of them?"

Jefferson shook his head and dumped a spoonful of sugar into his drink. "Shorty's not talking. In fact, I couldn't hold him on. Except for the land purchase, we're right back where we started."

"What about blackmail?" Cole asked. "If Aaron had something on Shorty and blackmailed him into doing his dirty work—"

"Then Shorty would have plenty of reason to keep quiet."

Cole nodded. "Exactly."

Jefferson rubbed his white beard and narrowed his gaze. "Or maybe Aaron really is innocent. Maybe purchasing the land from Ford is nothing more than a coincidence."

Cole hoped so, for Abby's sake and for the sake of any future he might have with her. But he still wasn't sure. There wasn't enough solid evidence either way, and rumors and speculations weren't enough reason to arrest someone.

"If Shorty is working for Aaron, we need proof." Cole stood and paced the room. Warming his hands in front of the wood-burning stove, he searched for a reasonable explanation. "We have to find something tangible that will hold up in a court of law."

"True, but what? Whoever's doing this is good. Six months and not a solid trace of evidence found." Jefferson let out a slow breath. "Did you find out anything about Shorty from your Chicago office? You Pinkertons are known for your vast records on criminals."

Cole shook his head and picked up his mug of coffee from the table. "I wired a detailed description, hoping to come up with a match, but ended up with very little information on the man. I do know that Shorty's real name is Horace Finkle."

Jefferson laughed. "A good reason to change one's name."

Cole took another sip of the strong coffee. "Five years ago, he spent time in jail for petty larceny."

"Hardly means for blackmail." Jefferson shook his head. "If you could get into Aaron's office and find something. Maybe he's having financial trouble, or someone's blackmailing him. A letter, a payment, any kind of discrepancy in his books might put us on the right trail. It might not be much, but it would be a start."

"I've already thought of that. It's just a matter of finding the right time. Aaron rarely leaves the house, and right now he's got Abby confined."

"He's afraid for her life," Jefferson said.

Aaron wasn't the only one afraid for Abby's life. Cole felt a deep frustration over the fact that she was in danger, and he had yet to stop the person involved. "That's what makes me tend to believe Aaron's innocent. Why would he harm his own daughter? I've seen them together. They're very close."

"We could be looking at two totally unrelated situations."

Cole nodded in agreement. "Meaning we've got more than one suspect to go after. Tomorrow's the orphans' Christmas Eve party. Bertie has the day off. If Aaron decides to go, then the place will be empty. Since I'm staying in the guest room, no one will be suspicious if they see me entering the house."

"Let me know if you find anything."

"I will." Cole stood and shook the older man's hand. "We'll catch this outlaw yet."

"I just pray it's before someone's killed. They might not miss next time."

~

Cole headed back to the ranch, frustrated that the lead on Shorty had proven futile. He'd been the number one suspect on his list. In the past two weeks, he'd managed to talk to all the cowhands individually, trying to extract any information that might be useful to the case. Each one had some aggravation over Shorty, but nothing he could connect to the cowboy being the saboteur. Carter complained about his lazy work habits and tendency to disappear for hours at a time—possible indications of something amiss, but it still wasn't enough.

Approaching the outskirts of the ranch, Cole regarded the brilliant black sky dotted with a mass of luminous stars. Despite Cole's years of unfaithfulness, God had remained faithful, waiting for his return like the Prodigal's father had longed for his son's return. Reading his Bible and talking with Abby encouraged him, motivated him, and showed him the reality of what had been missing in his life. Yet, had he totally let go of the bitterness from the past? Remnants of anger over his father's betrayal still haunted him.

Forgive him.

A whisper in the night spoke words he didn't want to hear. How could he forgive his father for murdering Sara and Mother?

I can't do it, Lord!

Forgive him.

I want to be Yours, Lord. I want to be filled with Your presence, but how can I forgive a dishonorable man like my father, who chose the coward's way out—taking his own life and the lives of those he claimed to love?

This time, there was no answer in the still evening. Ignoring the nag of guilt resting in the recesses of his mind, Cole turned his thoughts toward Abby.

If he could prove Aaron innocent, he'd ask Abby if he could court her. He'd thought of little else this past week. She felt so warm and natural in his arms the afternoon they decorated the tree together. She was the missing piece in his life, and her kiss had drawn him to her stronger than a forty-niner's quest for gold.

He couldn't have envisioned the changes that would take place in his life when he agreed to take this assignment. It had been close to a month, and he was no nearer to knowing who the saboteur was, but he knew that his heart would never be the same again.

The house was quiet when Cole arrived back at the ranch. Lit only by the silvery glow of the moon, he bedded his horse for the night before making his way to the porch. Shutting the front door quietly behind him, he glanced into Aaron's empty office. There was no time like the present.

Cole lit a candle and entered the small room. A brief exploration of the area showed Aaron to be an organized man when it came to record keeping. Opening a file drawer, Cole thumbed through letters and business correspondence. Aaron had kept paper receipts of everything from the Swiss music box in the parlor to cattle to the equipment in the barn, but strangely enough, Cole could find no record of the purchase of the Ford ranch.

In the back of the drawer, an envelope caught his eye.

Aaron's name had been scrawled in block letters on the front. Slipping a letter from the envelope, Cole began to read. His eyes widened as he scanned the revealing contents.

> *I know about your involvement with the string of "misfortunes" that has plagued our area. The cattle thieving and sabotaging . . . make no mistake, not only do I know you're behind it . . . I can prove it.*
>
> *I've seen you in the late evening as you watch the sunset with your daughter from your fine ranch house. There will be a price to pay for what I know, and you will pay. Unless you want your pretty little daughter to see you hang, leave one thousand dollars in the loft of your barn by tomorrow night.*
>
> *J*

Cole set down the letter on the desk and fought a wave of uneasiness. Had Aaron paid the man? Were these simply threats for money, or did Abby's life weigh in to the picture as insurance that the blackmailer would be paid? The biggest question still remained unanswered. Who had written the letter?

Needing to know if Aaron had paid the blackmailer, Cole searched until he found the account book in one of the desk drawers. Flipping to the first page, he searched for any discrepancies—large cash withdrawals or expenditures—anything that might allude to the fact that Aaron was paying a blackmailer or was in trouble financially. Fortunes could be spent faster than they were earned, and judging by the fine furnishings in the house, this ranch owner had already spent a great deal of his wealth.

Ten minutes later, he found what he was looking for. Three weeks ago, one thousand dollars had been withdrawn from Aaron's account and marked as a miscellaneous expense.

Cole shut the book. If Aaron was innocent, why would he have paid the blackmailer instead of going to Sheriff Jefferson?

A noise sounded in the hallway, and Cole's head shot up.

Abby stood in the doorway. The light of the candle caught the anger that flashed in her eyes. "What are you doing in my father's office?"

The trust he'd worked so hard to build with her vanished before him and was replaced with a look of startled dismay.

~

Abby stared at Cole, and a sick feeling of disbelief washed over her. It was happening again. How could she have played the fool to yet another gold digger? Another money-hungry con man who wanted nothing more from her than her father's wealth. The truth burned like a hot branding iron, but the reality that she'd fallen for Cole hurt even more. The tenderness of his kiss, the feeling of being in his arms . . . all of it had been nothing more than an act to win her over.

"Abby—"

"Don't even try to sweet-talk me." Her fists balled tightly against her sides. "You might have been able to gallantly account for the other coincidences, but not this one. I trusted you. My father trusted you."

The room closed around her, and she struggled to breathe.

"I can explain." Cole stood and took a step toward her.

Abby grabbed a tall, iron candlestick from a small marble table beside her and held it above her head. "Don't you dare come near me! There are half a dozen ranch hands who will be here the second I scream—"

"I don't want to hurt you, Abby."

She fought against the tears welling in her eyes.

"If you'll just let me explain."

"Why?" She wiped away an escaped tear of anger. "Why should I listen to you when I know all you're capable of is telling lies?"

"Please give me a minute to explain."

She gripped the candlestick tighter. "Don't come any closer."

Cole took another step, and she swung the candlestick. He ducked and it grazed the side of his head. He stumbled and fell against the edge of the desk. A trickle of blood ran down his face.

"Abby, listen to me! I'm a Pinkerton operative, trying to find out who's sabotaging the area ranches." He held a hand to his head, letting the words proceed in a rush as she posed to strike again if he made another move toward her. "Sheriff Jefferson knows who I am and can answer any questions you might have."

Abby blinked hard, trying to absorb what he said. Another one of his lies? "Who did you say you were?"

"I'm a Pinkerton operative. I've never done anything to hurt you, and I never will." He held up his hands. "Put down the candlestick and let me explain. Please."

She weighed the situation, hesitating with her response. "I'll listen for now. Sit down and talk."

Cole stumbled into the chair. "Like I said, I'm a Pinkerton agent."

"I should have known you weren't a cowboy." She hated the bitterness in her voice, but this second attempt at betrayal left her feeling like a maverick caught in a lasso.

"Abby, everything I told you was true. I'm no tenderfoot. I grew up in Montana just as I said. My parents owned a cattle ranch and did well for themselves."

She caught the look of sorrow in his eyes and wondered what secrets they held. But this wasn't about Cole and his past. This was about her—right now.

"Why Covington Ranch?" Ignoring his pained expression, she continued the questions. "Was a possible job opening the only reason you picked our ranch?" Anger roiled in her heart. Her gaze dared him to tell her anything but the truth.

"I was hired by two other ranchers in the area. They believe your father is behind the acts of sabotage and want him stopped. I thought working here would give me the advantage I needed to find out if your father was indeed guilty."

Abby dropped into the chair behind her and swallowed hard. "You're telling me you came here to convict my father?"

"I came to put the man responsible for the acts of sabotage behind bars." A slight hesitation registered in his voice. "If it turns out to be your father, then yes, I will turn him in to the authorities."

Abby felt her heart hammer within her chest. "And searching his office? What is that supposed to accomplish?"

"The sheriff told me tonight that your father recently purchased Jeremiah Ford's ranch."

Abby shook her head. This couldn't be happening. The rumors and speculations that he'd been buying up land couldn't be true, but if he'd bought Jeremiah's ranch . . .

"He never told me that."

Cole set a piece of paper on the desk. "In checking through his files, I found a letter from someone claiming they have proof your father is the man behind what's been happening."

She dropped the candlestick to the floor and fought against a strong wave of nausea. "I don't believe it."

"I don't want to believe it either."

"Why not?" Abby slammed her hands against the desk. "If the letter is right, you can send my father to jail and go on to your next assignment."

"I don't want to go on to my next assignment—"

"Don't!" She turned away from him and rubbed her temples, trying to stop the pounding sensation screaming through her head. Her father used to say her temper made her appear madder than a peeled rattler. Today, the expression didn't even come close to portraying the anger she felt. "How do you expect me to believe you?"

He shook his head. "I meant everything I ever said. The talks we've had, the realization I need Christ in my life, the kiss, dancing with you . . . it was all real. I was afraid you'd never trust me again once you found out the truth."

She couldn't stop the flow of tears. Couldn't stop the feelings of disappointment and loss. "You were right about my reaction."

"Can you forgive me?"

Abby drew a sharp breath, trying desperately to hold on to a semblance of reality. "You lied to me. Used me to get close to my father."

"Getting close to you was never an act, Abby."

She watched the trickle of blood on his face and felt a stab of guilt. Reaching inside the pocket of her robe, she pulled out a white handkerchief.

"Here." She moved to the other side of the desk and pressed the cloth against his temple.

"You have a pretty good aim."

He grinned, and she fought the swell of emotions that consumed her. He was close enough for her to inhale the familiar scent of aftershave, and for a brief moment her defenses began to crumble. If only things were different between them and he would take her in his arms, kiss her, and tell her everything was going to be all right.

But everything was not all right. How could it be, when his intentions were to convict her father?

Once the bleeding stopped, she moved back to the other side of the desk and sat down. "I just can't believe you're here trying to prove my father guilty."

"I don't want him to be convicted. Not after meeting you and knowing how much he means to you. I never wanted to hurt you."

She ignored his beseeching expression, the shock of the situation taking its toll. "Let me see the letter."

He handed the paper to her, and she read it. This couldn't be true. Her father wasn't capable of the crimes committed in the area. He loved the land and the people who lived here.

"I don't care what kind of information you have. My father's innocent, and I'll do whatever it takes to prove it." She threw the letter across the desk. "And even if this is true, then what about the wagon and the person who shot you? My father would never do anything to hurt me."

"I still don't know what the connection is, but I'm going to find out."

"Do you believe my father's innocent?"

"I've come to admire your father as a dependable, honorable, and godly man. I can't imagine him doing anything like this."

"Do you believe my father's innocent?" She repeated the question.

He hesitated briefly before responding. "Yes. Despite the evidence, my instincts tell me that your father's innocent."

Abby stood, pressed the palms of her hands against the edge of the desk, and leaned forward. "Then help me prove it."

CHAPTER

Eight

*C*ole sat at the long kitchen table and took a sip of Bertie's strong, black coffee. Bacon, potatoes, and eggs sizzled in the background, but this morning he wasn't interested in food.

Abby sat across from him, but in the light of day, he was afraid that granting her request to help prove her father's innocence was going to be difficult—if not impossible. Especially after what he'd discovered last night. Paying a blackmailer almost always meant that one was trying to cover up something.

Cole pushed his breakfast around on his plate then looked at her. He wondered if she'd slept any more than he had. Her red-rimmed eyes reflected a mixture of heartache and fear.

"I'll be right back, Miss Covington." Bertie wiped her hands on a dishcloth before setting it on the counter. "Help yourselves to seconds, if you like. There's plenty."

"You've been crying," Cole said once Bertie left the room.

Abby ran the back of her hand across her cheek as if trying to wipe away any leftover tears. "I was so angry at you last night when I found out who you were. A man sent to convict my father—"

"Abby, I'm sorry."

She held up her hand to stop him. "I was awake most of the night thinking and praying. I know I made you promise to help me prove my father's innocence, but, Cole, I'm scared. He paid off a blackmailer. Why would he do that if he was innocent? Why not just go talk to the sheriff?"

"I don't know. I thought the same thing." Cole reached out and squeezed her hand. He wanted so much to protect her, not only from whoever might want to take her life but from the emotional pain she felt.

Abby pulled her hand away, and a look of apprehension crossed her face. "After having time to think about it, do you still believe he's innocent?"

He knew he had to be honest with her. "I was up most of the night, too, trying to find a reasonable explanation for what has been going on. All the evidence points to your father."

"What if someone is setting him up?" Hope shone in her eyes as she sought answers that would absolve her father of blame.

"It's possible someone's framing him, but why, and more importantly, who?" Cole took a sip of his coffee and grimaced at the lukewarm liquid. "You know I'm going to have to talk to the sheriff about what I found last night. I have a job to do. I can't neglect my responsibility as an operative just because I've become personally involved." Especially when getting involved personally meant losing his heart.

Abby set her fork beside the uneaten food and shoved her plate aside. "Will you promise me one thing?"

He nodded, concerned at the intensity in her voice.

"Promise me you'll wait until after Christmas to confront my father about all this."

Cole wasn't sure about the wisdom of her request, but he agreed. "If that's what you want, I'll wait."

"If you need to tell the sheriff what you've found out, I understand, but please don't act on the information yet. I don't want anything to ruin the party today, and tomorrow *is* Christmas."

The soft squeak from the wheels of Aaron's chair turned Cole's attention to the doorway of the kitchen. Abby's father entered the warm room and stopped at the end of the table. "Morning, Abigail. Cole."

"Morning, Mr. Covington."

"Good morning, Father." Abby got up and placed a kiss on his cheek before going to the stove to make him a plate of food.

The tension in the room mounted. For over three weeks now, Cole had sat in this very same chair and eaten breakfast with them—as though he were a part of the family. Aaron shared story after story about his days back in Boston with Cole's parents, his search for gold near Pikes Peak, and the satisfaction in turning the land he loved into a working ranch. Surely this man he'd come to love and admire wasn't guilty of organizing the recent rash of crimes.

Cole turned his attention to Abby, and his yearning for her only grew as he watched her fill her father's plate. Her hair was pulled back, leaving soft wisps around her face. A frown tugged at her lips, reminding him that on this morning, things were not the same. Could she love him, even if he had to con-vict her father?

"How are you feeling this morning, Father?"

"This cold puts an ache in my bones, but I can't complain

too much." Aaron slapped his hands against the table. He seemed oblivious to the uneasiness that had settled in the room. "It is Christmas Eve, you know. We have a lot to be thankful for."

"Are you planning to come to the party at the orphanage, Father?"

"I'll ask Carter to take me later. You know how slow this ole body is in the mornings. In the meantime, Cole can drive you in the sleigh."

Abby set the plate in front of her father. "Of course."

Cole sensed a sad longing in her eyes. His determination to protect her at all cost rose.

Lord, I place Abby in Your hands. Please protect her and keep her from any harm. And if there's a chance for us . . . show me the way.

Thirty minutes later, Cole helped Abby into the sleigh. His heart quickened when her gloved hand took his. Once she was settled in the seat, he reluctantly let go and wrapped the buffalo-hide blanket around her. Gazing at her familiar face— pink cheeks, wide brown eyes, and narrow lips—he longed to gather her into his arms and kiss her. Instead, he got into the sleigh beside her and let the horse set off at an even pace along the icy path.

Her arm brushed against him, and he could feel the warmth of her body. Blowing out a frosty breath of air, he scanned the horizon for anything out of place. If Aaron was innocent, then one thing was clear: Abby's life was in danger. Even if Aaron was involved, the blackmailer's letter implied that he would use Abby to guarantee what he wanted if necessary. And a blackmailer's request rarely ended at one demand.

A piece of ice hit the dasher in front of them as they slid across a frozen stream, and Cole jumped. He looked at Abby, but she seemed lost in her own thoughts and unaware of the surrounding environment. Chastising himself at the reaction, he assured himself that nothing seemed out of place.

A clear blue sky made a canopy above them, dipping to the earth until it reached the snow-covered plain. The muffled plodding of horse hooves rhythmically danced before them. Sleigh bells rang out a soothing cadence. It was a perfect day for a romantic sleigh ride across the Colorado countryside.

As much as Cole wished this could be nothing more than a pleasure ride, there were more pressing matters at the moment. He decided to start with an obvious question. "Do you have any idea who would blackmail your father?"

Abby pulled her hooded cape closer around her face. "I've never known Father to have enemies. I'm sure there are those who are resentful of his wealth, but as for names . . ."

"Think, Abby." He had to get her to start somewhere, especially if she didn't want him talking to her father yet. In this case, time was not on their side. "Old business partners, disgruntled employees, anyone who might want to hurt him."

"I don't know!" She rubbed her temples with her fingertips. "I'm sorry. You don't deserve that. I'm just so worried about my father and the possibility that he might be involved."

He laid his arm across her shoulders and pulled her toward him. "You don't have to apologize. I know this is hard on you. We can talk about it later."

A few flakes of snow drifted toward them. Abby stuck out her tongue and caught one. "When I was a little girl, my father and I used to see how many snowflakes we could catch in our mouths. Silly, isn't it?"

"Not at all." Cole laughed, content to forget the situation

with Aaron and simply enjoy her company. He needed to know how she felt. "What about us, Abby? Is there a chance for something to develop between you and me?"

She turned to him, a slight blush covering her cheeks. She sat close enough for him to see the golden flecks in her dark eyes and the contrasting shade of brown that rimmed her irises.

"After Randall, I vowed I'd never fall for another man again, but then you came along. . . ."

Cole's heart quickened as she looked off into the distant mountains. "So does that mean there's a chance for us?"

She turned back to him, and he caught a look of hope in her eyes. "You're going to have to give me time. Trust is something I'm going to have to learn. Especially if my father is guilty. Right now I feel as though I'm having to choose between you and my father."

Something inside halted his response, and he waited quietly for her to continue.

"I'm just so afraid," she continued after a minute. "I can't believe my father's guilty, but if he is . . . I don't know if I can forgive him."

The sleigh went over a slight bump, and he tightened his grip on her shoulder to steady her. "Unforgiveness spreads hatred like gangrene."

"What do you mean?"

Cole swallowed hard, forcing haunting memories from his past to resurface. "I've never been able to forgive my father for killing my mother and Sara."

Abby turned to him, surprise registering in her eyes. "I thought your father died in the fire with them?"

"He did." Cole hesitated. There had never been concrete proof that his father was guilty, but that hadn't stopped Cole from blaming him all these years. "After the fire, I discovered some startling things about my father. I knew he'd started drinking, but he was also seriously in debt from gambling. The most troubling piece of evidence was a life insurance policy he took out on my mother only months earlier."

"But if he died with her . . . ?" Abby shook her head. "I don't understand."

"He must have felt an inkling of guilt and tried to save her at the last moment." He felt her shudder beside him. "How could you think that about your father?"

"He changed the year or two before he died."

"But my father talks about your father like he was such a wonderful, compassionate man."

Cole pulled back on the reins to slow the horse as they went down a slight incline. "Your father knew him before he ran up a gambling debt and lost everything."

Abby pulled the blanket against her chin as they turned and the wind shifted direction. "You said that not forgiving is like gangrene. Can you forgive him even if you never find out the truth?"

The straightforward question startled Cole. All these years he'd blamed his father and never stopped to recognize that he'd been the only one hurt by his refusal to let go of the past.

The righteous indignation he felt slowly began to slip away. He'd never told anyone about the anger he carried toward his father. But despite the truth of Abby's statement, years of hatred made forgiveness difficult.

Cole leaned against the back of the sleigh. Abby had told him that faith was a conscious belief. Wasn't forgiveness a conscious decision as well? Cole knew he needed to forgive, no matter what the circumstances—but could he?

"I'm not sure I know how," he said finally.

"Forgiveness is a choice."

"Just like obedience to Christ." *Show me how to let go, Lord.* "It's going to take time."

"Through Christ, all things are possible. Including forgiveness." She laughed rather solemnly. "Guess I should work on taking my own advice."

They topped a ridge and the orphanage came into view. "Before we get there, there's one other thing I need to talk to you about," Cole said. "We both know your life might be in danger. I want you to promise me you'll be extra careful. Stay with the group today. Don't go wandering off anywhere alone."

"You sound like my father. Think I should fire my current bodyguard and hire a better one?"

"I'm serious, Abby."

"I know." She tried to stifle a smile, but a light chuckle escaped her lips. It was good to hear her laugh after all that had happened.

"If your father's innocent, it means someone is out for revenge. And from what we've seen in the past couple of weeks, whoever it is will stop at nothing—even murder." He saw the fear in her expression and pulled her close. "Just promise me you'll be careful."

~

Abby stared out the kitchen window of the Meadow Springs Orphans Home and watched one of the younger children hit Cole in the forehead with a snowball. A dozen children, ranging from ages two to sixteen, had bundled up in cast-off coats, hats, and mittens. Their rosy cheeks and smiling faces showed nothing of the heartache they had experienced in their short lives.

Twenty years ago, Albert and Emma Turner had taken a run-down, two-story house and turned it into a home for young boys and girls in need. They'd never been able to have their own children, but God used them to bless the lives of dozens of youngsters who'd lost their parents.

Abby watched as Cole picked up the boy who struck him with the snowball and flung him over his shoulder. Even out of earshot, she could see the laughter emanating from the boy's smiling face as Cole ran around the yard, his own expression glowing with joy from the playful moment.

She continued to stir the hot chocolate, feeling the comfort of his presence nearby. Helping the Turners had become one of the highlights of Abby's week. It wasn't uncommon for her to come to the orphanage and assist the children with their homework and then stay for dinner, always bringing with her a plate of Bertie's homemade goodies.

This morning, though, she'd volunteered to make a pot of hot chocolate to warm the youngsters when it was time to return inside. She needed some time to sort through her troubled thoughts.

"There you are!" Abby's father entered the kitchen, pushing his chair across the wood floor. "Don't tell me you're ignoring me like Sheriff Jefferson is."

Abby lowered her brows in concern. "Of course not. Why do you say that?"

"He doesn't trust me." His eyes darkened for a moment. "But you know I have nothing to hide, don't you?"

She wanted to believe him—desperately—but could she? "You know I'll always love you, Father." Abby wondered if he realized that she hadn't answered his question. That she couldn't answer his question. She moved back to the stove. "I thought they might enjoy a bit of hot chocolate when they come in from the cold."

He moved to the window where he could watch the children play in the snow. "I believe you thought of everything today." He looked up at her and smiled. "You remind me so much of your mother. She was gentle and giving."

"I've always wanted to be like her."

Abby stood behind her father and looked out the window. Cole and the children had moved from throwing snowballs to building a snowman. Abby watched as Cole set his wool cap on the top of the pudgy, frozen figure.

"Father . . ." There were so many things she had to know. So many questions she needed to ask him, but she was afraid of the answers.

He turned from the window to face her. "What is it, Abby?"

"If you were in trouble or needed something . . . you'd come to me. Wouldn't you?"

"If it's Sheriff Jefferson and the others' accusations—"

She laid her hand on her father's shoulder and squeezed gently. "I just want you to know, I'm here, and I'll always love you."

Abby went back to stirring the hot drink, but her father leaned forward in his chair. "Why are you asking me these questions? If something's wrong, tell me, and I'll fix it."

Abby shook her head. There were some things her father just couldn't fix. She took the steaming drink off the stove, then sat beside him at the small table. "What do you do when you're afraid someone you love isn't the person you thought they were?"

"Like Randall?"

Part of her wanted to cry out, "No, like you, Father," but she bit her lip, not ready yet to confront him on the matter.

"Yes, like Randall." She was afraid of the truth. Afraid her father was involved in the sabotaging, and she would lose him.

"The Bible teaches that the truth will set you free." Her father grasped her hand in his and squeezed. "You know how much I love you?"

"I know." Abby kissed her father on the forehead.

"Are you sure you're all right?" He reached up and touched her cheek.

"I'll be fine. I promise." Abby grasped his hand in hers and smiled. "I thought you were supposed to be getting ready for a game of chess with one of the older boys?"

"I did promise Marcus I'd get the chessboard set up." He chuckled. "You know I never turn away from a challenge."

"You'd better go then."

Her father went into the parlor as the kitchen door leading to the outside banged open. Cole stood in the doorway, holding Timmy, one of the younger boys.

"What happened?" Abby jumped from the chair and rushed across the wood floor.

"He slipped on the ice and scraped his hand on a rock. I don't think it's serious, but it scared him."

"It's . . . bleeding." Timmy let out an exaggerated wail.

Abby looked at the injured area, then ran her hand down the young boy's tear-streaked face. "I think you're going to live."

Timmy continued to whimper. "But . . . it . . . hurts."

"Emma said you would know where something was to clean his hand," Cole said.

"Why don't you go sit at the table, and I'll see what I can find."

The young boy managed a small smile and nodded.

Abby found a clean cloth and washed the wound. When she finished, Timmy refused to get down from Cole's lap. Instead, he snuggled his head into Cole's shoulder.

"I think you've got a new friend here," Abby said, folding her arms across her chest.

Cole kissed the boy's wet forehead. "He is precious."

Abby ached for the three-year-old who'd lost his parents this past fall when cholera swept through a nearby community. He was blessed to have a home at the orphanage, but the young boy needed a loving family. A mother he could love as his very own and a father who could spend afternoons fishing and teaching him how to play ball. Someone like Cole.

Abby was startled at the thought. Cole would make a wonderful father. She'd been amazed at the way he interacted with the children throughout the morning. Some men appeared afraid of children, but Cole was different.

"Do you think you're well enough for a surprise, Timmy?" Cole asked.

The little boy's eyes widened, and he nodded.

"Then why don't you come with me, and we'll call the other children into the house."

Timmy pointed to the stove. "And we can have hot chocolate, too?"

Abby laughed. "Of course you can. In fact, if I'm not mistaken, there are quite a few more surprises in store for you today."

Cole winked at her then turned to leave. Her heart threatened to explode. As she watched Cole carry Timmy outside, she heard her father's boisterous laugh from the parlor, reminding her of the one haunting question that remained. Was she betraying her father by giving her heart to Cole?

CHAPTER Nine

C ole laid another log in the fireplace, then set up the painted screen to stop any shooting sparks. An evening of parlor games at the Meadow Springs Orphans Home was turning out to be a complete success. Twenty questions, I have a basket, and blindman's bluff had all been played with enthusiasm. Even Sheriff Jefferson had joined in the festivities.

Cole watched as Marcus waved his hands in front of him, snarling like a wounded creature as he attempted to act out a word in a lively game of charades.

"A bear?"

"A mountain lion?"

The audience shouted out their guesses, but Marcus only shook his head and continued his animated gestures.

Cole enjoyed playing with the children, but his awareness remained focused on Abby. She sat on a dark green couch across the room between two of the children. A familiar tug pulled at his heart as he watched her face light up when one of the youngsters climbed onto her lap and snuggled against her.

A cheer rang out as someone guessed Marcus's impression correctly.

The winner, a young girl dressed in a red jumper, turned to Abby. "It's your turn, Miss Covington," she said, handing Abby the hat. It was filled with pieces of paper with the names of famous people, books, animals, and other objects written on them.

"All right." Abby pulled out a slip of paper and held it up.

Cole stood beside the fireplace and watched her motions with amusement. She cupped her elbow with one hand, then swayed from side to side like a boat with a sail.

What will it take for me to win her heart, Lord? Is proving her father's innocence the only way? Once again, Cole found peace in conversations with his heavenly Father, but a measure of turmoil remained. What if Aaron Covington *was* guilty?

"Pilgrims!" someone shouted finally. Abby nodded, then proceeded with the third word of the phrase.

Cole let a slight grin cover his lips as he recognized her clue. *The Pilgrim's Progress.* John Bunyan's book was one they'd both read and discussed at length. Like his own life, Christian's journey to the Celestial City had been filled with temptations and trials.

He paused at the thought. Hadn't he given in to the temptation of holding on to bitterness? He'd asked for God's forgiveness but in turn had refused to forgive his father. A feeling of clarity encircled him as he realized what he'd done.

Jesus taught that only in forgiving others could one begin to understand God's complete forgiveness. He sat in a cushioned chair in the corner of the room, knowing what he had to do. Until he forgave his earthly father, he would never be totally free.

Lord, forgive me for holding on to the bitterness and hatred for so long. I need to let go and forgive my father.

The words felt awkward, yet he sensed a warm blanket of peace envelop him.

Only You know the truth behind what happened that night, but I forgive him and refuse to carry the anger any longer. And to You Lord Jesus, I surrender.

One of the children called out the correct answer, and Abby clapped her hands, bringing Cole's thoughts back to the warm parlor—and Abby.

Sheriff Jefferson walked up beside him. "Wondered if I could have a word with you outside before I leave."

"Certainly."

Sheriff Jefferson bid farewell to the Turners and the children. Shoving his hands into the pockets of his coat, Cole followed him into the crisp night air.

They strode inside the empty barn where Jefferson's horse waited. "You said you had some information for me?"

Cole slipped the blackmail letter out of his pocket and handed it to him. "I found this in Aaron's office last night."

Sheriff Jefferson read the letter then tapped the bottom of the page with his fingers. "Did you find any evidence that Aaron paid the blackmailer?"

Cole nodded and gave the sheriff the particulars of the rest of his findings at the ranch, including the fact that Abby now knew the truth about who he was.

"Did she tell her father?"

"No, but she will. She's asked that we wait until after Christmas to confront him. I think she's afraid he's guilty."

"Walt Madison had a dozen horses stolen last night."

Cole's jaw tightened at the information. "Carter told me he caught Shorty slipping into the bunkhouse in the middle of the night."

"If Shorty's the man Aaron's using to do the sabotaging, then who's the blackmailer?"

"There's still a chance that Aaron's innocent." Cole tried to put an inkling of hope into the words, but they fell flat. The evidence against him was too convincing.

Something hit against the side of the barn. Cole's head shot up in surprise. "Wait here."

Cole stepped into the darkness to see what it was. He shivered as an icy gust blew against his face, and he struggled to catch his breath. He watched for movement in the shadows along the side of the barn. After a moment, he decided nothing seemed out of place, and he reentered the barn.

"Must have been the wind," Cole said, blowing on his hands for warmth.

"I've got to go, but let's pray you're right and Aaron is innocent." Jefferson mounted his horse and set his Stetson firmly on his head. "Arresting her father isn't a Christmas present I want to give Abigail."

~

Abby entered the parlor an hour later, carrying a large bowl of popcorn she and Emma had drizzled with butter. A loud bang exploded from across the room, and she jumped. "What in the world?"

Timmy ran across the room, his eyes wide with excitement. "Look what Mr. Ramsey just gave us. Christmas crackers!"

His exclamation was followed by a dozen more loud bangs

from the holiday noise poppers. The children squealed in delight as they pulled on the paper tubes and found pieces of candy inside.

She set the bowl of popcorn on a table and scooped up the boy whose eyes gleamed with excitement.

"Would you like a piece?" Timmy asked.

Abby smiled and held out her hand. "Why, thank you, Timmy."

"Are you going to marry Mr. Ramsey?" he asked, popping a piece of chocolate in his mouth.

Abby felt her mouth drop open at Timmy's words and tightened her grip around his waist, hoping no one had heard the question. Out of the corner of her eye, she caught Cole's amused expression.

"Mr. Ramsey is just a good friend, Timmy."

"Too bad." Timmy jumped out of her arms and ran toward the popcorn. "He's nice."

Slipping the wrapped candy into her skirt pocket for later, she felt a stirring in her heart, followed by a deep physical ache as her gaze shifted from Cole to her father. She reached down and picked up one of the empty noise poppers. Rubbing the bright, shiny paper between her fingers, she looked around the cheerful parlor decorated with handmade ornaments, popcorn strings, and boughs of blue spruce.

The entire day had worked out perfectly, but the possibility of her father's guilt remained disconcerting. The lights of a candlelit chandelier hanging from the middle of the room flickered against the flowered wallpaper, giving the room a festive glow. Struggling to push aside her fears, Abby proceeded to announce the next event of the evening.

"Gather round, children. It's time for Mr. Turner to read the story of the birth of Jesus."

Mr. Turner, a tall, lanky man, stood and cleared his throat. "If you don't mind, I've asked Mr. Ramsey to do the honors this evening, and he agreed."

The children congregated around the Christmas tree where Cole sat. Timmy shimmied onto his lap while Cole tried balancing a candle and a Bible in his hands.

Abby's stomach fluttered as he looked at her and grinned. "This has been a wonderful day of fun and games, and I want to thank each of you for letting me be a part of your celebration."

The children smiled and clapped their hands before he continued. "The Bible says that Jesus is the light of the world."

Cole struck a match, and a golden flame appeared. He lit the candle and handed it to Marcus. "As I read the account of Jesus' birth from the book of Luke, we're going to light the tree, letting its radiance remind us of the importance of allowing Christ's light to shine in our own lives."

One by one, Abby helped the children light the candles on the tree. The dimly lit room gradually took on a yellow glow as Cole recounted the visit of the angel to Mary, the tiring journey to Bethlehem, and finally the long-awaited birth of the Savior in a simple stable.

Abby watched the children, amazed at their intent interest. As Cole read the last verse of the biblical account, Mr. Turner lifted Timmy so he could light the final candle. "'And the shepherds returned, glorifying and praising God for all the things that they had heard and seen, as it was told unto them.'"

The poignant image of Cole telling the story of the Christ child remained fixed in Abby's mind minutes later as she slipped into the frosty night to get the children's Christmas stockings, which she'd left in the sleigh. Cole's words of concern over her safety had not gone unheard, but surely there was little danger of anything happening so close to the house. The sleigh wasn't far, and she'd be back inside before anyone noticed her absence.

She took in a deep breath, her lungs filling with the crisp night air. The hanging of the children's stockings would be the last part of a wonderful day. Carter had come for her father earlier in the wagon, and her heart skipped a beat anticipating the sleigh ride home with Cole.

His reading of the birth of Christ reminded her why God had sent His only Son to earth to seek and save those who were lost and to grant them forgiveness. And as painful as it was to realize what might happen with her father, forgiveness was something Abby must be willing to give as well.

Careful not to slip on the packed snow, she made her way from the house toward the sleigh that sat outside the barn. A thousand stars lit the night, casting a soft blue light across the distant plains. There was something magical about Christmas Eve. It was a night where anything could happen.

Even love?

Resting her hands on the side of the sleigh, Abby glanced back at the house where the silhouettes of the children danced in the shimmering candlelight. Faint strains of "Silent Night" floated through the breeze as Emma played the piano-forte. Abby touched her pocket and felt the crinkle of the wrapped candy from one of the noise poppers Cole had bought each of the children. Was God giving her the opportunity to share her life with Cole?

Despite the anticipation she felt over a possible future with him, the situation with her father left a damper on her mood. *I'm afraid of what might happen, Lord. Give me the strength I need, and bring all hidden things to light so that the truth will be known.*

A horse whinnied behind her, and Abby spun around. A gun cocked, stopping within inches of her face.

"Abigail Covington. We finally meet."

A web of fear spread as the man pointed the gun at her temple. Her eyes focused on the barrel, then moved to the figure standing in front of her illuminated by the pale light of the moon. The stranger's long, black coat couldn't conceal his thin form, nor could his black Stetson hide the pastiness of his hollowed cheeks. But despite his apparent weak stature, a fierce determination shone across his face.

Was this the man blackmailing her father?

Abby pressed her back against the side of the sleigh. She had to run. She could scream and pray that in the cover of darkness his bullet would miss her. Her foot crunched in the snow as she leaned forward.

A firm hand gripped her arm and shoved her against the sleigh. Pain shot down her back, and she realized she'd miscalculated the man's strength.

"Don't even think about it. I've waited years for this moment. Ending your life would bring me nothing but pleasure. But first I want your father to pay."

He took a step back, a bony finger resting on the trigger of the revolver as he held his aim steady. Her mind went to her father—then to Cole. Suddenly she knew, no matter the outcome of her father's guilt or innocence, she loved Cole. *Oh, Lord, give me a chance to tell him how I feel. Don't let my life end like this.*

"The Lord will also be a refuge for the oppressed, a refuge in times of trouble." Abby took a deep breath, clinging to the promise of the psalm that flashed through her mind. "What do you want?"

The man's hollow laugh sent a renewed sliver of fear down her spine, but she refused to panic.

"Something only you can give me, Abigail. Or does your father call you Abby?"

"Who are you?"

His eyes narrowed into a beady stare. "Jeb Maddox."

She shook her head at the unfamiliar name.

The man frowned and loosened his tight grip from her arm. "Don't tell me your father never mentioned me."

"No, he hasn't." *Jeb Maddox.* Her mind whirled, trying to come up with a clue as to who the man was and what he wanted with her.

"It's a shame your father never mentioned me." He pushed the gun closer to her temple, until she could feel the cold metal pressing against her head. "I've thought about him for the past thirty years. That much time gives a man plenty of time to think about revenge."

Frustration rose in Abby's throat. "Revenge for what?"

When he ran his free hand down the side of her face, she recoiled from his touch. "You know, you look like your mother."

Her eyes widened in disbelief at his implications. "You knew my mother?"

He coughed, but his callous gaze never left her face. "Planned to marry her until your father came to town and stole her from me. I had a small fortune stashed away and could have provided for her . . ."

How could her mother have been in love with this man? "I just came to get something out of the sleigh. I need to go—"

"And miss everything I have to tell you?"

Abby glanced at the house. Would Cole hear her if she screamed?

Jeb cocked his head, and his lips curved into a malicious smile. "Didn't your mother ever tell you the truth about who you are?"

An icy fear swept over her. "What are you talking about?"
"Aaron Covington is not your father."

CHAPTER

Ten

$\mathcal{C}$ ole searched the room for Abby, a vague sense of anxiety gnawing at him. He'd seen her chatting with Mrs. Turner a few minutes earlier, but now the older woman stood beside the Christmas tree, visiting with one of the children.

He crossed the room. "Mrs. Turner, have you seen Abby?"

The plump, matronly woman smiled at Cole but shook her head. "She told me she left the stockings for the children in the sleigh and needed to get them. I thought she'd be back by now."

A knot hardened in the pit of Cole's stomach. Hadn't he specifically told her not to go anywhere alone? Grabbing his coat and gun, he ran down the steps of the porch toward the barn where he'd left the sleigh.

An icy gust of wind blew against him, but the scene playing out beside the barn struck fiercer than any winter storm. Abby sat astride a horse in front of a man dressed in black. The barrel of a gun resting in the man's hand glimmered in the bright light of the full moon.

"Abby!"

He noted the glimpse of fear in her expression as her captor dug his boots into the side of the horse and galloped away. Running to the barn, Cole mounted one of Turner's horses. It had been years since he'd ridden bareback, but there was no time for a saddle. His wounded shoulder burned as he grabbed the horse's coarse mane and mounted. Ignoring the dull pain, he pushed the mare as fast as he could.

Lord, please protect her!

He studied the tracks heading south, thankful for the white glow reflecting off the snow, and managed to keep the villain's horse in his range of vision.

What does he want with her, Lord?

He had no doubt that Abby's kidnapper was the blackmailer. Familiar feelings of unforgiveness reared inside. How could Aaron have put his daughter in a position like this? Conviction tugged at his soul. Hadn't he just learned the importance of forgiveness with his own father?

But this was the woman he loved. The realization came with great clarity. He loved Abby. He knew that now. Knew he wanted to spend the rest of his life with her beneath the shadow of the Rocky Mountains. If anything happened to her . . .

They galloped past a neighboring ranch house and continued toward a barn and several smaller buildings. Coming around the corner of one of the structures, Cole kicked his boots against the sides of the horse. There was no sign of Abby and her kidnapper on the other side.

Had they turned off the main path? A hundred yards later, he pulled back on the reins and turned the horse in a slow circle, desperate to pick up her trail again.

Lord, I need a miracle. Where is she?

Cole went back to the buildings where he'd lost them and searched each direction. Panic began to rise. The wind whipped against his face. The tracks he'd been following blended with a dozen other hoof marks. He needed something . . . anything.

A shiny object caught his eye just past one of the buildings. Dismounting quickly, he bent to pick it up. It was one of the candies from the Christmas crackers. He'd seen Timmy give one to Abby.

"Good girl!"

Remounting the horse, Cole rode hard toward the east, his eyes scanning the flat horizon for any sign of Abby and the horseman. Finally, he caught sight of the silhouette of a horse with two riders. They were stopped at the top of a slight ridge.

"Abby?" he called.

"The horse stepped in a hole and can't walk," she yelled to him over her shoulder.

The man aimed his gun at Cole and fired, missing him by inches. Cole pulled his gun out of his holster. He pointed it at Abby's kidnapper then hesitated, afraid he might miss and hit Abby. The man fired another shot. A searing pain shot through him. He gripped the horse's mane. Steadying himself upright atop the mare, he clutched his arm and struggled to focus.

"Cole!" Abby jabbed her elbow into her captor's ribs and pushed against him. He spit out a curse then fell back, tumbling to the ground. The downed man grabbed for his gun. Weapons fired in unison. Abby screamed as her kidnapper gripped his leg and rolled onto his side.

Cole watched as Abby dismounted and ran toward him— then all went black.

~

Abby poured two cups of steamy coffee and handed one of them to Cole, thankful to be back at the Covington ranch house after last night's alarming confrontation with Jeb Maddox. Thanks to ranch owner Matt Leland and his sons' help, they'd been able to quickly get Cole and her assailant to the doctor.

"You know you've got to stop doing this." Abby said as she sat down at the kitchen table beside him and added a spoonful of sugar to her drink.

"Doing what?" Cole took a sip of coffee and raised his brows in apparent amusement.

"Getting shot every couple weeks."

Cole let out a deep chuckle. "I don't know. Look at all the attention it gets me."

Abby's heart fluttered at his nearness, but she added a note of seriousness to her tone. "Next time it might get you killed."

"It was nothing more than a flesh wound. Doc said I'll be as good as new in a few days."

"You might not be so lucky next time."

Cole set down his drink and took her hand. "Abby, there's one thing I learned as I was trying to find you last night."

"What?"

"I couldn't imagine life without you. I realized I love you."

Sheriff Jefferson entered the kitchen behind her father, and Abby frowned at the interruption. While her heart soared with the knowledge that Cole loved her, the sheriff's presence in the room reminded her of just how close last night's confrontation had been. Jeb Maddox was bent on revenge, and if the Lord hadn't been protecting them, she and Cole might not be sitting here together this morning.

"Can I get you some coffee, Sheriff?" Abby stood, but he

motioned her to sit. "Thanks, but no. I need to head back to town. Just wanted to let you know that Jeb Maddox won't be causing problems around here anymore."

"How is he?" Despite the evil the man had done, Abby felt a measure of compassion for him. He was a man who needed to forgive—and be forgiven.

"Doc says Maddox will make it, but he'll limp the rest of his life."

"What will happen to him?" Abby asked.

"That will be up to a judge in Denver." Sheriff Jefferson tapped his Stetson against his leg. "And one more thing . . . I need to apologize for suspecting your involvement, Aaron. You're a fine man and to even think you could have been mixed up in such a matter—"

Aaron waved a hand in protest. "You were just doing your job, Sam. I'd think less of you if I thought friendship would stop you from doing your work."

The sheriff nodded. "I'd best be getting to town now. I'll see you folks Sunday at church."

Abby brought her father some coffee, watching as he gripped the sides of the mug.

"We need to talk," she said, sitting back down at the table.

Cole cleared his throat and stood to leave, but Abby reached up and touched his arm. "Please stay."

He sat down and took her hand, giving her the courage she needed before she turned to her father. "Jeb Maddox said you weren't my father."

Aaron took a deep breath. She saw the pain her words inflicted, but all she wanted was the truth.

After a moment, he looked up again, struggling to speak. "I . . . I promised your mother years ago I would never tell you about her past."

Abby leaned forward. "Father, it's time I heard the truth."

Sighing deeply, he nodded. "I know. There have been too many lies and deceptions. Look where they have brought us. I might never have seen you again if Cole hadn't stopped him."

Aaron leaned back in his chair and took a deep, labored breath. "Your mother told you she first came to Denver to look after a sickly aunt. That's what everyone thought, but the truth is . . . she was expecting you."

"So it's true." Abby's heart hammered, and she fought the tears threatening to erupt. "You're not my father."

"Oh, Abby." He reached out and ran his hand down her arm. "I've always loved you like a daughter. It didn't matter to me that you weren't my own flesh and blood."

Abby clung to Cole's hand. "Tell me everything, Father. I need to know."

Aaron's lips trembled, but he continued. "Your aunt told everyone your mother was a young widow whose husband had died in a hunting accident, and people accepted that explanation. But the truth was your mother had lived a promiscuous life.

"When she gave birth to you, she realized for the first time that there had to be more to life than parties and drinking and men. She began talking with her aunt, who had been trying for months to influence her toward Christ."

"What about me?"

"Your mother was an only child, but her parents disowned her and refused to accept you as their grandchild."

An ache formed in Abby's heart over the loss of a family she never knew. How could they have renounced their only daughter?

"Your aunt let you both live with her. You were about six months old when I first saw you." He smiled. "You were so adorable. Dark eyes and hair . . . you were a beauty. Anyway, your mother had recently become a Christian, but she was also engaged to Jeb. They planned to marry the following spring. No one knew, though, the kind of man Jeb really was. Your mother's father was a wealthy man, and I've always suspected that was the reason he wanted to marry her."

There were so many questions she wanted to ask, but one in particular haunted her. "Is Jeb Maddox my father?"

Aaron shook his head. "Your father was a blacksmith your mother knew back East. When you were two years old she received word he'd been killed in the War Between the States."

Abby waited for feelings of sadness over the loss of a man she'd never met, but felt nothing. Aaron Covington was the one who had raised her, nurtured her, and given her everything she needed.

"I met your mother at church about a month after I arrived in Denver. I think I fell in love with her that first day." He sighed, struggling to finish his story. "I was a widower who'd recently lost my wife of ten years. We'd never been able to have children. Believing I couldn't have my own biological children made falling in love with your mother—and accepting her child—seem perfectly natural. I never meant to steal her from Jeb, but that's what happened.

"When she told me the truth about her past, I assured her it didn't matter. In Christ, she was a new creation, and the past was exactly that—the past. All that mattered was that I loved her and she loved me, and we'd start a new life together.

"We married, and I legally made you my child. Your mother didn't want anyone to know you were illegitimate. We moved away from Denver and settled in Meadow Springs.

A year later, I struck gold, and that's when Jeb Maddox entered our lives again."

He shook his head. "Jeb never got over your mother jilting him. One afternoon, a heated argument broke out between us, and in a fit of rage Jeb tried to kill me. He shot me in the back, leaving me crippled. That's when we found out Jeb had his own disreputable past and was wanted by the law for several other crimes. He was arrested and sentenced to life in prison."

"And he blamed you for ruining his life," Abby said.

"Sheriff Jefferson told me Jeb confessed that his scheme to destroy my life was because he felt his own life had been ruined," her father continued. "He tried to frame me by sabotaging the surrounding ranches and spreading rumors. Even buying the Ford ranch in my name was part of his plan to ensure my guilt. Then he went after what I loved most—you."

"Why did you pay his blackmail demands?" Abby asked.

"I knew it was Jeb and foolishly thought if I paid him off, no one would ever find out about your mother's past. I promised her I'd protect you. . . ."

"Secrets never protect, and knowing the truth about my mother's past doesn't change my love for her." Abby squeezed her father's hand. "Cole once told me that denying forgiveness spreads hatred like gangrene. As hard as it is at the moment, we have to find a way to forgive Jeb and what he's done."

"What about me, Abby?" Her father leaned closer to her. "I've failed in numerous ways, but for thirty years I've loved you like a daughter. I can't imagine life without you."

Abby got up from her chair and knelt beside him. "You are my father and nothing will change that. Not the past, not Jeb Maddox . . . not anything."

Grasping her father's hand again, she stood and turned to

Cole. "It's time to put the past behind us and move toward the future."

A future she prayed included Cole.

The snow had melted, leaving only traces of white patches on the ground. Abby let Cole take her hand as they strolled away from the ranch house, her heart soaring with the knowledge that he loved her. They stopped beside the fenced corral to watch the sun slip behind the mountains as it scattered waves of color across the sky in its final performance for the day.

Abby leaned against a wooden post and rested her chin against her hands. In spite of the startling revelations her father told her today, she felt a warm peace covering her. She would not be the product of an unforgiving heart.

"How's your arm?" she asked, turning her head to watch Cole. He smiled and she was lost in his tender gaze, a place she'd like to stay for the rest of her life.

"Better." He reached out and took her hands, pulling her toward him. "I meant it when I said I loved you."

She let out a sigh of contentment. "I remember standing outside last night with a gun at my head, and all I wanted was a chance to tell you how I felt. I realized it never was a choice between you and my father. Even if he had been guilty, I knew then that I still would have loved you."

Cole pulled a small package out of his coat pocket and handed it to her. "I was hoping you'd say that."

Carefully, Abby unwrapped the paper. Inside was a delicate glass ornament in the shape of a heart. "Cole, it's beautiful!"

"I bought it to remind you of our first Christmas together."

Abby felt her heart overflow with happiness as she held it up to catch the light of the fading sun.

"And I'm hoping it will be the first of many Christmases together." Taking the ornament back, he carefully set the gift on the fence post and encircled his arms around her waist. "I don't want to lose you, Abby. Will you marry me?"

"Oh, yes!" Tears of joy formed in the corners of her eyes. "I'll even follow you back to Chicago if that's what it will take for us to be together? You are a Pinkerton, remember."

He pointed to the latest wound on his arm and chuckled. "I've known for some time my days as an operative were numbered. I think it's time for me to retire. Besides, I hear Covington Ranch has a position I might be interested in."

"What do you know about working a ranch?"

He cocked his head slightly and smiled at her. "I was born and raised on a ranch in Montana, remember. Lived half my life in the saddle."

"And the other half?" she asked, recalling the conversation they'd held after her accident in the wagon.

"I'd like to spend the second half growing old with you." His lips brushed hers.

Resting her hands against his chest, she lost herself in his kiss, knowing she'd found the place where she belonged—in the arms of the undercover cowboy who'd stolen her heart.

POPCORN CHRISTMAS ORNAMENTS

12 cups popped popcorn
1½ cups white granulated sugar
⅓ cup water
⅓ cup corn syrup
2 tbsp. butter
1 tsp. vanilla

Preheat oven to 250°. Grease a large shallow pan and add popcorn. Set in oven while making caramel mixture.

Place sugar, water, and corn syrup in a heavy 2-quart saucepan. Stir over low heat until sugar has dissolved and mixture comes to a boil. Continue to cook over low heat, without stirring, about ten minutes or until candy thermometer measures 280°. Sugar crystals that form on the sides of the pan can be brushed down with a pastry brush that has been dipped in warm water. Remove from heat and stir in butter and vanilla until smooth.

Pour syrup mixture slowly over popcorn, turning to coat kernels evenly. Set aside until the mixture is cool enough to handle but still warm enough to shape. Lightly butter your hands, then quickly press warm mixture into 2-inch balls. Let cool completely.

Wrap each ball with enough colored plastic wrap to pull together at top. Lastly, secure with a colorful ribbon and form a loop to hang on the Christmas tree as a decoration.

＾ **A Note from the Author**

Dear Reader,

I hope you've enjoyed reading Abby and Cole's story. I had so much fun getting to know them as they worked to resolve difficult spiritual issues and faced danger and uncertain peril together. One of the most satisfying parts of an inspirational romance to me is the happy ending, and as Abby and Cole discovered, there is nothing more valuable in a relationship than to have it based on the foundation of Christ and His example of unfailing love for us.

For me, writing has become a place of self-discovery. I never know what lesson I will learn along with the characters. I was recently reading in Matthew 18 where Jesus tells Peter to forgive not seven times, but seventy times seven. I was reminded again of the spiritual lesson Cole learned. Jesus knew that forgiveness is for us, as well as for the person who wounded us—a lesson often difficult to achieve, and yet what a blessing when we can finally let go of hurts from the past. And the biggest blessing of all is being reminded that we have a heavenly Father who loves and forgives us daily!

My prayer for each of you is that you might always find rest and peace in His arms regardless of the circumstances in your life.

Blessings,
Lisa Harris

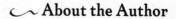

Lisa Harris is a wife, mother, and author who has been writing both fiction and nonfiction for the Christian market for the past four years. She and her husband, Scott, along with their three children, live outside Johannesburg, South Africa, as missionaries.

After graduating from Harding University with degrees in Bible and in family and consumer sciences, Lisa spent several years living in Europe and West Africa with her husband as church-planting missionaries. They have traveled to more than twenty countries, including France, Kenya, Japan, and Zambia.

Lisa's previously published works include over fifty articles, short stories, and devotionals as well as "Rescuing Sydney," a novella in the anthology *To Catch a Thief*, and *Michaela's Choice*, a historical novel.

Lisa welcomes letters written to her in care of Tyndale House Author Relations, P.O. Box 80, Wheaton, IL 60187-0080.

The Outlaw's Gift

LINDA GOODNIGHT

Oklahoma Territory
October 1888

*H*efting the old Henry repeater to shoulder level, Raven Patterson took aim at the big red dog and fired one shot. A pair of trusting brown eyes stared at her, puzzled, then glazed over as the old hound crumpled to the bed of dry autumn leaves.

"You killed him! You killed him!" Twelve-year-old Fanny flung herself out the front door of the cabin and flew over the yard toward the grove of bare oak trees fifty paces away, her calico dress whipping around her bare legs as she came. Quickly, Raven lowered the gun and whirled toward the screaming voice. With sure, no-nonsense steps she strode toward her younger sister, taking the brunt of her anger head-on, shielding her from the dead animal.

"I hate you." Fanny's pale, narrow face twisted in pain. "You are the meanest person on earth. You don't care about nothing anymore, not even poor old Red."

Raven swallowed back the heavy, sick despair that lay on her shoulders day and night. Fanny was so wrong. She cared all right, but caring hurt too much to let on most of the time. Since the day Ma and Pa died of the fever, leaving her with a younger sister and brother to raise on this lonely patch of Oklahoma prairie, all she'd done was care.

"He was old, Fanny. And suffering. I can't abide suffering."

Goodness knows she'd seen enough of it.

"You killed him 'cause he ate too much. You'll be killing one of us next."

Raven sighed. Fanny had her own way of seeing things. "Go back to the house. Joshua will be upset."

Grief-stricken and furious, Fanny stomped back to the cabin, her wail ebbing to a sustained moan.

Raven turned her attention to the fallen dog, shutting out the sound of her crying siblings. Old Red had been a good buddy, and she'd miss him. He was the only one she could talk to most times. Talking to Fanny or little Joshua only scared them and made her load heavier to bear. Only Red and the Lord had listened without fear. What would she do without that faithful old dog?

She pulled herself up tight at the notion. No use getting sloppy and weepy. People died. Dogs died. All leaving you with nothing but an empty hole inside to fill with work and worry.

Stiffening her resolve, Raven went to work. Pa's shovel made feeble scraping sounds against the stubborn Oklahoma earth. Thanks to the lack of rain, the ground was hard and dry and unforgiving. Twice daily she'd hauled buckets of water from the creek to water the withering peas and squash—bucket after bucket until she thought her back would break right in two. Now with winter just over the horizon, the pitiful joke they'd called a fall garden hadn't produced enough food to last a month, much less all winter.

She heaved a weary sigh—heartsick, tired, lonely, and scared, though she hated admitting the last one. Nine months of trying to keep things together with hungry mouths crying for their ma and she herself wanting to do the same was enough to scare anyone.

She looked skyward, where the gray November clouds obscured the sun. "Lord, if You're not too busy, I sure could use some help right now."

She poked at the ground again. As if dead set against taking in the gentle old dog, the hard earth refused to budge.

"Ah, Red." What if she couldn't dig the hole? Raven glanced over to see a swarm of insects already buzzing around her old friend. She shooed them away and dragged a broken tree branch over to cover his lifeless body until she could scrape out enough dirt to make a grave. She had to do it. Had to for Red.

The hound had been a gift from the man she'd always called Pa. She'd never known for certain who her real father was, but she'd been proud to call Benjamin Patterson her pa. She'd been ten when Ma had married Ben and come west. Along the way, they'd picked up the fat, wiggling puppy at a stagecoach station, and she'd immediately christened him Red.

"Good hunting dogs, they are," the stationmaster had promised Pa when he'd asked about the litter of squirming pups. And he hadn't been lying about that. Red had treed more than his share of possums and coons, and been a fine rabbit hunter to boot, putting food on the table in those first lean years before the land started to yield strong fertile crops. No one could ever say the old hound hadn't earned his keep.

Raven jabbed harder at the rigid soil, dismayed to see only a shallow indentation in the ground for all her effort. Tears prickled the back of her eyes. She jabbed the shovel a little harder, determined not to cry. Crying over Ma and Pa hadn't made the past months a bit easier.

"You deserve a proper burying, Red, and I aim to give it to you if it kills me."

Frustration mounted higher than the pitiful scoops of dirt. After twenty minutes of digging, the grave was only deep enough to bury a bird—if it was skinny.

A squawking cry overhead drew her eyes upward. Buzzards.

"No, you don't." She gritted her teeth in anger. "Not Red. You'll not get Red."

As if to mock her, a hungry vulture swept from the overcast sky, black wings *flap, flapp*ing as he landed on the protective branch covering the dog.

With a cry, Raven rushed toward it, shovel swinging. Squawking in protest, the bird lifted off but remained overhead, circling, biding its time.

She went back to shoveling. In seconds, the vulture returned and this time jabbed his beak at the fallen animal before Raven could reach his side. With a wail of despair, she threw herself over the dog, shielding his body with her own. The stench of blood and death assailed her. She clenched her teeth and gulped, swallowing the saliva that pooled beneath her tongue.

"I won't be sick. I won't," she declared only seconds before the spasms racked her body, spilling the contents of her meager breakfast.

When the awful moment passed, Raven spat and wiped a shaky hand across her mouth. With a trembling sigh, she closed her eyes and rested her forehead against the brittle leaves covering the dog's lifeless body, wishing she'd died instead of Ma and Pa.

"Have you thought of burying the animal closer to the creek? Ground might be softer there."

At the unfamiliar masculine voice, Raven's head snapped up, heart thudding wildly. Other than her four-year-old brother, there wasn't a male within three miles.

Less than six feet away stood a lean, duster-clad cowboy holding a big bay horse by the reins. She hadn't heard his approach, but then she'd been busy . . . and old Red hadn't been able to warn her this time.

Jumping up, Raven straightened her skirts, eyeing the stranger with distrust. How long had he been there? Had he witnessed her humiliating sickness? And where had he come from? She knew all the homesteaders round about, and he wasn't one of them. Granted, cowboys, drifters, and new settlers came through occasionally, stopping to rest a spell or to fill canteens from her spring. Maybe he was one of those.

His sun-darkened face was friendly enough, set off by eyes as green as elm buds in the springtime. Something she recognized as pity lurked in their depths.

Raven stiffened. She wasn't having pity from anybody. "I'll manage," she declared, waiting for him to either state his business or disappear as quickly as he'd come.

He did neither. Without another word the stranger removed his long duster and tossed it across his saddle. Then he fetched the shovel from where she'd flung it, walked to a spot nearer the creek, and started digging.

"Didn't you hear me?" Raven followed, indignant.

"Keep the buzzards away."

Though it raised her hackles to be bossed by some stranger, the request made sense. She certainly wasn't making any progress on the grave. With a huff of self-disgust, Raven went to stand guard beside the fallen dog. The man

LINDA GOODNIGHT

went to work, his back to her, giving Raven ample time to study him.

He wasn't too old. A little older than she, but less than thirty she'd say, though his surprisingly clean-shaven face made him look much younger. If he were a woman she'd have called him pretty, so clear and defined were his features. Beneath a wide-brimmed hat, his sandy hair was long enough to pull into a short ponytail at the nape of his neck. It was tied with a strip of rawhide.

He was simply dressed like a dozen other wandering cowboys who'd passed this way in the years gone by. His trousers were heavy denim, worn and faded. His blue shirt stretched across his back as he wrestled the soil from its confines. Lean, hard muscles bunched in the arms driving the shovel deep into the earth. He wasn't oversized, but he was as strong as a young mule, and Raven knew a moment of envy. Why hadn't God given her the strength of a man? She had a man's work to do. Why not the strength to do it with?

"You got anything to wrap him in?" he asked without turning. "Or you just want me to toss him in and cover him up?"

"There's some old feed sacks."

"Get one." When she hesitated, he glanced over one shoulder and said, "I'll watch out for the buzzards."

In short order, old Red was wrapped and buried beneath a mound of fertile Oklahoma dirt. The north wind kicked up, as it always did out here on the prairie, and Raven pulled her father's old work coat a little tighter, the chill in her heart more pronounced than that of the autumn weather. Overhead the barren tree branches clacked against one another as wind hummed through them.

The young cowboy turned from the grave, wiping a sleeve across his now sweating brow. "You want to mark the spot?"

"No." She'd never forget where Red lay buried. Never. "But we need to pray over him."

The man hesitated. "Go ahead then," he said gruffly, then walked a little distance away. He propped the shovel beside the tree, retrieved his duster, and leaned his broad back against the rough post oak. One booted foot propped behind him, he crossed his arms and waited.

"Don't you pray?" Raven called after him.

"No." His expression was distant.

"Why not?"

He shrugged. "Don't figure it does any good to talk to somebody that never listens."

Wondering about the wounded expression in the stranger's green, green eyes, Raven bowed her head. "Lord," she said, self-conscious to know the man must be staring and listening. She cleared her throat. "Lord," she started again, "old Red's been a good friend. I don't know if dogs go to heaven, but I know You'll take care of him for me. And I thank You for it."

Keeping her eyes squeezed tight, she silently offered a prayer for the rambling cowboy who'd come to her aid. Something had hurt him, and she knew for certain only the Holy Spirit could penetrate that kind of desolation. No matter how difficult times might be, she couldn't imagine life without hope in the Lord.

When she raised her head, the man had disappeared. Whirling, she saw him amble toward the house, his loose duster making *pop-pop* noises above the spurs on the back of his worn boots.

Her stomach lurched. She didn't know this cowboy and didn't want him anywhere near her little brother and sister. Grabbing the Henry repeater, she hurried after him. "Hey!"

Her shout turned him around. Standing with one hip lower than the other and the pearl handle of a six-gun riding on one thigh, he looked relaxed and dangerous.

"Who are you?"

"Name's Seth Blackstone." His green gaze moved to the rifle in her hands. "Can a man get a drink of water?"

She lowered the gun, feeling foolish. Of course, he was thirsty. No matter that the wind was chill and the sun only a weak glare behind gray clouds, the man had just dug a grave in very hard soil. What was wrong with her, getting all nervous this way? He had done her a kindness. She owed him the courtesy of a cool drink of water and a few minutes' rest before he continued his journey.

Torn between the hospitality spoken of in the Bible and the safety of her family, she considered sending him to the creek. *"Some have entertained angels unawares."* The familiar Scripture played through her mind.

The man's duster blew open and again Raven caught a flash of the six-gun. She scoffed at her fanciful thoughts. *Angel, indeed.*

"I'm Raven Patterson," she said. Then attributing her sudden shiver to the cold wind, she led the stranger up the wooden steps and into her house.

CHAPTER
Two

*O*ver a dipper of cool, clear water, Seth watched the slim, dark woman move with graceful efficiency around the clean kitchen. Raven. That was her name, and aptly so, for her long, flowing hair was as black as a raven and her exotic, almond-shaped eyes almost as dark. She didn't fit society's idea of beauty, but Seth found her darkness interesting. She was tired too, bone weary and worried sick about something.

"Who's that man, Raven?" From near the fireplace, a red-haired boy no more than four gazed at him with curious eyes. In a chair by the single window, with her rigid back turned, sat a young girl, her hair equally as red as the boy's. Odd that Raven was so dark and the little ones so pale.

"His name is Mr. Blackstone," Raven answered over her shoulder, then returned to the task of scrubbing away the dirt and unpleasantness of the grave digging.

Blackstone. Even now the name sounded strange to his ears, though he'd claimed it as his own for over two years. Ever since Stephen and Cleo had turned him into a hunted man.

Cleo, with her soft blonde hair and winning smile, had played him for a fool. He never should have let her talk him into—

Seth slammed the door on that thought. For two years now, he'd been on the run, searching for the two people who had destroyed his life. He'd find them. He clenched his teeth. And they would pay.

"Why is he here?" the blue-eyed boy asked, gazing up at Seth in a kind of awe. One cheek glowed pink with heat from the small fire crackling beside him.

"He helped me bury Red."

"Oh." The child's face clouded. "You killed Red."

Raven's dark eyes filled with tears. She turned away abruptly. "I had to."

Pity pulled at Seth. He'd seen her tears. He'd observed her sickness as she battled the elements to give the dog a proper burying. The little ones might not understand how badly she ached over what she'd been forced to do, but he knew.

Settling the dipper back into the bucket, Seth strode across the room, his spurs jingling loudly against the wooden floor. He crouched down to eye level with the boy. "What's your name, son?"

"Joshua." The child sniffed, the corners of his bow mouth turning down.

Though Seth had no experience with children, he had plenty with suffering.

"Well, Joshua, old Red was tired. Raven didn't want to lose him anymore than you did, but he was sick and suffering." He tilted the boy's chin upward. "Do you know what that means?"

"No." Blue eyes drilled holes in his composure. Poor little fella. Seth searched for a way to make the child understand. "Did you ever stump your toe real bad?"

"Yeth." The flame-colored head bobbed. "It hurted too."

"And you wished it would stop, didn't you?"

"Uh-huh."

"That's how Red felt. Like he'd stumped his toe and it wouldn't ever stop hurting. Now he's not hurting anymore."

"'Cause he's with Jesus?" the guileless boy asked.

Seth gulped, the heavy load of sick despair slamming down on him like an iron stove lid. Oh, for the simple childlike faith of his boyhood. How could he tell this innocent, sad little fellow that God played favorites, that He'd let you down when you needed Him most?

Gazing into the hopeful face, he couldn't do it. "Yeah, buddy. Your dog's with Jesus now."

A radiant smile, so sweet it made Seth's teeth ache, crossed Joshua's face. "Then I'm glad. Jesus will take good care of him, and Mama and Papa will be so happy to see him again."

The small body catapulted into Seth's chest. In reflex, Seth grabbed for the boy and found himself engulfed in a miniature bear hug. Riding back on his heels to take the child's weight, he breathed in Joshua's warm, puppy scent. A deep yearning started inside him. How long had it been since any human had touched him in affection?

More than a little discomfited, Seth let the boy hug his fill, then awkwardly patted his narrow, cotton-clad back. The child was thin, too thin, just like his sisters.

The thought had him giving the house a quick survey. The furniture was solid and sturdy. A nice store-bought rug circled the center of the living room where the younger girl sat. A comforting fire crackled in the fireplace, though he saw very little reserve wood for fuel. The cookstove was a good one, but above it, the rows of shelves were nearly empty. He'd noticed a smokehouse out back, but from the looks of the kitchen, it would be just as bare. The scent of this morning's bacon was the only hint of food in the house.

Something was amiss.

The children couldn't be Raven's, could they? She looked older, midtwenties or so, but not old enough to have a near-teenage daughter. And he hadn't seen a single sign of a man around.

Keeping one hand on Joshua's bony shoulder, he rose. "You folks alone here?"

His question brought Raven spinning around, her exotic eyes wide. She held a washrag against the side of her tear-stained face.

"My—my—husband's gone to town," she stuttered, hands clenching and unclenching the cloth. Catching his glance at the empty pantry, she hurried on. "For supplies. He's gone for supplies."

The two younger children stared at her.

"But, Raven—" The little boy blinked.

"Joshua," the woman interrupted, "you get on out to the chicken house and make sure they have water. Go on now."

"But, Raven—" The boy seemed determined to say something.

"Mind me, Joshua."

With a baffled expression, the boy slid from beneath Seth's hand and took a jacket from a peg by the door, pulling it over his skinny arms. He opened the door, went out, then reappeared just as quickly, blue eyes round with fright.

"Those mens are coming again."

The woman closed her eyes, shoulders slumping for a moment before she stiffened her back and commanded, "Get back in the house this instant."

The boy needed no cajoling. He scampered inside and hid behind her skirts.

Raven was clearly distressed at the arrival of visitors.

Seth moved to her side. "What men?" He frowned down into a pair of worried brown eyes. "Trouble?"

"The sheriff."

Seth jerked, his hand going automatically to the revolver. Dandy. Just what he needed. A lawman.

Raven saw his reaction and studied him for a long moment. She gnawed at her lip before coming to a decision. "You can wait in there if you'd like." She hitched her chin toward a closed door at the end of the kitchen. "This shouldn't take long."

If he had a lick of sense, he'd take advantage of the woman's willingness to shield him. He wasn't a coward, but he was so close to finding Stephen and Cleo. He couldn't risk getting caught now.

The pounding horses' hooves helped make up his mind. Swiftly, he entered the bedroom and closed the door. Moving to the window, he eased back the cheery yellow curtain to see three riders lope into view.

Wearing an old denim coat three sizes too large, Raven met them in the yard. The two children followed her like chicks beneath a hen's wing.

"Sheriff," he heard her say, her husky voice stiff with discomfort.

"Afternoon, Raven." The florid-faced lawman touched the brim of his hat. "How are you and the children?"

"We're fine, as you can clearly see. Yourself?"

"The boy there don't look none too fine to me. Kinda skinny and frail." The sheriff leaned forward on the saddle horn and motioned to Joshua. "Come here, boy."

"Stay put, Joshua." She forestalled him with a palm to his shirtfront.

"Now Raven, there ain't no need of getting high-headed. We're just interested in the boy's welfare. You three been out here on your own for coming on a year soon. Winter's fast approaching, and you ain't got enough supplies laid by to feed a mouse, much less a family. There's no need for these children to suffer because of your stubbornness."

Seth listened with interest. So, there was no husband. And no supplies coming from town.

"You're wasting your time here, Sheriff." Visible only to Seth's watchful eyes, Raven's fingers trembled against her brother's chest. "I can take care of my family."

The sheriff shifted in the saddle as he turned to the man beside him. "Parson, maybe you can talk some sense into her."

"Now, Raven dear," the black-suited reverend began, motioning at the third man who sat low in the saddle, his coat pulled up around his ears and mouth. "George Johnson and his wife are a fine Christian couple who would look after Joshua and Fanny like they were their own blood. You know your mama and papa would want these children to have a good home with plenty of food and warm clothes."

Raven's elegant chin shot up. The wind caught her long black hair and whipped it back so that she looked as proud as a warrior queen. Admiration filled Seth. The woman wasn't about to let the sheriff see how frightened she was. "God will supply our needs," she answered.

With a disbelieving snort, George Johnson looked around at the weary little farm. "Well, He better hurry." Then glancing at the preacher, he added, "No disrespect meant, Reverend."

The preacher pushed at his wire-rimmed spectacles. "We've missed you at church lately, Raven, and that worries the congregation that things out here are not going well. We wouldn't be very good Christians if we weren't concerned for these children. You have to understand that."

Seth smiled grimly at the little scene being played out beneath the gray Oklahoma clouds. One thing for sure: Raven had grit, but he doubted that was enough to stop these three men. He knew how towns worked. If the preacher and the sheriff and a few old busybodies convinced each other that the children's welfare was at stake, one stubborn woman wouldn't change their minds.

The sheriff sighed. "You ain't gonna make this easy, are you?" He started to dismount. "As sheriff it's my duty to see these children are well cared for. I ain't trying to hurt you, girl. I knew your papa for years, but a young woman out here alone can't make a go of this farm. And without this farm, you can't care for these children."

The two young ones clung to Raven's skirts as she clasped them to her. "We've been through this before, Sheriff. Joshua, Fanny, and I are a family. They stay with me."

Seeing the intent of the men, Seth slipped to the opposite side of the room and eased open the back window. Dropping silently to the ground, he worked his way to the corner of the house, listening. The scent of woodsmoke curled in his nostrils, and oak leaves crunched beneath his feet, but his attention remained on the scene in the front yard.

The sheriff yanked at little Joshua, who was stuck tight as a dog tick to Raven's leg. Raven gripped the child with one hand, while hammering at the sheriff with the other. Her cry of anguish drove Seth out of hiding.

"What's going on out here?" Seth asked, ambling forward with a puzzled frown, hoping against hope that the lawman didn't recognize him.

"Who are you?" the sheriff demanded.

"Didn't Miss Raven tell you?" As casually as a man could with his heart in his throat, Seth stuck out a hand, effectively freeing Joshua from the sheriff's grip. The child scrambled onto the porch. "I'm Seth Blackstone, the new hired man. Figure as how this little farm can be mighty productive with a man to turn the plow again."

"Hired man?" The sheriff glared at Raven. "Why didn't you tell me?"

"I—you didn't give me a chance." Raven's hands twisted in her plain brown skirt.

Seth stood his ground while the sheriff eyed him suspiciously. If he hadn't quit praying long ago, Seth would have asked the Lord for help right then and there. If the sheriff recognized him, he'd be swinging from a rope before the week was out.

"Where you hail from, mister?" The wily lawman's gaze fell to the holster tied around Seth's thigh.

"St. Louis," Seth answered honestly, though he hadn't been home in more than seven years, and Papa and Amanda had probably long since forgotten his name. He'd shamed them, shamed himself, and as much as home pulled at him sometimes, he could never return.

"What's a city boy doing way out here?"

Casually, Seth lifted one shoulder. "I hear the government's planning to open up some territory in these parts pretty soon."

The sheriff took his measure. "So you're sticking around then?"

"Maybe." The lawman's questions were starting to rankle. "As long as Miss Raven and the young'uns need a hand."

"This sounds fishy to me, Sheriff. She never said nothing

before about no hired man. And what good will he do them now with winter coming on?" This from the man called Johnson.

"That's a fair enough question, Mr.—what did you say your name was?"

"Blackstone. And there's plenty of work on this place to keep a man busy the rest of the winter."

"That's right, Sheriff." Raven came to life, spilling out a list that made his head reel. "Hogs to butcher, wood to chop, pens to fix, and soil to turn. By spring, this farm will be running itself again."

Johnson stretched up out of his coat and glared at Seth. "I got plans for those young'uns. My wife ain't gonna like it one bit if I come home without 'em."

Something in the man's insistence didn't set well with Seth. "What's the matter, Johnson? Losing a couple of cheap farmhands?"

The sheriff looked from Johnson's livid face to Seth's hand riding lightly above the pearl-handled gun. Finally, he settled on Raven. "I don't know what's going on, girl, but I aim to keep my eye on you. If things don't perk up around here by Christmastime, I'm coming back for those youngsters. And next time, your hired man won't stop me."

Measuring Seth one more time, the sheriff mounted his horse. "You mark what I say, Raven Patterson. If I find this man staying anywhere but the barn, it'll be my duty to remove your brother and sister from his presence. I can't leave them in an indecent situation."

At Raven's sharp gasp, Seth stepped up beside her. "You've insulted the lady, sir. I suggest you apologize and be on your way."

The sheriff had the grace to flush. "No insult meant."

Briefly, he touched the brim of his hat, then slapped the big roan and cantered away, stirring the leaves in his wake. The other two men followed—one sour and muttering, the other shaking his head in worry.

"Oh, dear Lord in heaven." Trembling, Raven collapsed on the front-porch step and dropped her head into her lap. "Thank You, Jesus. Thank You, Jesus."

The children stood around her, uncertain.

"Raven." The little boy pushed at the long hair covering her face and spilling down the steps. "Is he really going to be our hired hand? Is he?"

Raven lifted her head, dark eyes pleading. "Will you, Mr. Blackstone? Will you stay? I can't pay you anything but room and board and a part of the profits if they come. But this would be a warm place to winter."

"No, ma'am. I can't stay."

"Why not? The snow and ice will come soon. Surely you don't want to be out in the weather."

He shook his head, glancing away from the pitiful little trio huddled on the porch steps. He knew enough about farming. He could help her. Hadn't he started his own ranch down in Texas? Ah, Texas. Exactly why he couldn't stay. "I'm sorry. No."

Her voice took on a tone of desperation. She rose from the steps and touched his arm. "Why? I don't understand. Is there some place you have to be?"

"You might say that." The bitter gall rose in his throat. "Some people I'm looking for are reported to be in this area." Teeth clenched, eyes narrowed, he said, "And I won't stop until I find them."

Raven's gentle touch dropped away. Her eyes searched his. "Or until someone else finds you?"

With a shock he stared into those intelligent eyes. She suspected the truth about him, reason enough to get on his horse and head west. "You don't understand—," he started.

She held up a hand to silence him. "We're desperate enough not to care."

"Why would you take such a chance?"

"I asked God to help us and now you're here."

Bitterness rose in Seth. "Don't be thinking I'm anyone's answer to prayer."

"I reckon we'll let the Lord decide on that." Something about the way her chin rose in stubborn commitment to her faith reminded him of his sister, Amanda. The never-faraway ache for family gnawed at his insides.

"Please, mister." The boy flung his arms around Seth's legs. "I don't want to live with anyone but Raven."

A lump the size of Texas filled Seth's chest as he looked down at the small redheaded boy, then up into Raven's anxious face.

The hope and need he saw in her—in all three of them—clawed at him. He knew how desperation felt. He knew something else, too. For two long years he'd roamed the borders of Texas and Oklahoma, following the trail of the devious pair who'd destroyed his life. Though he couldn't pretend that God had sent him, he was bone tired and soul weary, and the notion of spending the cold months in a warm place tugged at him like the memories of boyhood Christmases.

With a certainty that he would live to regret his rash decision, Seth nodded his head. "All right, then, I'll stay. Until spring, if I can."

Or until the sheriff figures out who I am and comes for me instead of these children.

CHAPTER

Three

$\mathscr{R}$aven tromped halfway up the ladder to the barn loft and paused. "Mr. Blackstone?"

"Yes."

Raven hesitated, unsure whether to wait or go on up. Pa had allowed many a wayfarer to rest a night in the barn, but she'd never been allowed to disturb them. She bit back a sigh of loneliness. Pa wasn't here anymore to protect or advise. She'd have to make her own decisions about proper decorum with a strange man.

"I've brought you some blankets."

Hay rustled, then two boot toes appeared at the ladder's edge. "I'm obliged." He bent forward. Long, strong fingers reached for the bedding.

Handing them up, she offered, "Supper's on. I expect you're hungry after all the work you've done this afternoon."

From the moment Sheriff Clifford rode away, Seth Blackstone had set to work. He'd repaired the barn door broken in a sharp gust of wind months ago. He'd checked and straightened one segment of fence, inspected the cow, the hogs, and the chickens, making tight, concise recommendations about each, and then he'd spent the remainder of the day chopping firewood.

All the while, Joshua had trailed him, scurrying to hold a post or hand up a hammer or carry in armloads of wood, his hunger for a man's attentions almost painful for Raven to watch. To her relief—and Mr. Blackstone's credit—the stranger had patiently encouraged the small boy. More than once she'd raised her head from a mountainous pile of mending, certain she'd heard the boy's childish peal of laughter lifting on the chilly wind, and her heart lifted along with it.

"Well. Are you hungry?" Wondering if his hesitation was due to their shortage of supplies, pride took over and she hastened to add, "We've plenty, you know. Biscuits, gravy, and cold buttermilk."

When the scuffed brown boots began their descent, Raven quickly retreated, stopping at the barn entrance. The cowboy stepped around her, politely pushed the door open, and held it against the wind until she slipped passed into the waning twilight.

Drawing his coat around him, Seth remarked. "I've never seen a loft so snug and tight, as fine as most houses. The man who built it did an excellent job."

Raven blamed the cutting north wind and the swirl of dust and leaves for the sudden sting of tears. "My father was a carpenter. He took pride in everything he built, but especially in that loft. Papa always said we might someday house an angel unawares and we wanted him to have good lodging."

Seth Blackstone shot her a sharp look, then set his face toward the cabin.

She knew he didn't appreciate her talk of angels and

prayers and the Lord, and she wondered again what had turned his heart so cold.

They said nothing more until they reached the house, where the pleasant heat of the cookstove and the aroma of hot biscuits met them at the door.

Joshua, hair neatly combed and face washed, carefully set out the plates. Fanny, still in a snit, poured buttermilk into tall glasses with the air of a wounded queen. "Is *he* eating in the house?"

"Fanny Clarice!" Raven stood stock-still at her sister's impudence.

Fanny's nose shot into the air. "Papa never let vagabonds inside."

"Papa never allowed his children to behave rudely either. He'd be heartbroken."

Fanny's arrogance faded. She dropped her head. Tears gathered on the pale blonde lashes surrounding her green eyes. "I'm sorry, Mr. Blackstone."

Seth stepped into the kitchen, bringing with him the scent of the outdoors, of hay and cold and hard work. He removed his hat. "No offense taken, Miss Fanny. I'm a stranger to you folks and rightly should take my meals in the barn."

"You'll do no such thing." Raven marched around and pulled out Papa's chair. No one had sat in that chair since the night Papa, feverish and weak, had eaten his last meal. But Raven was nothing if not practical. She sent Fanny a stern look, daring her to make a comment, but Raven's anger disappeared like woodsmoke in a whirlwind when Fanny's lip began to quiver.

"Why does everything have to die?" the twelve-year-old whispered as Seth's hand touched the back of Papa's chair.

Raven's heart twisted. If only she had an answer to that one. First Mama and Papa and six-year-old James. And now old Red. "I don't know, Fanny. Dying is as much a part of living as living. That's the way God made it. They're all in a better place. Remember the Scripture Mama taught us?"

Fanny nodded. "'To be absent from the body, and to be present with the Lord.'"

"That's right. Mama and Papa and little James are walking on streets of gold with Jesus Himself right this minute." These were the words Raven had used over and over to comfort herself and her siblings. Sometimes they worked.

"But I miss them all so much."

"I know." Drawing in a steadying breath, Raven patted her sister's hand. The subject hurt too badly and Raven determined to move past it. "Bow your head for grace and let's eat. Mr. Blackstone is near to starving."

When they were seated, she wrapped one hand around Fanny's and out of long habit extended the other in the direction of Papa's chair. As soon as she'd done it, she wanted to yank her hand away, but that would be far more rude than Fanny's remark. Peeking from the corner of her eye, she watched the man's surprised reaction. When she fleetingly hoped he'd refuse to join hands in the family circle of prayer, conviction overcame her. He was a lost and lonely soul. That was all. A man in need of the Lord and a filling supper same as anyone else.

After a long moment, a warm, calloused hand, masculine like Papa's but very different too, grasped hers.

As she prayed, distracted by the unfamiliar experience of holding hands with a man, the heat of a blush crept up her neck. "There," she declared when the prayer was over, sliding her hand from his to the biscuit pan. "Have a biscuit."

That suddenly fascinating hand reached out and took a golden piece of bread, neatly slicing it down the middle before applying a slice of fresh butter from Sadie. Seth bit into the biscuit, then closed his eyes and sighed appreciatively. "I haven't had a biscuit this light and tasty in a long time."

His compliment didn't do a thing to take Raven's foolish mind off the feel of his hand in hers. Furthermore, his impeccable table manners, an oddity for a wanderer, increased her curiosity about him. More than once she tried to ask about his life, but each time he steered the conversation back to the farm, the work that needed doing, or to questions about community life in nearby Riley's Fork.

"If the townsfolk are so worried about you, why haven't any of them been out to help butcher one of the hogs?"

"I didn't ask." Raven spooned a dipper of thick, white gravy onto Joshua's biscuit. "I was afraid they would see it as a sign that I can't take care of this place by myself."

"You can't."

Raven bristled, letting the dipper clatter against the glass bowl. "Yes I can."

Laying his fork aside, he quirked an eyebrow. "Then why haven't you butchered a hog?"

"I was getting around to it." She'd already made up her mind to kill the hog even if she had no idea of how to go about the actual process.

As Seth reached for yet another biscuit and sliced it in two, an amused twinkle lit his face. "Ever butchered one before?"

Raven squirmed. "Well, not exactly."

Leaning forward, he propped an elbow on the table and aimed half a biscuit in her direction. The corner of his mouth quivered suspiciously. "Have you ever even watched while one was butchered?"

Suddenly she realized this stranger was teasing, and the notion sent a feeling, warm as gravy, coursing through her. "Not yet." Raven pressed a hand against her lips, covering the grin that quivered there. "But I'm planning to right away. Just as soon as you're ready to let me."

Laughing outright, Seth leaned back in his chair. After a moment, he sobered. "Butchering hogs isn't a woman's job, especially a woman alone."

"I'm big now," Joshua piped up. A buttermilk mustache coated his upper lip. "I can help; then Raven won't be so tuckered out all the time."

Raven's heart twisted with love for her baby brother. Sweet little Joshie. His head barely reached above the table-top. But already he shouldered a load of responsibility, carrying firewood, taking care of the chickens, and was even learning to milk old Sadie. Nobody was going to take this precious little boy from her as long as she had breath in her body. Maybe someone else could give him more material goods, but no one could love him more than she did.

To his credit, Seth Blackstone recognized Joshua's longing to be grown-up. "I could use a man's help, Joshua, if you're willing."

"Yes, sir!" Joshua's narrow chest swelled with pride. "I'm sure enough willing."

Since their parents' deaths, Fanny had been anything but cooperative, so Raven could hardly believe her ears when her sister joined in. "We can all learn. I'd much rather butcher a hog of my own than be farmed out to George and Agnes Johnson."

A slow smile eased up Seth's face as he settled back against Papa's chair. "Miss Raven, with these good workers, I do believe you'll make a go of this place."

His gentle encouragement, the moment of shared laughter, and the memory of his warm, calloused hand in hers, filled Raven with a sense of security long missing. For all his secrets, Seth Blackstone was a gentle man. Maybe the Lord really had sent him along to help them. And maybe things were about to take a turn for the better.

Stomach full and feeling more optimistic than she had in months, Raven rose to clear the table.

"Thank you for the fine supper." Seth swigged the last of his buttermilk. "I'll say good night and head to the barn."

Joshua clambered up from the table and hurried around to Seth's chair. "Don't go yet. Raven's going to read to us."

The man looked at her quizzically.

"Devotionals," she clarified, setting the two remaining biscuits in the breadbox for breakfast.

Instantly Seth stiffened, then scraped back from the table. "Thank you again for the meal, Miss Raven." He nodded toward the children. "We'll get started on that work first thing in the morning."

He turned toward the door.

"Mr. Blackstone."

One hand on the door handle, he hesitated, looking back over his shoulder. Gone was the laughter they'd shared only moments before.

Something in his expression tore at Raven. She asked the question that had nagged her since the moment he'd refused to pray over old Red. "Aren't you a God-fearing man at all?"

He let two beats pass. The green eyes that had twinkled with kindness all through the meal suddenly grew distant and sorrowful. "Oh, I fear Him all right." His mouth turned down in a hard line. "I fear Him plenty."

With that curious declaration, Seth Blackstone turned on

his heel and disappeared into the darkness of the night—and the far more terrible darkness of his soul.

CHAPTER

four

The smell of hot grease permeated the house as huge chunks of white fat slowly melted in the black kettle hanging from the fireplace. Chilly as the weather had turned, Raven wiped a sleeve over her perspiring forehead. Rendering lard was slow, hot work, but she wasn't complaining. The much-needed fat would serve them well in the coming winter months. For the hundredth time in two weeks, she thanked God for sending Seth Blackstone her way.

Using a thick rag, she reached for the kettle to drain the melted fat.

A lean, masculine arm, clad in faded chambray, reached around her. "I'll get that."

Fighting down the strangest urge to tidy her hair, Raven admired the ease with which Seth lifted the kettle and tipped it up, holding the lid with one hand as the liquefied contents flowed into freshly scrubbed storage buckets.

He'd spent the better part of the day butchering an overgrown hog, and now here he was offering to do her work too.

But that's the way he'd been ever since the day he'd agreed to stay, working like a man who wouldn't be here long enough to get it all done.

"I've got the meat hung and the smokehouse fires started. Fanny and Joshua can keep an eye on them."

They both well knew that the preservation of the pork depended on keeping the little building out back filled with smoke for at least the next week. The children's help was essential.

Raven took the kettle from him and rehung it, adding more thick strips of fat. "Did Fanny agree to that?"

A small smile lifted the corners of Seth's mouth, and his eyes caught the light from the crackling fire. "Fanny wants to do her part."

Raven had her doubts about that, but Seth seemed to have a way of getting the most and the best out of both the younger siblings, easing Raven's load considerably. With him in the house, she not only felt safer and less frightened that the sheriff would take Joshua and Fanny, she was almost rested for the first time in months.

"Would you like some coffee?" she asked, wiping her hands on Mama's white apron. "The wind out there is pretty cool."

"Coffee sounds good. But I'll be hoping for some of this pork later on." Holding cold hands toward the fire, he sniffed the air appreciatively and eyed the pot of ham boiling on the cookstove. "Smells good."

Raven laughed, something she did more often these days. "I don't know how you could smell the ham over this melting fat. Shoo-wee." She waved a hand in front of her nose, then filled two thick mugs with hot coffee and thumped them onto the table.

Seth scraped back a chair and sat, his hat hanging behind his back from a string. "Smells like success to me."

"You're right. I should be thankful. We've needed this lard for weeks now."

"Thought you were going to watch me butcher the hog so you could learn how," he teased, wrapping strong, lean fingers around the coffee cup.

Enjoying the novel experience of lighthearted banter, she quipped, "A hired hand's got to earn his pay."

Seth laughed outright, fully aware that she couldn't pay him a cent. "One of your buttermilk pies is pay enough for me."

Unused to compliments, Raven felt a swirl of pleasure dance through her. She was fast growing to like Seth Blackstone, an attraction that could be as dangerous as it was foolish. For all his hard work and quick wit, he was in some kind of trouble, a drifter with a secret past whose heart was cold toward God. But Raven had been struggling on her own too long and relished the strong, adult company. In addition, some part of her—the Christian part, she was certain—yearned to break through Seth's protective wall and see him happy again.

"If a pie is all you require, I'll bake two and get twice the work from you."

"I'd better get busy then." Swigging back the last of his coffee, Seth pushed away from the table. "Don't want the boss woman to fire me and renege on those pies." Grinning, he pressed his hat in place and slid the long duster over his lean shoulders before disappearing out into the cool, cloudy day.

Heart suddenly buoyant, Raven checked the rendering fat, then collected the ingredients for buttermilk pie.

Seth Blackstone, for all his secrets, made the farm feel like a home again. If not for his steadfast refusal to remain in the house during devotionals and the way he always kept one eye on the horizon, Raven would have considered life near perfect. But something dark and frightening haunted her hired hand. She'd thought God had sent Seth to help her and her family, but now she wondered if the sending had been more for him than for them.

~

"Joshua, stop that whining right now." The minute Seth stepped inside the house, he heard Raven's husky voice rise in agitation. "Tomorrow is church and you're taking a bath."

Seth flinched. Except for her constant reminders of the faith he'd left behind in St. Louis, he liked Raven Patterson. She was strong, taking on the most unpleasant tasks without a word of complaint. She was kind and generous to a fault, scrimping on her own food while plying him and the children with more than they could eat. And she was as much a mother to the younger ones as possible, taking them through their nightly lessons, hearing their prayers, cleaning their ears. He just wished she'd stop talking so much about the Lord.

"I don't want to, Raven." Joshua's bottom lip stuck out in a pout as he backed away from the galvanized tub of water parked near the fireplace. "I'm clean. See?" Standing in his red union suit, Joshua offered a pair of questionably clean hands.

Seth's lips twitched. No little boy ever wanted to take a bath, especially on a frosty autumn night. "What's the matter, partner?" Seth asked as he stepped into the kitchen. "Afraid you'll melt?"

Raven, holding a bar of soap and a washrag, looked up and

smiled. The sight shot an inexplicable shaft of sunlight through Seth's darkness. "He's of the mind that real men don't bathe, only helpless little boys who are forced by their big sisters." She pulled Joshua up to her and began unbuttoning his suit.

"Ah, leave him be, Raven. You and Fanny can use the tub."

"Seth! He needs a bath for church. I won't have townsfolk thinking he's not well cared for."

Greatly relieved to be rescued, Joshua tried to wiggle out of Raven's grasp. "Us mens don't need no bath."

Seth pulled out a chair and straddled it, folding his arms across the top. He liked teasing Raven, liked the moment when she recognized the joke and her black eyes lit up with laughter. "He'll get his bath."

"When?" she asked doubtfully, trying to hang on to the boy who danced back from her touch.

"After supper. When I head to the creek for mine."

Joshua stopped squirming and aimed a wide-eyed look in his hero's face. "The creek? But it's cold, Seth."

"Sure is. *Brrr.*" Seth faked a shudder. "Freeze the hairs on your mustache."

Joshua giggled. "I don't have a mustache."

"You will if you do much bathing in the creek. You'll grow hairs on your ears and your nose—" He poked a finger at Joshua's button nose.

"I will not. You didn't."

"Well, you see, that's the problem. I nearly freeze my ears off. You, on the other hand, can stay right here in this warm house . . . if you've a mind to."

Raven rose and turned her back, laughter threatening as Joshua made a quick decision and began fumbling with his buttons. Suddenly, the four-year-old's eyes lit up. "I don't want you to be cold neither, Seth. Why can't you take a bath in here with me?"

"Well, I—" Seth felt the heat rise along his cheekbones. Much as he'd enjoy a hot bath, there were ladies present.

"That's a grand idea, Joshua." Raven whipped around. "Fanny and I will go out to the barn and milk Sadie. You can call us when you're finished."

"I can't take you ladies' bathwater," Seth protested.

"Why, Mr. Blackstone, a man's got to have a bath now and then, and there's plenty of water in the creek for the rest of us."

"I'll be getting it then."

"You certainly will. Right after you and Joshua get all spiffed up." Her eyes twinkled with merriment as she slipped on the oversized coat and took the gleaming milk bucket from its nail. Fanny followed suit, donning a shawl.

Seth considered Raven's innate kindness, thankful that he'd stumbled upon this place and agreed to stay. He'd needed this. Needed to feel like part of something again. Needed to feel like more than a man with a hole inside his chest that could only be filled by the deaths of his enemies. There were even days when determined Raven and her redheaded family almost made him hope again. Almost. Then he remembered that hope was long gone.

Only the weather kept him here. Not Raven. Not the children. Knowing Cleo's penchant for comfort, he figured she and Stephen were holed up somewhere for winter too. But come spring, no matter how much he liked this little family, he'd be gone. He'd hunt down the pair who'd ruined his life, who'd stolen his hope . . . and satisfy this festering need for revenge.

~

Raven trekked across the backyard toward the barn, carrying a mended chambray shirt. Soft moonlight lit her way, and a pale glow of lantern light seeped around the barn door in greeting.

Sliding back the grating door, she called, "Seth."

He appeared at the top of the ladder in an instant. "Something wrong?"

Pearl-handled pistol at the ready, his face was grim, cold, unfamiliar.

Raven took a step backward. "Uh, no. I . . . uh—" She held up the mended shirt.

Seth caught the direction of her startled look. Contrite, he holstered the gun. "Sorry."

"No, I'm the one to apologize for surprising you. I thought you might need the clean shirt."

He ran a hand over his head, the slicked-back hair still wet from his bath. "Would you like to come up?"

"I shouldn't."

"I'll come down." Turning, he clambered down the ladder and across the straw-covered floor to where Raven waited just inside the door. Seth's freshly scrubbed fragrance mingled with pleasant scents of hay and warm animals.

"Thank you." He took the shirt. "I could have gotten this in the morning at breakfast."

"Yes, but I wanted to talk to you—away from the young ones. I've been wondering about something . . ."

His face closed up again.

Not wanting him to draw inside himself, Raven laid a hand on his arm. Her touch was met with tensed muscle, tight enough to snap. "I wasn't going to pry, if that's what you're thinking."

"Good." He relaxed a little. "There are some things I won't discuss."

"Some things will fester when bottled up too long."

He glanced off, scraping fine-boned fingers over his smooth cheeks. For a man he had elegant hands, clean with trimmed nails that didn't belong to a wandering cowboy. She often wondered what he was running from and what had hurt him too much to forget. But she'd promised not to pry, and as much as she longed to help, she'd keep silent until he was ready.

"Would you come to church with us tomorrow?"

His eyes narrowed. "Is that why you came out here?"

"Yes. Joshua thought since you'd had a bath . . ."

Amusement flickered then died, to be replaced by resignation and something Raven thought was despair. "Tell Joshua I can't."

Disappointed, she spoke without thinking. "Seth, whatever has happened, whatever is wrong, the Lord is the answer."

"I don't want to hurt your feelings, but you're wrong."

"God is faithful, no matter what you think."

"I believed that once, a lifetime ago." He turned toward the ladder. "Give Joshua and Fanny my apologies."

"Wait, Seth. Please listen."

He paused, one booted foot on the bottom rung, lean hands gripping the ladder. Raven moved closer, hay stirring softly beneath her heavy boots.

"I don't pretend to understand God. Sometimes I even get angry because He seems slower than molasses in January. And when an answer does come, it's never in the way I expected. But there's more to being God's child than having every prayer answered the way I'd like." She tapped at her chest.

"There's this peace deep inside that says no matter what happens, no matter how hard life is, God is there, working all things to my good."

Shaking his head, Seth spoke so softly she barely heard the words. "There's only one thing that will bring me peace, Raven. And it isn't God."

CHAPTER

five

$\mathcal{T}$he days flew by in a blur of readying the farm, as much as possible, for the winter ahead. By late November, with Thanksgiving only days away, Raven had begun to believe she could hang on to to her homestead as well as her siblings.

Sometimes she thought Seth Blackstone really was an angel sent by God in answer to her prayers—a handsome angel who always had an eye on the horizon even while lifting the heavy load of work from her tired shoulders. Other times she saw him as a lost and broken soul. Since that night in the barn, when he'd rebuffed her attempts to talk about her faith in the Lord, she'd prayed unceasingly for his heart to be softened. To her amazement, her own faith grew stronger as she sought the Lord on behalf of her troubled hired hand.

Raven looked up, saw Seth standing in the open doorway wearing a triumphant grin, and got that little catch beneath her ribs again. Disturbing how it came more and more often lately. Had it not felt so pleasant, she'd have wondered if she'd developed a touch of pleurisy.

"Come outside. I have a surprise." The scent of cold, damp air swirled around him.

In their weeks together, she'd learned that his surprises were invariably good—a mended harness, a newly built wood box, a basket of persimmons for pies and jellies. This one was even better.

"Oh, Seth. Praise the Lord! Venison."

Cheeks reddened from his first hunting trip, Joshua danced around the base of the big oak out front where a large buck hung from a rope tossed across a tree branch. The child paid no attention to the two adults who stood grinning at one another with delight.

"Thanksgiving dinner will be a feast."

~

And she was right. Two days later, the house redolent with the scent of his venison, Raven's corn-bread dressing, and cinnamony pumpkin pie, Seth pulled up to the table. He'd agreed, just this once, to leave his firearms in the barn. The familiar weight of holster against thigh was missing, and he felt more than a little vulnerable without it.

He glanced around at the little gathering. Everyone was shined up like a silver dollar. Joshua's red hair, wet and slicked down, smelled like Simpson's Manly Hair Tonic—a remnant, Raven told him, of her father's belongings. Fanny, whose gaunt face grew plumper and prettier every day, had pulled her fiery mane into a bun and donned her Sunday best, a rich blue cotton dress that turned her eyes to emeralds. The girl would soon be a lovely young woman, and the notion worried him. Who would protect flighty Fanny from the wrong kind of fella? Her big sister?

At the thought, his gaze moved to Raven, who ladled

brown gravy into a bowl. Though he doubted Raven gave much thought to how exotic and pretty she looked in her simple calico with her dark hair pulled up on each side, Seth noticed and imagined her in bright colors to set off her dark skin and doe eyes.

Catching his stare, Raven smiled. "Hungry?"

Giving himself a mental shake, he pulled his mind back to the feast. Raven Patterson occupied his thoughts too often these days.

"Starving." Reaching for a platter of roasted venison, he paused when Raven sat down and thrust an upturned palm in his direction. Stifling an inner sigh, he took her hand. Warm and smooth, her fingers fit neatly into his palm. With effort, he ignored the sudden lift of his stomach.

"Lord," she said, husky voice rich with honest gratitude, "we are so blessed this year. Blessed with food. Blessed to be together as family. Blessed to have Seth share our table. We pray for those who hunger and ask that You send them our way so we can share. We also pray for those who hurt, that You will heal their hearts. . . ."

Battling an inexplicable ache in his chest, Seth blocked out the prayer. He needed to get out of here soon. Raven's sweetness and her steadfast faith hammered at him, made him wish for the impossible. If he stayed much longer, he'd get soft and grow careless. Careless men got caught.

~

At the meal's end, Seth pushed back, replete. "Fine meal, Miss Patterson."

Raven tilted her head prettily. "Why, thank you, Mr. Blackstone."

Joshua's curious smile swung back and forth between the adults. "How come you're talking fancy like that?"

"Good manners, my boy." Seth tweaked the button nose. "Always compliment the cook."

"Why?"

"So she'll keep cooking, silly," Fanny answered.

Everyone laughed, the pleasantness of the day hovering over the room.

"What we need now is some entertainment," Seth suggested.

"Raven can read to us."

Seth knew where that invariably led—the Bible. "Actually, I was thinking of that fiddle up there." He pointed to a well-used instrument on the wall.

Three suddenly serious faces gazed at him. "Papa was the only one who could play the fiddle," Fanny said. "I tried to learn, but it's hard."

"Do you mind if I give it a try?" Long ago, he'd squeaked and squawked his way through lessons with Mr. Plumley, but he hadn't played since leaving St. Louis.

"You play? How wonderful." Raven lifted the instrument from its hanger on the wall and handed it to Seth.

"I'm a bit rusty, but if you sing loud enough you won't even notice." Tilting the fiddle to his chin, he drew the bow across the strings in several hesitant attempts before breaking out in a scratchy version of "Skip to My Lou."

Fanny leaped up and pulled Joshua into the game, singing and clapping. At the song's completion, they begged for another and then another. Raven clapped and sang, watching the children's fun with joy on her face.

The sight caused Seth to keep playing long after his neck and arms grew weary. At last, to the moans and protests of the youngsters, he laid the fiddle across his lap. "I've insulted your papa's fiddle long enough."

"Please one more," Joshua begged, blue eyes adoring Seth in a way that made him sorry he wasn't a decent man.

"All right, then. One more. But Raven gets to choose this time." He recognized his mistake the moment he spoke.

She leaned forward, black hair spilling around her shoulders, face aglow. "That's easy. 'Rock of Ages.' Can you play it?"

He considered saying he couldn't play the tune, but what would it hurt to do this one thing for her? With a tilt of his head, he lifted the fiddle. Slowly, softly, the melody eased from his bow.

Raven's smoky voice joined in, her face growing radiant, eyes closed. "'Rock of Ages, cleft for me, let me hide myself in Thee. . . .'"

The familiar words pierced his soul. How desperately he wanted to hide himself in a loving God instead of on a small homestead on the edge of the Oklahoma prairie.

When the final strains echoed in the now quiet room, Raven opened her eyes and beamed at him. "That was wonderful."

She could have preached at him again, but she chose not to and he was grateful. His conscience was doing enough of that lately without her help. He started to rise, to replace the fiddle.

"Careful," Raven warned and motioned downward.

Joshua was sprawled on the floor, cheek resting on Seth's boot. He hadn't even noticed the child's weight.

"Look at him. Sleeping like a log." Seth gently eased the child off his foot.

"I envy him," Raven declared with an amused shake of her

head. "But I'm afraid my nap will have to wait. The water's boiling and the dishes won't do themselves."

"I don't have to help, do I?" Fanny declared. "I did them yesterday."

"I'll help your sister." Seth went to the empty water buckets stacked in one corner. "You can go to the spring for water."

He extended the two pails. For a moment, Fanny looked as though she might argue, but Seth only stood there, quietly insistent.

"I wanted to check the pecan trees anyway," Fanny said, taking the buckets and flouncing away.

After the door closed, Raven shook her head. "You're amazing with her."

"Ah, Fanny's just suffering growing pains. And losing her mama and papa made the growing that much harder to face."

After adding soap to the dishpan, Raven filled it with steaming water from the pot on the stove. "I don't remember going through such a thing. Do you?"

Seth handed her a load of plates, a dark cloud of regret passing over him. "Oh, yes. I strained at the bit, arguing with my father day and night after Mother died."

"About what?"

"He wanted me to stay in St. Louis and join him in the mercantile business, but I wanted the excitement of carving out my own future here in the untamed West." He smiled ruefully, surprised to be telling this much about himself. "Easterners have a romantic view of what life out here is all about." Taking a clean dish towel from the shelf, he began to rinse and wipe the cleaned dishes.

"They must." Metal clattered against metal as she fished in the bottom of the dishpan for forks and spoons. "Are they still there, then? Your family?"

"As far as I know. I haven't been home in seven years."

She looked up from her work. A tiny appealing frown puckered between her dark eyes. Seth resisted the urge to smooth a finger across it. "So, you really have a family back East?" she asked.

"What did you think? That I was hatched beneath a toad-stool?"

She wasn't going to let him tease his way out of this one. "That's not what I mean and you know it. You have a living, breathing family in St. Louis, and you've chosen not to see them for seven years? Surely, you hear from them."

Her tone shamed him. Raven would never have left her family, no matter the circumstances. But then, she'd never disgraced her people the way he had.

He rubbed a circle in the plate, paying too much attention to a hairline crack along the edge. "No."

"Not even a letter now and then?"

"I'm never in one place long enough to get a letter." That much at least was true.

"But you do write to them, let them know that you are well."

Suddenly his fine meal lay in his stomach like iron. He could almost hear the sound of his sister, Amanda's, laughter and see his father, head bent over the *St. Louis Dispatch*. He missed them both with a palpable ache. "Papa and Amanda wouldn't want to hear from me."

"Nonsense." Water dripped from her hand and ran down her arm as she plunked a pot into the rinse water with a little more force than necessary. "They're your family. They're probably worried sick."

He didn't tell her that the truth would worry them more than the silence. "They wouldn't be pleased with the life I chose."

She paused, elbow deep in suds, to gently ask, "And what kind of life is that?"

He'd said too much and wished he'd learn to keep his mouth shut, but Raven had a way of making him feel safe. Time to steer the conversation in another direction. "Here. Let me wash awhile and you dry."

Raven placed a bowl in the rinse water, then turned toward him, drying her hands on her apron. "Seth, your past is not as important as your future. God can wipe it all away in an instant."

"If only that were true."

"But it is!" She laid a hand, warmed from the dishwater, against his arm. "God loves you."

She kept coming back to that. Once he'd believed it as steadfastly as she did, but experience had proved him wrong. If God loved him, He wouldn't have allowed Cleo and Stephen to destroy his reputation and his hard-earned livelihood. And he wouldn't be a fugitive running from the law.

Seth clenched his jaw and turned away. "I reckon I better get back down to the barn."

He moved to the door, acutely aware of Raven's hurt silence behind him. He didn't want to hurt her, would do almost anything to see her happy. But her words were a bitter reminder of all he'd lost, including his faith.

Hand on the door, he dropped his head for a second, then turned back. "Thank you for the finest day and the best meal I've had in two years."

Stubborn tears, unshed, darkened Raven's eyes. It was his undoing. He started across the floor, to pull her into his arms and apologize.

The door flew open with a gust of wind and a breathless Fanny. Her coat pockets bulged with pecans. Water sloshing, she stepped inside, clunked the buckets on the floor, then quickly slammed the door behind her. "Someone's coming."

"Who?"

"Looks like Sheriff Clifford."

Seth stepped around her and pulled the door open. The sight of a lone rider bowed against the wind chilled him to the bone. His hand automatically went to his gun and came away empty.

"What could he want?" Raven asked, moving up beside Seth. "I'm taking the children to church most every Sunday. He could ask anyone there how we're doing if he had a mind to."

"Maybe it's not the children he's interested in."

Raven sucked in a hissing breath, pushed the door closed, and leaned her back against it. "Don't you have some work down at the barn?"

She indicated the back door, her warrior-queen stance saying she'd protect him. Seth felt a wave of regret at putting her in this position, especially now. But she needed him here, couldn't risk losing his help. That was the only reason he could think of for her actions.

But if the sheriff found out she was harboring a criminal, he'd take the children in an instant. The dilemma tore at him. Setting her aside, Seth stepped out onto the porch. Throat as dry as Raven's fall garden, he said, "Afternoon, Sheriff."

"Where's Raven and the children?" He rode alone this time.

"Inside. Would you care to come in for some of Miss Raven's pumpkin pie and coffee?"

The saddle groaned as the sheriff dismounted and tied the horse to the porch rail. "Don't mind if I do." His heavy boots clomped across the porch.

Seth pushed the door open, stepping in first with a warning glance. "Sheriff Clifford's had a long ride and could use some coffee to warm up."

"Sit down, Sheriff." Raven bustled around the kitchen, cutting pie, pouring coffee as if the lawman was a favored guest, but Seth noted the tremble in her hands as she set the refreshments on the table.

"Mr. Blackstone, would you mind carrying Joshua up to his bed?" She indicated the ladder to the loft where the children slept. "He's plum tuckered out from all the food and frolic today."

Seeing her intent to protect him, Seth turned his back to the sheriff, effectively hiding his face as he lifted the sleeping boy into his arms. Taking his time, he started up the ladder, both ears trained on the conversation.

He heard the scrape of a chair and imagined Raven perched at the table. "What brings you out our way on Thanksgiving Day, Sheriff?"

At the top of the ladder, Seth paused, turning where he could look down without being seen.

"Some of the townsfolk are worried the young'uns might not have enough to eat." The florid-faced lawman forked a bite of pie, talking while he chewed. "They sent along some extra vittles just in case."

"Well, as you can plainly see—and taste—we're doing fine. We don't need charity."

"Don't matter, Raven. Folks think the children would be better off with the Johnsons than out here alone. Ain't safe. Too much riffraff drifting into Oklahoma Territory to hide out."

"We're not alone."

"Hired man planning to stay forever?" Something in the

way he asked the question set Seth's teeth on edge. Placing Joshua on his bed, he clambered down the steps, wishing every step of the way that his pistol was hanging from his hip.

"No, sir, I'm not." If he'd been born with a lick of sense, he would have stayed safely hidden, but he didn't much care for the insinuation in the sheriff's voice. He started around behind Raven's chair, then thought better of that action. No use giving the sheriff fodder for his imagination. "But before I go I intend to see that the Patterson farm is self-sufficient."

"Fancy words. Hope you can do it." The lawmen stood, adjusting a wide belt around his girth as he moved to the door. "Things still look a mite thin around here. Woodpile's nearly empty, too."

"Farming takes time." Something he didn't have much of, from the looks of this suspicious lawman. Seth eased him out into the yard.

Throwing a thick leg over his horse, Sheriff Clifford settled into the saddle and squinted down. "What was your name again, fella?"

Seth held his gaze. "Blackstone."

"You sure remind me of someone, Mr. Blackstone." He removed his hat and scratched at his balding head. "Wisht I could remember who." Then he clapped the hat back on, pulled the bay around and rode off, leaving Seth with a sense of foreboding too real to ignore.

CHAPTER

Six

*R*aven had expected Seth to leave after the sheriff's visit. He hadn't. He'd stayed on deep into December, and her foolish heart had leapt at the notion of keeping him around a while longer. She realized then what she'd been trying to ignore: She was falling in love with Seth Blackstone, a man who was most likely an outlaw, a man who denied the Lord as surely as Simon Peter had.

Still, for the sake of her brother and sister, she needed Seth to remain here. At the slightest indication that she was struggling, Sheriff Clifford would remove the children and farm them out.

She might be desperate, but she was also a Christian woman who knew the danger of being yoked with an unbeliever. Not that Seth had shown any indication of returning her feelings, but she had to make certain she kept her emotions under tight rein. He was her friend, her hired hand, and that was all he could ever be without the Lord.

Leaning her forehead against the warm side of the milk

cow, she silently prayed for God's wisdom and direction. Cold December had arrived and Christmas was only two weeks away. Christmas, the time when Sheriff Clifford had threatened to take the children unless he was satisfied that all was well.

"We need to have the best Christmas ever," she declared to the cud-chewing Sadie.

"I couldn't agree more."

The unexpected sound of Seth's voice startled her. She made a grab for the milk bucket, saving a spill in the nick of time. "My. You'll give a body apoplexy sneaking up that way." Breathless, she blamed her thundering pulse on the scare instead of on her hired hand's nearness.

Leaning his lanky frame against the stall, he crossed his arms and smiled. "My apologies, Miss Patterson, but I've been doing some thinking about Christmas myself."

"You have?" With a tilt of her head in his direction, she stripped the last few drops of milk from the cow, hearing the welcome *splish* in a full bucket.

"Yep." He leaned around her to take the bucket. "Christmas was always a big event when I was a boy. Figure as how Joshua feels the same."

"I'm not certain how much he remembers of last Christmas, but he and Fanny are so excited about this year." She hung the milking stool on a nail and backed Sadie out of the stall. "I heard them whispering and giggling over some Christmas secret yesterday. Who knows what mischief they're concocting."

"Where is the boy? I expected him and Fanny to be down here milking instead of you."

"Fanny and I traded chores. She's making breakfast while I milk." Raven fell into step beside him, ready to share her worry with someone. "Joshua came down with a cough in the night so I put a hot rag on his chest and left him in bed."

"Nothing serious is it?"

She shook her head. "I don't think so."

"Good." His relief was genuine, his deep affection for Joshua as plain as the secrets in his eyes. "I've been wanting a chance to talk to you about the animals."

"What about them?"

"We're running low on feed. There is no possibility of wintering all of them."

Alarm shot through her. "But we can't have a farm without animals."

"Hear me out." They'd made the house by now. Seth pushed open the door with his free hand and let her go inside first. Bacon scented the air. "Consider this. Sell the two younger pigs and keep the sow for breeding purposes next spring. The money will buy grain for the other animals."

"I don't know."

"You don't have much choice. I can make a moveable pen for the sow so she can root for most of her food, and we can stake the cow and horses out in various places to graze."

She knew he hadn't arrived in time to put up much hay, and the cornfields had lain fallow this year. All her energies had gone into the pitiful garden that yielded only enough beans, pumpkins, and turnips to last until spring.

With a resigned shrug, Raven took the milk bucket and strained the contents through a clean cloth. She was so weary of worrying and scrimping. When Mama and Papa had been alive, there was always enough, and any worries had been theirs, not hers. Christmas was a happy time, a time for joy in the Savior's birth, not a time for wondering if this was the last Christmas your family would be together.

A sturdy hand grasped her shoulder. "Don't fret, Raven. We'll make it."

We'll. A deep longing stirred. How nice it would be to have Seth here forever, to have someone to lean on, to help carry this load. He was so strong, had been a rock for her. If only . . .

Shaking off the melancholia, she straightened. Only God could change Seth. And only God could change their abysmal situation. When would she ever learn to put things in His hands? "Of course we will. Christmas is the best time of the year, and this one will be no different. We'll sell the animals and not give the problem another thought."

The sound of coughing had both of them turning toward the loft.

"He's been coughing like that all morning." Fanny plunked a stack of pancakes on the table next to a plate of bacon.

"All night too." Raven frowned. "You two go ahead and eat. I'll check on him."

"I'll go with you." Seth led the way, taking the ladder two rungs at a time.

Joshua lay on the straw ticking, a patchwork quilt up around his ears. He sat up the minute he saw Seth.

"Hey, partner. Are you sick?"

"Nah, but Raven won't let me get up. Says I'll catch 'moany."

"Pnuemonia?" Seth shot her an amused wink.

"I won't though, will I? We mens are too strong."

"Sometimes a man has to take care of himself. You got to get better so you and me can find us the perfect Christmas tree."

"Today?" Joshua's eyes grew round and excited. He shoved

back the covers. "I'm better enough. Let's go. I know where some pretty ones are."

"Whoa now." Seth pressed him back onto the bed and snugged the covers up around him. "You stay in this bed and do as your sister says and I'll bring up some wood chunks."

Joshua frowned. "What for?"

Seth put a finger to his lips and looked sideways at Raven. "Shh. Don't let Raven hear us, but we'll carve a Christmas surprise for her."

"Yes! A surprise. Raven likes surprises." He cast a furtive glance in her direction. "Shh. Don't tell her."

"And you know what else?"

"What?" Joshua wiped the sleeve of his union suit across his nose.

Seth yanked out a kerchief and handed it to the boy. "A gentleman uses this."

"Are we gentlemens?"

With muffled laughter, Raven listened to Seth's amused affirmation, then backed down the ladder, relieved that Joshua seemed no worse this morning. Seth was right about one thing. He might be an outlaw with a terrible secret, but he was a gentle man. No wonder the Patterson family had come to love him in such a short time.

~

After finishing the day's chores, Seth had returned to Joshua's side as promised. As he showed the boy the proper use of knife and wood, Raven and Fanny sang and worked below, decorating the house for Christmas.

At suppertime, he'd taken his plate up the ladder and encouraged Joshua to eat. Then they'd resumed their carving.

Joshua's little fingers must surely ache, but he kept on, tongue poking out the corner of his mouth as he concentrated on peeling the wood away. From the kitchen came the fragrance of cedar boughs mingled with the hot, enchanting scent of fresh popcorn. That and the sounds of Christmas carols stirred memories of his boyhood in St. Louis.

When he'd come down much later, he was both amazed and discomfited by the changes. Cedar boughs tied with gaily colored strips of cloth and ribbon hung above the crackling fireplace and the doorways. A crocheted angel at least a foot tall sat in the center of the table. And the pair of ladies, gilded by the lamplight, bent over a bowl of popcorn, threading kernels onto thick string.

The need for home and family slammed into Seth like a fist. This home and this family. The notion filled him with anxiety. He had no business thinking this way. For two years all that had kept him alive and moving was the quest for vengeance. He wouldn't give that up. He couldn't. Not even for Raven.

"I think the boy could use some rest," Seth said.

Raven laid aside her popcorn string. "And so could you. You've entertained him all evening." She went to the mantel and took down the Bible. "We'll have devotionals up in the loft." She made a point to aim her remark at Fanny, knowing Seth wanted nothing to do with her Bible reading and prayers.

The realization hurt him for some odd reason. "I'll see you ladies in the morning."

Raven's dark eyes studied him; then she nodded and went up the ladder.

He started toward his coat hanging by the back door.

"I want Seth. I want Seth!" Joshua's cry turned to a harsh fit of coughing.

Seth took the ladder rungs in three leaps. "Hey, pard, what's wrong?"

"Us gentlemens don't read the Bible, do we?"

Raven's eyes accused him.

"Sure they do."

"You don't never. And I ain't if you ain't."

Responsibility tore at Seth. Whether he'd intended to or not, he'd become a father figure to this boy. The child looked up to him as a man. And he could no more deny the plea in Raven's crestfallen face than he could rise and fly.

He eased onto the edge of Joshua's bed, the straw ticking crinkling beneath his weight. Swallowing a wad of dread, he said, "We gentlemen are ready, Miss Raven."

"We're reading in the book of James. James 1." And she began to read the familiar Scripture about patience and wisdom and the dangers of being double minded.

Head pounding with the need to escape, Seth blotted out as much as he could.

" 'Let no man say when he is tempted, I am tempted of God: for God cannot be tempted with evil, neither tempteth He any man. But every man is tempted, when he is drawn away of his own lust, and enticed. Then when lust hath conceived, it bringeth forth sin: and sin, when it is finished, bringeth forth death.' "

Was that what had happened to him? Had he been drawn away by his own lust? His desire for adventure, for a wealthy business, for Cleo? He fisted his hand, gripping the straw ticking. No. It wasn't his doing. If God had cared . . . if God hadn't let Cleo and Stephen cheat him—

" 'Do not err, my beloved brethren. Every good gift and every perfect gift is from above.' "

Raven's warm voice broke into his tumultuous thoughts.

If God sent such good and perfect gifts, where were his? Why did he have nothing but emptiness to show for all his hard work?

A small hand crept out from under the quilt and wrapped around his fist. The answer to his question hit him right in the heart. He looked at the trio gathered around the bed. Here were his perfect gifts, the gifts he wanted but could never have.

When Raven finally closed the Bible, he'd never been more relieved in his life. He stood on weak knees, eager for escape.

Joshua's hand still clung to his. "You can't go yet. I have to say my prayers."

Seth wasn't sure he could take another moment of this. "Go ahead then."

Joshua slipped from the bed to his knees and looked up expectantly. Raven and Fanny followed suit, leaving only Seth standing awkwardly in the low-ceilinged loft. He'd lived through a lot of bad moments in his life. Surely he could get through this one. Resigned, he went to his knees beside the boy.

Joshua folded his hands, squeezed his eyes shut, and recited the "Now I lay me" prayer. At the end, he began a round of "God blesses" that included every human and every animal within five miles.

"And Jesus, thank You for sending Seth to be my friend. Please make him stay here forever. And don't ever let anybody hurt him anymore. Oh, yeah, and send him a good Christmas present. Amen."

Seth was certain he would die right there in Raven's loft. Insides twisted into a knot, he raised his head to find Raven staring at him with compassion and a deeper, richer emotion he dared not acknowledge.

She and her family had done the impossible. They'd made him feel something other than hate and anger. They'd brought sunlight into his dark soul. And though he fought against it, unwilling to turn loose of his hatred, the warmth of their love washed over him like a cool summer rain.

CHAPTER
Seven

$\mathcal{R}$aven sat in the rocker, fingers moving the needle swiftly in and out of Fanny's Christmas gift. Across from her, sandy hair glinting in the firelight, Seth carefully fashioned bits of tin into various shapes. Since that night in Joshua's room, a subtle change had occurred in him. He was more relaxed, less watchful, even though the pearl-handled six-gun remained on his hip. And though he'd said little about it, he now stayed in the house during devotionals, then sat talking with Raven and making Christmas preparations long after the young ones had turned in.

"Fanny is going to love those." Raven nodded to the glittering stars dangling from strands of wire.

"My mother loved wind chimes, too." When Seth held up the partial set, six tiny stars played a sweet melody. "Once Father ordered a set for Christmas all the way from China."

"China?" Raven couldn't imagine a place so far away and so foreign. "What were they like?"

"Tiny white birds that tinkled in the breeze. Mother was certain they sounded like the angels."

"You must have had some happy Christmases as a boy."

"The best." Firelight captured the sudden spark of memory that flared. "My favorite time was caroling on Christmas Eve. Amanda and I would bundle up with our friends and stroll the streets of St. Louis, feet aching in our boots, throats so cold we could hardly carry a tune."

"That was fun?"

"Oh, yes." He shot her a grin. "People would come out on their porch to listen or stand in open doorways wearing the happiest smiles. Afterward, we'd all head back to the church or someone's home for hot cocoa and fresh-baked cookies. And more singing, of course."

"I've never heard you sing." The idea of hearing his voice lifted in song thrilled her.

"Lucky woman."

She laughed, delighted to have him sharing so much of himself. "Tell me more of your Christmas memories."

"Well—" shoulders rounded in consideration, he stared at the shadows playing over the floorboards—"there was always the food. Mother and Amanda baked for days, torturing us poor men with mouthwatering smells but no tastes. Fruitcakes and cookies and candies—you name it, they baked it. Then on Christmas afternoon, we'd drive out to the orphanage. Father would have fruit from the mercantile, Mother had her baked goods, and Amanda with her needlework."

"They sound like wonderful people."

"They are. Were."

"It's clear you love them and miss them. Why don't you go back?"

"I can't." Growing solemn, he fiddled with the chimes.

"Would you? If you could, I mean?"

He inhaled deeply, then exhaled in a long breath. "Yes. If

I could I'd go home, set things right with my father, tell him I didn't mean half the foolish things I said."

"You were young. Your father knows that."

"That doesn't matter."

"Of course it does. When you love someone, you look past their mistakes. You forgive them because that relationship means too much to let anything stand in the way. Remember the story of the prodigal son? After all he'd done, his father welcomed him with open arms."

For once, he didn't shy away from her talk about the Bible. "I wouldn't want my father to know about some of the things I've done."

"Your heavenly Father already knows that something is terribly wrong, and He'll forgive you if you ask."

"Would you forgive me, Raven? If you knew?"

She never hesitated. "In a heartbeat."

"But I don't want you to know." Regret pulled his lips down at the corners. "The truth could hurt you, maybe even put you in danger."

"I don't care." She stopped short of what she wanted to say. That she loved the man he was *now*, and no unsavory revelation would change that.

Firelight flickering in his eyes, he battled the temptation to share his burdens, but caution won out. "I do. I care too much."

Those words hung between them, full of meaning. Was he saying he cared for her as she cared for him? His actions said he did. She felt loved by him and ached to see him find his way back to the Lord. Because no matter how much she loved Seth Blackstone, she loved the Lord more.

A cinder snapped, shot from the fireplace to the wood floor. Seth pushed the toe of his boot against it.

Raven resumed her sewing, looking for a new topic of conversation before she said too much. "Did I thank you for helping Joshua with his shepherd's costume for the church program?"

"I didn't do much. A feed sack and a stick."

"He was thrilled with the crook you carved." She laughed softly. "He chased the rooster all over the chicken pen trying to capture it with that hook."

Seth's quiet laugh joined hers. "A shepherd has to have a proper staff."

"He adores you. Fanny, too."

"They're fine children. I like them."

"You must. Anyone who'd listen to Fanny practice her solo for days on end has the patience of Job."

"That song has lost some of its former appeal." His lips twisted wryly.

She lowered the lacy collar into her lap and looked across at him, happy. "Will you go next Sunday and watch? The children would be so pleased. So would I."

He didn't answer at first, only bent his head to the wind chimes and twisted on two more stars. "I'll think on it."

Sweet peace flooded Raven. At least he hadn't refused outright. The Holy Spirit was at work in Seth's life whether he acknowledged it or not.

~

He couldn't do it. As much as he wanted to please Raven and the children, Seth couldn't make himself go inside that church. God might be there for someone else, but not for him.

The afternoon was cold and still, the sky as clear as an angel's conscience. Beside him on the wagon, Raven sat in her Sunday finest, the worn muslin breaking his heart. She deserved velvet and silks. Yet she'd used what little fabric and money she possessed to make Christmas special for the young ones, and to remake one of her mother's dresses for Fanny, adding ribbons and lace so that her sister preened and twisted with delight.

Unable to stop himself, he reached over and adjusted the quilt across her lap. "Warm enough?"

She nodded. Regardless of her own lack, she sparkled, glowed with the excitement of the evening ahead. He wanted to stay in that spot, his shoulder pressed to hers, close enough to hear the soft puffs of her breath.

"You look pretty," he said, shocking both of them.

Twin spots of color darkened her cheekbones. "Why, thank you, Mr. Blackstone," she said, resorting to formality to cover her discomfiture. "I don't think anyone has ever told me that before."

"Must be a lot of blind men round this parts." Rattling the reins, he urged the horses forward.

Fanny poked her head between the two adults. "Oh, I'm so worried I'll forget my song." Frosty air puffed from her lips. "May I practice a few more times?"

Seth didn't know if he was annoyed or relieved for the interruption.

Raven's tone said she felt the same ambivalence. "Fanny, you know that song as well as you know your name. Think of the Lord's birthday, not of your nerves."

"I know my part too." Joshua sat in the back of the wagon surrounded by a pile of quilts. He leaned forward, coat gapping to reveal the gunnysack costume underneath. He pointed his crooked staff toward the sky and shouted, "Hark! A heavy host of angels!"

The adults exchanged amused smiles. *"Heavenly* host," Raven corrected.

"That's what I said. See?" And he shouted the line again.

Relenting, Raven clapped her hands, gloves thudding softly. "Wonderful. You'll be the finest shepherd ever. And Fanny's solo will bless the Lord."

"I just want to impress Thomas Bentley."

"Fanny!"

Seth nearly choked on his laughter. "Looks like I'll have to keep an eye on this Thomas fella."

They jostled along, past stands of blackjack and cedar and long expanses of open field. By the time they reached Riley's Fork, the sun edged down the western horizon. From every direction came the *clip-clop* of horses' hooves, the rattle of wagons and carriages, and the excited echo of voices gathering at the small whitewashed church that doubled as the school.

Seth pulled the wagon around to the side, letting the others disembark. A black buggy bearing Sheriff Clifford and his wife rumbled into the yard.

"Come on, Seth." Joshua's expectant face titled upward.

Seth's hands tightened on the reins. He couldn't go inside, no matter how disappointed the Pattersons would be. "Sorry, pardner. I'd better stay with the horses."

"It's too cold out. Please come in." Dismay dimmed Raven's excitement.

"I'll be fine." He hitched his chin toward the heap where Fanny and Joshua had spent the ride. "Plenty of quilts. Go on now. You can't be late."

Dejected, the trio left him. He hated himself for hurting them, but he could no more be a hypocrite than he could chance being recognized.

Dusk descended as the Christmas program began. Congregational singing filtered through the walls and then the muffled words of the preacher. Seth slouched on the wagon seat, hat drawn low over his ears, trying to tune out the sounds, as chilled in soul as he was in body.

The horses shifted, jingling the harness, reminding him of childhood Christmases. Golden lamplight spilled out the windows while high above stars began, one at a time, to pop into view. Seth shifted his attentions upward, counting the silver diamonds as they poked holes in the black velvet sky.

From inside the church came Fanny's sweet soprano, and "O Little Town of Bethlehem" pierced his cold, dark silence. Drawing the blanket tighter around his shoulders, he thought of little Joshua kneeling in the church, all innocence and joy, doing his simple part in the play.

Then Seth's imagination drifted to another time and place when real shepherds in a field experienced what no other mortals ever had, and angels had filled the sky with glorious singing. What that night must have been like when God came down as man. When a simple teenage girl wrapped her baby in rags because she'd had no fine, knitted blankets, and then watched in silent amazement while shepherds came to worship on the straw floor around a manger.

A yearning strong enough to make him shiver pulled at him. He squeezed his eyes shut against the cold, blaming the sudden burning in his throat on the frigid air. "Oh, God, are You up there? Do You hear me? If You do, show me what to do." He felt foolish whispering such a thing into the night, for God had turned His back a long time ago.

How had he gotten so lost? so empty? He wanted to weep from the terrible darkness of his own soul, and prayed that his father and sister would never know how far he'd fallen.

With immense relief, he heard the church doors open, and the townspeople began to leave the building. Some stood outside in small clutches, talking in animated voices, while others boarded their lantern-lit conveyances, calling "Merry Christmas" as they left for warmer confines.

"Seth, Seth!" Joshua and Fanny tumbled out the door, running toward him. "We got a peppermint stick."

Sure enough, they each carried an apple and a peppermint candy. They bounded into the wagon and snuggled down into the bed. "Brr. It's cold out here. You must be freezing."

Seth leaped from the seat to assist Raven into the wagon, denying his hands the right to linger on her small waist. "How was it?" he asked when she'd settled in beneath the quilts.

"Wonderful." Even in the moonlight, her eyes glowed with a heavenly radiance. "I almost imagined myself there on that holy night."

So she had felt it too. He pulled the wagon onto the hard-packed dirt street and headed home. After much excited conversation, the younger ones soon fell asleep. Raven hummed snatches of carols, breaking off now and then to share special moments of the evening with him. Her tone warmed him but did little to assuage his awful longing.

The cloak of night wrapped around them. The horses knew the way home and Seth gave them their head. An occasional rabbit darted across the road and coyotes howled in the distance.

Raven shivered and he couldn't bear to think of her warm heart growing cold like his.

Before he could reconsider, he reached out and pulled her close to his side, spreading quilts around them both. "Let me block the wind," he said, but there was no wind to speak of.

She didn't argue. Her warm side meshed with his and, though he should have removed his arm from her waist, he didn't. They were cold, he reasoned. Sharing heat was not the same as sharing love.

She snapped her peppermint stick in two, handing him half. He smiled his thanks, broke off a piece which he popped in his mouth, then stuck the rest in his pocket.

"Look at the heavens." Raven's peppermint-scented breath puffed softly against his neck. "Aren't they lovely tonight?"

He thought so too, but he thought she was lovelier.

They rumbled into the yard. He drew the wagon up close to the porch, reluctant to leave the pleasant cocoon that included only Raven and himself. He felt almost content, a foreign condition for him and one that confused him no end.

"Joshua," Raven whispered, smiling at the sleeping boy.

"I'll carry him in." But he made no move. His own voice was languid, soft. "Raven." He leaned closer, so he could read her eyes, he told himself.

"Yes?" She lifted her face, expectant.

"Whatever happens, I want you to know something."

"What is it?"

The words struggled upward. Oh, how he longed to say them and then to kiss her sweet lips and hear her say the words back to him. But what good were words of love when he was a dead man? when he would ride away from this farm someday and never return, knowing what he had to do?

"Seth?" She moved closer, shivering, and he recognized her longing coupled with indecision, for it matched his own.

As if he'd taken a blow, Seth pulled back, shaking his

head. Guilt rippled through him like a shudder. His very presence endangered her. "Better get you inside."

Slipping away from the promise he couldn't make, Seth leaped from the wagon and bundled the sleeping Joshua into his arms, knowing Raven deserved better than a murderer.

CHAPTER

Eight

Christmas Eve dawned, cold and overcast. Seth squinted up into the blinding white sky and loaded the hundred-pound bag of pecans into the back of the wagon, then sat the bucket filled with shelled nut meats next to it.

Snow would come soon and with it the harsh, bitter days when a man could barely care for his stock. He was thankful to have such a comfortable place to spend the winter. Thankful too for the hours spent around Raven's fireplace shelling pecans that Fanny and Joshua had gathered to sell in town. Hopefully, they'd bring a good enough price to trade for some much needed flour and other supplies.

Part of him dreaded the trip into town, knowing he might be recognized. Though he'd been there a couple of times with Raven, she'd done most of the talking while he stayed in the shadows. Another part of him thought the probability of recognition unlikely. After all, he'd faced the sheriff several times without giving himself away. And today he wanted to go alone. There were presents yet to buy.

He hummed under his breath, surprised at the content, excited buzz in his blood. Not since Mother was alive had Christmas thrilled him. But after so many years of bleak Christmas Eves when he'd missed his family in St. Louis and longed to return and make things right, this place and this family felt like home again. Leaving next spring wouldn't be easy, especially leaving Raven.

As if she'd heard his thoughts, Raven appeared, holding something wrapped in a towel. A luscious aroma emanated from it. "You'll get hungry before you get back home."

"Thanks." He took the warm package, peeked inside at the thick ham slices and fresh-baked bread, and groaned his approval.

Raven laughed. "You'd eat my cooking even if it was awful."

"I'm glad we'll never have to put that theory to the test." He stepped up into the wagon seat and took the reins. A horse whinnied his impatience. "I should be back before dark."

"We'll wait to read the Christmas story until then."

He couldn't wait for her to see the small créche he'd helped Joshua carve. She'd love it. But the créche was Joshua's gift, not his, and he hoped to remedy his giftless state in town today. Somewhere the perfect Christmas present awaited. This was the only Christmas he and Raven would spend together, and he planned to make it as special as the woman he'd fallen in love with.

There. He'd admitted it. Seth sucked in a deep, satisfied breath while studying Raven's lovely upturned face. He loved Raven Patterson, with her warm, giving heart and her strength and determination. Not that he'd ever tell her. He couldn't, but they could have this one special Christmas together. And for the rest of the winter, he'd work his fingers to the bone getting this farm in shape. Then, come spring, when he left her behind, he'd know she could make a go of it on her own. He couldn't give her his love, but he could give her that.

"I'll check around with some of the men in town. See if I can find a man willing to take a piglet in exchange for the use of his boar next spring." Funny how he could talk about such mundane things when what he wanted to do was leap off the wagon and kiss Raven good-bye.

"Fine. You might ask about a bull too. Sadie's plenty young enough to raise some more calves."

"I'll do it." With that, he snapped the reins and set the team rattling toward Riley's Fork.

By the time he reached town and sold the pecans at the general store, occasional bits of light snow swirled in the slight north wind. The store was full of people, a fact that discomfited him no little bit. Women buying last-minute goods for tomorrow's dinner. A girl about Fanny's age counted out handkerchief-wrapped pennies in exchange for a box. Seth overheard her whisper it contained a new pair of sewing shears for her ma. Men huddled around the potbellied stove, talking weather and crops and Christmas Day.

After he'd loaded the necessary supplies in the wagon, Seth moved past rows of yard goods, considering each color and texture, wondering which Raven would like. But somehow fabric wasn't special enough. He peered into a silver-handled mirror, but when his own outlaw's face peered back, he moved away.

Discouraged at not finding the right gift, he headed toward the men gathered around the stove. The least he could do was inquire about the bull and boar.

Soft grunts and whines issued from a crate next to the stove. Inside, a litter of fat pups wiggled and played. Seth hunkered down beside them, lifting the nearest one against his chest, stroking the warm fur with one finger.

Conversation swirled around him.

"Ought to see that place," Seth heard someone say. "Ain't no fancier house this side of St. Louis."

"I heard the woman was mighty fancy too. Named after some queen in Egypt or somewhere."

Seth stilled, listening now.

"Woman's name is Cleo," the storekeeper called from behind the counter. "I know 'cause she ordered one of them newfangled phonographs from the Sears and Roebuck catalog. Man's name is Stephen Seifer. Seem like decent folks. Paid cash money."

The man named Ben laughed. "You think any of 'em's decent that pays cash."

The storekeeper joined in the good-natured ribbing.

Seth's hand froze on the side of the box. Blood pounded in his ears. Cleo and Stephen? Here?

Slowly, he eased the pup back into the crate and stood. As casually as he knew how, he joined the conversation. "I knew a couple with those names once. Down in Texas."

"That a fact?"

"Yep. Friends of mine, though I didn't know they'd moved into these parts." He swallowed the lie, tense as a fiddle bow. "Wouldn't mind seeing 'em again. Where'd you say they built this fine house?"

"About three hours north of here, near Fool's Gully. Big, fancy house. Cain't miss it."

"I might just mosey over that way and give them a Christmas surprise." They'd be surprised all right.

Ben, a wiry fellow with a missing front tooth, leaned toward Seth, frowning. "Say, where do I know you from?"

"I work out on the Patterson place." Adjusting his hat a little lower, Seth averted his face. "Good talking to you gents. Reckon I better get back to the farm before this snow worsens."

Forgetting all about the intended gift for Raven, Seth forced his legs to walk calmly out the door and climb onto the waiting wagon. Blood pounded in his ears, and his fingers shook as he gathered the reins. At long last he'd found the pair who'd destroyed him. He hoped they'd done plenty of celebrating last Christmas. They wouldn't live to enjoy this one.

As he pulled away from the store, the gap-toothed Ben clomped out onto the boardwalk and stared after him. An icy shiver ran up Seth's spine that he couldn't blame on the winter wind. Time was running out. For Cleo and Stephen . . . and for him.

~

The loud rumble of a fast-moving wagon brought Raven outside to see what all the commotion was about. She threw a shawl over her shoulders, drawing the soft wool together at her throat with one hand. Snow fell in spits and spurts, sprinkling the hard, packed ground like sugar. Pushing the horses hard, Seth rolled into the yard and leaped from the wagon seat. Expression hard, his face was set. He didn't even look her way, just hurried to the back of the wagon like an angry man on a mission.

Alarmed, she rushed to his side. "Is everything all right?"

"Help me unload the supplies." He grabbed a flour sack, toting it into the house before she could follow.

Raven's insides trembled. Something was wrong. Seth had drawn inside himself again, his eyes full of fire. Reluctant to press him, she prayed silently as they emptied the wagon.

Once the task was complete, he stalked into the barn

without a word. She followed to find him tossing his saddle on the buckskin's back. Unable to keep quiet any longer, she asked, "Seth. Talk to me. What's wrong?"

"I'm leaving."

Shock and pain slammed into her like a blow. "Now?" she whispered. "On Christmas Eve?"

Back turned, he flopped one stirrup atop the saddle and jammed all his worldly goods into the saddlebags. Tension etched his strong shoulders. "I have no choice." He rammed the rifle into its holster.

"We always have choices."

He paused, one foot in the stirrup, hands on the saddle, ready to mount. "You don't understand."

"No," she cried, trembling. "I don't. You can't just leave without an explanation."

"You knew I couldn't stay."

Raven didn't deny the truth. Though she'd prayed and pleaded with the Lord to change Seth's heart, she'd always feared he would leave. Raven shuddered violently in the warm barn, her legs barely holding her up. Tears clogged the back of her throat.

She wouldn't cry. She wouldn't.

When she didn't speak, Seth's chest heaved once in a gusty sigh and he turned. When she saw the devastation in his face, Raven's tears broke free, tumbling down her cheeks. Tears, not for her own heartache but for Seth, for the terrible black void in him.

"Raven." His voice gentled. He stepped toward her. "Don't cry. Please don't."

"Can't you wait until after Christmas?" She struggled against the sobs welling in her chest. "The children will be brokenhearted." *And so will I.*

"No. I'm sorry. I truly am."

"Why? Why can't you at least stay until tomorrow?"

He shook his head. "Don't ask me that."

"I'm asking, Seth. Tell me what you're running from."

His head dropped back and he stared up at the barn rafters. His chest heaved raggedly.

Raven longed to touch and comfort him. Whatever had hurt him was eating him alive.

When he began to speak, his voice was as soft and cold as snow. "I trusted them."

"Who?"

"Cleo and Stephen. Stephen and I were partners in a growing cattle-brokering business. Then Cleo came along. Beautiful Cleo."

"You loved her." Jealousy ripped at Raven like wolves' teeth.

"I thought so at the time. Funny how stupid a man can be."

"What happened?"

"Our operation was known for its unflagging honesty. I was proud of that. We could do business on a handshake. Cleo took advantage of that trust and cooked up a scheme to bilk our investors. I was blamed for all of it because my name was on every document. Their names were on nothing. Clever Cleo had seen to that. They even testified against me in the trial, then left town, claiming they couldn't bear to watch me hang." His mouth twisted in a bitter smile. "But they didn't plan on my escape."

Raven's heart thudded painfully. Seth was an outlaw, a wanted man. "Did someone recognize you in town today? Is that why you're leaving?"

He jerked. "What? No." He shook his head. "I'm not sure."

LINDA GOODNIGHT

"Then why not stay until after Christmas?'"

"Because I know where Cleo and Stephen are." Cold rage emanated from him. "And I've waited too long to take a chance of losing their trail. It's time they answered for their crimes."

A sudden chill prickled Raven's skin. "What are you planning?"

Jaw clenched hard enough to break rock, his handsome face was as empty as a beggar's pockets. "Justice."

"What kind of justice?"

"The only kind that matters now." He tried for a smile and failed. "Don't fret, Raven. I'll be fine."

"No you won't." Terror drove her to speak her mind. "You're talking about murder. I can see it in your eyes."

He blinked those eyes and looked away. "I've murdered them in my heart every day for two years."

"But you're not a killer. Let the law take care of this."

"They already have, Raven, and they found me guilty. Listen to what I'm saying. There's no other answer. There's no hope for me anyway. One way or another, I'm going to hang."

"Seth, I'm begging you not to do this. You're a good man."

His lips formed a grim line. "I wish that were true."

"Stay here. Let me help you. Together we can find a way to prove your innocence."

"It's only a matter of time until Sheriff Clifford recognizes me." He started to step away from her.

"Seth." Pulse drumming wildly, she stopped him with a hand on his duster-clad shoulder. "You're not leaving until I tell you something. You have to know. I can't let you go without knowing."

"Don't say it, Raven." Anguish flashed in his eyes. He lifted a hand to silence her. "Not now. I can't bear to hear it now."

302

But she would not let him leave empty-hearted. "I love you." She tossed her chin up, daring him to accept what she offered. "Take that with you."

The words drove his eyelids into a pinch. With a groan of surrender, he pulled her to him and lowered his head, brushing his lips reverently across hers. His arms trembled. Then just as suddenly, he pulled away, and without another word or look, he mounted his horse and rode out of the barn.

Raven ran after him, heart shattering, and watched him ride into the north wind, his sandy hair whipping out behind him. Certain that something terrible lay ahead, she fell on her knees in the snow. Only God's grace and mercy could help him now.

When the awful storm of grief finally passed, Raven pulled herself together, dried her eyes, and went back to the house. She had no idea how she'd tell the children, but she could not let them see her deep despair. Not today. Not on Christmas Eve.

Fanny looked up from a pot of stewing apples. Cinnamon spiced the air. "I saw Seth come in and then ride out again. Where's he going?"

"He—" Raven hesitated, unwilling for the children to know the terrible truth about the man they'd come to love and trust—"he had some business to take care of."

Fanny frowned. "But he just came from town."

"His business isn't in town." She busied her hands, taking out flour and lard to make piecrust.

Fanny set the spoon aside. "Is something the matter, Raven?"

"I—Seth needs our prayers, that's all."

"He is coming back, isn't he?"

She couldn't lie. "I don't know. I hope so."

Joshua left the building blocks Seth had made him and came into the kitchen, little lips quivering. "He'll come back. Tomorrow is Christmas. He has to come back, don't he?"

She knew she should correct his grammar, but her heart wasn't in it. Out there in the snow and wind a fine man rode toward the unspeakable. As much as she wanted him back, she wanted him to find his way back to God even more.

Two sets of solemn blue eyes stared at her, awaiting an answer. What could she say? How could she break their hearts on this of all days?

Leaning the fork in the bowl, she forced a smile. "I have an idea. Let's pray that he will find a faster, better way to take care of his business, so that he can return safely home by tomorrow. And while we're praying, let's ask the Lord to touch his heart and renew his faith." She stretched a hand out to each of them. "Come on. Prayer changes things."

And so the little group clasped hands and sought the Lord. Though she prayed aloud, choosing her words carefully so as not to alarm the younger ones, in her heart Raven cried for God's mercy and deliverance.

They'd no more finished praying than the thunder of horses' hooves broke the solemn mood.

Joshua rushed to the window with a cry. "Maybe it's Seth. Jesus sent him back already."

But when Joshua's little body grew rigid, Raven knew it was not Seth. "It's those mens," he said.

"Those mens" could only mean one thing. The sheriff had returned.

"But he promised not to bother us until after Christmas," Fanny cried, rushing to Joshua's side.

Anger surging, Raven stalked to the door. "You two stay in this house. I will not allow him to take you anywhere."

Grabbing a shawl, she yanked the door open and stormed out to meet the riders. A gust of wind ripped into her, whipping her hair and dress in wild circles around her body. To her surprise, the men with Sheriff Clifford were not George Johnson and Parson Watley. They all wore badges.

A ripple of fear replaced the anger. "We're doing well, Sheriff. Fanny and Joshua are fine. You can't have them."

Taken aback, a frown creased the sheriff's brow. "We didn't come for the children. We came for Barringer. Where is he?"

Raven blinked, the awful knowledge seeping into her. Seth's name must be Barringer. Someone had recognized him in town, and his crime was bad enough to bring a posse out on Christmas Eve. "I don't know anyone named Barringer."

"Don't lie for him." The sheriff's thick jaw tightened. "The law doesn't hold with folks who give aid to wanted criminals." He waved to two men behind him. "Look around, boys."

Relenting, Raven stepped in front of them. Having the deputies prowling the farm would terrify Joshua and Fanny. "You have my word of honor, Sheriff. Seth, if that's who you mean, is gone. He left about an hour ago."

His shrewd gaze measured her and found her truthful. "Must have got wind that Ben here recognized him from the poster in my office. Did he say where he was going?"

"No. Just that he had some unfinished business to see to."

"Did he mention any places or names? Ben says he was mighty interested in a couple over by Fool's Gully. Guy's name is Seifer. Barringer ever speak of them?"

"No."

Ben Thomas edged his roan closer to the sheriff. "First names was Stephen and Cleo. That ring a bell?"

A sinking motion turned Raven's stomach. "Seth is innocent. Those people framed him."

"So you knew all along he was an outlaw and still allowed him to live here around these innocent children?"

Tiny bits of snow pelted her cheeks, and the wind blew clear through her. If they thought she'd endangered Fanny and Joshua by keeping Seth on as a hired hand, she'd have no chance of keeping her family intact. "No. He never told me until today."

The sheriff pressed. "But you knew he was hiding something, didn't you, girl?"

Raven swallowed a knot of anxiety. "Perhaps I suspected. But he was good to us, Sheriff. He didn't commit that crime."

"I figured you'd say that. Barringer, with his pretty face and good manners, plays up to women, gets them to do anything he asks. That's what he did to that poor little gal down in Texas. You were no different."

"That's not true! Seth isn't like that." But inside, she ached with the suspicion of what Seth might do when he found Cleo and Stephen. Maybe it was best the sheriff caught up with him before he did something he would forever regret.

"Come on, boys, let's get moving." Ben Thomas spat a stream of tobacco at the horses' hooves. "Barringer's got a head start on us, but now that we know where he's headed, we can make Fool's Gully and be back by morning if we ride hard."

"Yeah," another deputy put in. "I promised my wife and boy I'd be home in time for Christmas."

The saddle creaked as the sheriff leaned forward, piercing Raven with a glare. "We got an outlaw to catch, but the way I see it, you've put those young'uns in danger. I got no choice but to come back for them once Barringer is behind bars where he belongs."

Tears sprang to Raven's eyes, burning as she held them back. "Please don't do that. Please. It's Christmas. If your concern is for Fanny and Joshua, at least let them have tomorrow."

A horse stomped and whickered, tossing his head. Leather and metal clanked together as the sheriff shifted his weight and pointed a fat finger at Raven. "I can't get back here until after Christmas anyhow, but I will be back. That's a promise." With a jerk of the reins, he turned the impatient bay, motioned with one hand, and loped the posse into the north wind.

Fighting an overwhelming despair, Raven looked into the heavens and cried out. "Please, Lord, don't let them tear my family apart. Help me. Help us all."

Behind her, Joshua opened the door. His voice quavered. "Raven?"

She filled her lungs with cold, moist air, shivering. How could she do this? How could she face Christmas now, knowing the man she loved was a hunted criminal and the children she adored would be gone in two days' time?

CHAPTER Nine

Seth drove the horse hard for a while, trying to blot Raven from his mind. Finally he'd slowed, not wanting to destroy the best horse he'd ever owned when no amount of running could erase the hurt he'd left behind or the task that lay ahead.

Even now, he tasted the salt of Raven's tears, his mouth tingling with the sweet warmth of her lips. Both had stricken him to the core. He'd looked back once and seen her there, praying in the snow, and he'd almost turned around. Almost.

The horse puffed breaths of smoke that rose and mingled with his own. Cold as he was on the outside, he burned on the inside. Hatred was a powerful taskmaster. Hatred so contrary to the love Raven offered. Love of God, love of a good woman. He was tormented by all three.

As the sun slowly faded to his left, he approached Fool's Gully, a travelers' landmark. In the distance, faint light dotted the horizon. He rode on, certain he'd found his prey.

His eyes adjusted to the descending darkness. Cleo and Stephen would never see him coming.

Around a bend, past some woods, a three-story house came into view—stately, queenlike, befitting Cleo's opinion of herself. Golden candles flickered a welcome from the windows.

Seth pulled his horse to a halt and leaned forward in the saddle, staring at the house that deceit had built. A chandelier sparkled, radiating through a huge front glass window. A giant tree, decorated with so many gifts and candies the green had disappeared, stood like a laden sentry in the room's center. Above the fireplace mantel hung a gilded wreath decked with stuffed birds and fancy red bows.

Raven's little house flashed through his mind—the simple fireplace, the small cedar he'd cut for her, and the even simpler wreath she'd fashioned from cedar branches. But Raven's had been done in joyful celebration of her Savior's birth while Cleo's was all for show. And that made Raven's all the more beautiful.

Perhaps when this was over, he'd go back, tell her what she meant to him. He rubbed a weary hand over his face. What was he thinking? He could never go back. He'd still be a wanted man.

Only this time you'll be guilty.

The thought jolted him. "They deserve to die."

You don't have to do this. There's still time to change your mind.

Seth stared up into the dark sky. Tiny snowflakes kissed his face. "Is that You, God? Finally talking to me?"

I've always been here. Listening. Waiting.

Lips rigid with cold, Seth's breath puffed out before him. An inner battle raged as he remembered the feel of handcuffs around his wrists, the sense of brokenhearted betrayal, the loss of everything he'd worked for, and the scorn. "I won't change my mind. They took everything from me. Everything."

Not everything, Seth. One thing you gave up freely. What good is it if a man gains the whole world and loses his own soul?

"You don't understand, Lord." His words crackled in the silent darkness. Normally, he'd consider talking aloud as foolish babble, but not tonight. "I never wanted to give You up. I need You in my life. Raven made me realize that."

But you need revenge more?

"Yes!" he shouted and spurred the horse forward toward the moment of truth before he could relent. His yell echoed back to him a dozen times, but the voice in his head fell silent. Seth shivered, suddenly very alone, as if a warm, comforting presence had departed.

Outside the mansion he slid from the horse's back and strode to the door, gun drawn beneath his duster. Lifting the brass lion's mouth, he knocked.

The huge doors swung back and Cleo stood there, as radiant as her chandelier. The golden hair that had once reminded him of his sister and mother flowed in soft waves over her shoulders.

Seth felt nothing but icy contempt. Shouldering his way into the lighted room, he pushed the door shut behind him. "Hello, Cleo."

Eyes widening in horrified surprise, she stumbled backward, hand over her heart. "I thought you were dead."

He winced. She still had the power to wound him. But where the foolish youth had once seen beauty, the man now saw hard, glittering eyes, the cold blue as different from Mother's as they were from Raven's black ones.

"I am. But I've come back to haunt you."

Her frightened gaze flickered to the gun pointing at her heart. "What do you want?"

"You. Stephen." Seeing her fear, grim satisfaction shifted through him. "Where is he?"

At that moment, Stephen came down the winding staircase. Wearing a brocade vest and ruffled shirt, he was every inch the gentleman. "I thought I heard voices, Cleo. Who's—" Stephen froze as Seth waved the gun in his direction.

"Come on down, Stephen. Have a seat. Both of you." He motioned to a horsehair sofa and waited; he remained standing while the two of them sat. With a sense of gratification, he noticed they chose opposite ends. He looked around the fine room, beautifully furnished with stolen money. His money. "Cleo and I were just getting reacquainted. Nice place you have here."

"What do you want?"

Seth laughed, a bitter, harsh sound that had his prisoners shrinking back against the couch. "Seems to me you should know what I want."

"The money's gone. We spent it all on this ranch."

"I figured as much." He eyed Cleo, beautiful Cleo with the empty heart. "It's not the money I'm after."

"What then? Cleo?" Stephen grabbed the woman by the arm and pushed. "Take her, then. Embezzling that money was all her idea in the first place."

Cleo slapped at Stephen, rose, and came within two feet of Seth. "Don't believe him. He forced me to do it." She ran long, dainty fingers over his sleeve, her voice growing silky. "I've missed you. I was hoping you'd rescue me from this madman."

Seth stared down into the petulant face and compared it to the pure, open honesty in Raven Patterson's. How blind he'd been to ever trust this woman. "Sit down, Cleo, and make your peace with God." He motioned with the pistol.

Understanding dawning, she staggered back. "You're going to kill us."

"As surely as you killed me. Only I won't leave your walking corpse."

Cleo began to cry, whimpering sobs. "He made me do it. Kill him. Let me go with you. We can be happy again. I promise."

"Shut up, Cleo." Stephen's face distorted in disgust. "It's your greedy whining that got us into this. Can't you see he's after blood, and all your conniving ways won't change his mind?"

"Smart man." Seth cocked the gun. The sound shattered the quiet. "Too bad you didn't think of that when you and I were partners, running a decent, respectable business."

Cleo slithered down onto the couch, trembling and moaning. "Don't kill me. Don't kill me."

"Seth, wait." Panic stripped Stephen's skin of color. "You can have this ranch and everything on it. You can even have Cleo. Let me walk out the door and you'll never have to see me again."

Had Seth not been so heartsick, he would have laughed. They were pathetic, both of them. Blaming each other, looking for the easy way out. Godless, worthless scraps of humanity, not worthy to lick Raven's worn boots.

For two long years he'd waited for this moment, planned their deaths right down to who would die first. He'd expected elation, joy, relief. Instead he ached when he realized that they were as lost as he was, maybe more so, for they'd never known the Lord at all.

But they deserved to die, he told himself. And he needed this absolution, this revenge.

Don't do it, Seth.

So, You're back. I'd thought You'd abandoned me again.

Never.

Let me do it. Let me put them out of their misery.

Look at them. Pitiable. Sick and so full of sin they hate themselves. They're miserable. Tell them about Me.

No. They don't deserve to know.

Deserve? What does that have to do with Me? My love is unconditional. I love you, Seth. I love them. All any of you have to do is choose My Son over your own desires. Old things will pass away, and all things will become new. Trust Me, Seth. Prove Me.

Seth's insides began to tremble as he looked first at Stephen and then at Cleo. To think he'd held this woman in his arms, wanted her for his wife. She reminded him of the Scripture Raven had read in James. And as clear as sunlight, Seth suddenly saw the truth: Lust—for adventure, for worldly gain, for this woman—had led him down the dark path of destruction. The Lord hadn't forsaken him. He'd forsaken the Lord.

"Oh, God. I'm so sorry." And a light, long quenched, flared to life in his soul. He wanted to fall to the floor and weep. "I've been such a fool."

"I'm sorry too, darling," Cleo cried, completely misunderstanding. "I always loved you, not Stephen. Without him, the two of us can finally share all of this." She indicated the fine house, the rich furnishings, and the elegant decorations.

Keeping his gun trained on the pair, Seth shook his head. "Don't you see? It's not things you need. It's Jesus." True relief exploded in his chest. He longed to shout, to cry, to fall on his knees and worship.

"Jesus?" Cleo said, horrified. "What kind of religious nonsense is that?"

"Not nonsense, Cleo. Jesus can take away the insatiable need for all this." He swept the gun around the room.

She tossed her head. "You've gone clean out of your mind."

Seth sighed and eased the hammer down on his pistol. "You think about what I've said. Someday you'll realize how much you need the Lord. Remember that He's there, waiting for you, same as He was for me. I finally had sense enough to realize it."

Cleo's puzzled eyes shifted from Seth to Stephen. "I don't understand. I thought you wanted to kill us, and now you're preaching Jesus. What kind of game are you playing?"

"Get a piece of paper."

"What for?"

"The two of you have a confession to write."

Thirty minutes later, feeling freer than he'd ever felt in his life, Seth tied the pair of outlaws onto their horses and turned them all west toward Riley's Fork. Fat snowflakes danced in the air while Cleo whined about the cold, huddling deeper into her elegant velvet cape.

Halfway to Riley's Fork, five riders appeared on the horizon, riding hard. Even after he recognized the sheriff and his posse, Seth held his course, determined to set things right. No matter what happened to him with the law, the Lord would be with him, even in a prison cell.

Cleo set up a howl the moment she saw the posse. "Help! Help! We've been kidnapped."

Seth reined the horses to a stop and waited. Frosty breath circled the horses' heads as the posse thundered to a halt in front of them.

"Hold it, Barringer." Five gun barrels aimed at Seth's heart. "You're under arrest." The sheriff motioned to a deputy. "Untie those people."

"Wait, Sheriff. Before you do, maybe you should read this." Seth withdrew the confession from his pocket and handed it over.

With a curious frown, Sheriff Clifford called for a lighted lantern, then unfolded the paper and studied it carefully.

Seth shifted nervously in the saddle, aware that his future hinged on the next few moments.

Finally, the sheriff looked up, face orange in the light, and addressed Cleo and Stephen. "I reckon you folks got some explaining to do."

"I'm innocent, Sheriff," Cleo insisted. "You have to believe me. Scamming those investors was all Stephen's idea."

"Shut up, Cleo." Scowling, Stephen settled deeper into his saddle. "Do you want to make this any worse?"

"Well, little lady, looks like you just confirmed your confession." Clifford refolded the paper and stuck it inside his coat. "Barringer, I owe you an apology, and I'm man enough to admit it. You and Raven both."

Seth sat up straighter, not sure whether to be relieved or worried. "What does Raven have to do with this? Has something happened?"

"Settle down, son. Nothing's happened, except she's one worried little gal. When you get home, tell her that I won't be coming after those young'uns after all. That is, if you're planning to stay on as her . . . hired hand." The wily sheriff's face broke into a knowing grin.

"Yes, sir." Seth relaxed and returned the smile, chest bursting with the knowledge that he was not only a free man in the natural sense, but he was free in the spiritual. Free to tell Raven of his love for her. "I'll tell her."

"Well, get on home, then. I know where to find you for

the trial. We'll take these two from here." He motioned to the deputies who surrounded Stephen and Cleo. "And tell the Pattersons Merry Christmas for me."

Christmas. In a few hours the sun would rise on the Lord's birthday. In all the turmoil Seth had nearly forgotten. With a joyous shout, he slapped the reins against his buckskin and headed home, hard and fast. *Home*. Home to Raven and the children and to a celebration of his Savior who'd been patiently waiting a long, long time.

~

Christmas morning broke cold and clear with glorious sunshine glistening off the pristine snow like jewels. Raven awakened exhausted, having spent most of the night in prayer. She felt as though she'd wrestled the devil himself for Seth's soul.

Now, this morning, she struggled to celebrate Christmas, feigning a joy she didn't feel. Fanny and Joshua moped, refusing breakfast, refusing to open the small pile of packages beneath the tree.

"We'll wait on Seth," they said, breaking Raven's heart anew.

"Today is our Lord's birthday. Even if Seth can't make it back home, we have a reason to celebrate."

"But I don't feel like cebelating," Joshua said. He sat on the floor by the fireplace, listlessly staring at the door. "My stomach hurts."

Raven knelt beside him. "I know, baby. Mine does too."

"I thought Seth liked me."

Raven swallowed the knot that threatened to choke her. "He does like you, Joshua. He loves you."

"Then why did he go?" Fanny came to join them, settling

morosely in the rocker. "Was it because of me? Did I run him off with my hateful tongue?"

"No, Fanny, no. Nothing like that. He always told us he would leave someday. The time just arrived sooner than we expected."

"I miss him." Joshua's lips quivered. Tears gathered in his blue eyes. "I didn't want him to ever go."

Raven pulled the child's little body onto her lap and held him close. He smelled of tears and peppermint candy. "But we have to remember that no matter who else we lose in this life, Jesus will never leave us. He'll always be here."

Raven fought back her own tears. They'd lost so many since last Christmas. How could they bear any more? How destroyed would these children be to learn they would also soon lose her?

With a final hug, she set Joshua on his feet and rose, straightening her skirts. "Now, listen here, you two. Seth wanted us to have the best Christmas ever. We're letting him down by moping around this way. So—" she drew in a fortifying breath—"let's sing."

Her two siblings eyed her doubtfully.

"Singing lifts the spirits," she insisted and launched into a halfhearted "O, Come All Ye Faithful." By the time they finished and started "Joy to the World" the mood was growing lighter.

Voices raised, they hadn't heard the horse or the barn door, but they did hear the jingle of spurs on the wood porch and the rich male voice raised in exuberant song.

"What in the world?" Oh, Lord, could it be? Dare she believe her prayers had been answered?

The trio around the Christmas tree froze as the door burst open and Seth entered, the picture of joy unspeakable. He stopped singing and stood there, cheeks red with cold, green eyes dancing, and smile wide, his long duster floating around him like an angel's robe.

He took in their shocked expressions. "What? You've never heard a man sing before?" And then he laughed, full-hearted as he tossed his hat into the air. "Merry Christmas, everyone!"

"Seth, Seth, Seth!" A mad scramble occurred as Joshua catapulted into Seth's stomach and Fanny grabbed for his arm.

"Whoa there, partner. You're smashing Raven's present." He looked at her then, over the children's red heads, capturing her with his elm-bud eyes.

In those eyes she witnessed a peace that had been missing yesterday. Hope flared. What miracle had God wrought?

Unwinding himself, Seth reached inside his coat and withdrew a fat, redbone puppy, his gaze never leaving hers. "Merry Christmas, Raven."

She came to him then and reached out to take the pup. Seth's hand grazed hers. "He reminds me of old Red," she said.

"I thought he might."

As she drew the puppy against her neck, a warm, pink tongue licked her cheek. She laughed, feeling as happy as she had the day Papa had given her old Red. "Thank you. But I don't understand. What's happened?"

"The Lord and I had a long time to talk last night. I finally had sense enough to listen."

A thrill exploded inside Raven. "Oh, I'm so glad! I prayed and prayed."

At her cry, the pup startled and wiggled to be free. She handed him to a bouncing Joshua.

"I know. I could feel those prayers. Sit down and let me

tell you everything." He shucked his coat, pulled up two chairs, and told her of his recommitment to the Lord, of Cleo's and Stephen's confessions, and of the sheriff's apology.

"So you're a free man now?" Raven's heart danced with joy. *Thank You, Lord. Thank You.*

"In every sense of the word. Free from prosecution for a crime I didn't commit and free from the load of sin and revenge I've carried far too long."

"What the Son sets free is free indeed."

"Amen to that. This is truly the most blessed Christmas of my life." He laughed again and rubbed his hands together. Then he moved to the floor beneath the Christmas tree. "Are we going to open these presents or not?"

And so they did. With great exuberance and much laughter, paper flying, ribbons carefully preserved for reuse, they shared their carefully chosen gifts. Seth opened his, saving Raven's for last. Withdrawing the hand-stitched shirt, he fingered the fine, soft material and grew thoughtful.

"Raven," he said quietly, drawing her full attention to him. "I like this very much, but I really had something else in mind."

Raven sat in the rocking chair, stroking the new puppy as she watched the people she loved most enjoying their gifts. Having Seth alive and home was enough present for her. "What?"

Going to his knees in front of her, Seth set the puppy on the floor and took her hands. "You've already given me back my faith, and now that I'm a free man, there is one other gift I'd ask of you. I love you, Raven. I want you to marry me."

Joy bubbled up inside her, too wonderful to contain. As Seth's strong, calloused hands gripped hers, she remembered how struck she'd been by his touch that first night. She remembered, too, how she'd wondered if he was an angel sent by God to help them through their bitter trial. Not an angel, she knew now. But a helpmate.

"Say yes. Say yes!" Fanny and Joshua joined forces to dance around the rocker, clapping and shouting.

"God knew all along what each of us needed most," Raven murmured.

Seth quirked an eyebrow. "Is that a yes?"

She drew his hand up to her face and pressed it against her cheek. "On one condition."

"Name it."

"Come spring I want to take a wedding trip. To St. Louis to meet your father and sister."

"Aw, Raven. My sweet, sweet Raven." He pulled her out of the rocker then and into his arms. "No wonder I love you so much."

"We'll write to them first. And tell them everything that's happened. And then they'll welcome you home with open arms."

"I believe they will. Thanks to you."

Overcome with joy and peace and renewal, Seth stared into the ebony eyes of the woman whose strength and faith had been his lamp in the darkness. Quietly he rejoiced, thanking God for sending him along this path that had led him to the Oklahoma prairie . . . and to the greatest Christmas of his life.

Unlike many bread recipes, this one does not require precise measurements—or even kneading—to turn out great. Makes good cinnamon rolls, too!

EASY YEAST BREAD

3 cups warm water
3 pkgs. dry yeast
1 egg, beaten
½ cup sugar
½ cup oil
1 tbsp. salt (omit if using self-rising flour)
6–7 cups flour

In a large bowl, sprinkle yeast over warm water, then mix in remaining ingredients, except flour. Add flour until dough forms a very soft ball. (It will be a little sticky and you will not be able to handle it at this point.) Cover and let rise in a warm place until double.

When double, punch down, divide into two parts, and work with one part at a time. Sprinkle with flour and roll the dough out to about an inch thick. Cut out like biscuits or slice with a knife. Place pieces about an inch apart in two 9 x 13 baking pans. Let rise in pan until double, about 45 min. Bake at 375° for 15–20 minutes or until golden brown.

Dear Reader,

I hope you've enjoyed "The Outlaw's Gift," my first novella for HeartQuest books. Though the characters are purely fictional, they became as real to me as living people, and I am delighted to have this opportunity to share them, their struggles, and their faith with you. I trust that the message of God's ever-abiding love has ministered to you in some way. Truly, as Seth finally learned, God never leaves us nor forsakes us, no matter how dark our situation seems.

Like Raven, I love the Scripture passage Romans 8:28: "We know that all things work together for good to them that love God." It's a verse I often meditate on in times of storm. The world is an uncertain place, and difficulties most surely will come. But we can rest assured that God is constantly working on our behalf. I don't know about you, but I am so encouraged and comforted in knowing that the Master of the universe, the God who measures the oceans in His palm and hangs the stars in the heaven, has my best interests in His thoughts at all times.

May you always feel the peace that comes from God's abiding love.

All the best,
Linda Goodnight

ᕙ About the Author

A *native Oklahoman,* Linda grew up in the small ethnic town of Prague, where she idled the summers away eating Dreamsicles and sitting beneath the magazine racks of the Sooner Café reading *Superman* and *Archie* comics. A shy child, she loved books and to this day would rather have a new book than a new wardrobe. (You can tell it, too!) Her own writing reflects her small-town roots and the warmth and humor of simple country folk.

After being nominated for the prestigious Golden Heart Award in 1999, Linda sold her first novella to Barbour Publishing. That book, *Prairie Brides,* made the Christian Best-sellers list in July 2000 and again in April 2001. She has also published novellas in the anthologies *Lessons of the Heart* and *Love Afloat,* as well as several full-length books in the general market.

A nurse for many years, Linda later became an elementary teacher and now teaches fifth grade in a small rural school. She and her husband, Gene, have a blended family of six terrific kids. They make their home on a small cattle ranch with a dog that climbs trees and a cat that doesn't. Linda loves chocolate, long walks, football, and especially hearing from readers.

Linda invites you to visit her Web site at www.linda goodnight.com. She also welcomes letters written to her in care of Tyndale House Author Relations, P.O. Box 80, Wheaton, IL 60187-0080 or by e-mail at linda@lindagoodnight.com.

Turn the page for an exciting excerpt

from Catherine Palmer's book

Prairie Rose

Book 1 in the best-selling series A Town Called Hope.

(ISBN 0-8423-7056-0)

❖ ❖ ❖

Available now at a bookstore near you.

HEART
QUEST

Prairie Rose

Kansas City, Missouri
May 1865

Talking to God from the outstretched limb of a towering white oak tree had its advantages. For one thing, it meant that Rosie Mills could see beyond the confining walls of the Christian Home for Orphans and Foundlings, where she had lived all nineteen years of her life. For another, she had always felt like she was closer to God up in the old tree. That was kind of silly, Rosie knew. God had lived in her heart ever since she gave it to him one night at a tent preaching service, just before the War Between the States. But the best thing about praying in the oak tree was the constantly changing scene that unfolded below.

Take these two men coming her way. The first—a dark-haired fellow in a chambray shirt and black suspenders—minded his own business as he drove his wagon down the dusty street. He had a little boy beside him on the seat and a load of seed in the wagon bed. The other man followed on a black horse. All the time Rosie had been praying, she had been watching the second fellow edge closer and closer, until finally he was right behind the wagon.

"Seth Hunter!" the horseman shouted, pulling a double-barreled shotgun from the scabbard on his saddle. "Stop your mules and put your hands in the air."

The command was so loud and the gun so unexpected that Rosie nearly lost her precarious perch on the old limb. The milkman across the street straightened up and stared. Down the way, the vegetable seller and his son halted in their tracks.

"I said stop your team!" the horseman bellowed.

The man on the wagon swung around and eyed his challenger. "Jack Cornwall," he spat. "I might have known."

He gave the reins a sharp snap to set his mules racing lickety-split down the road. Jack Cornwall cocked his shotgun, lifted it to his shoulder, aimed it at the fleeing wagon, and fired. At the blast, Rosie gave a strangled scream. A puff of pungent gray smoke blossomed in the air. A hundred tiny lead pellets smashed into the seed barrels on the back of the wagon. Wood splintered. Seeds spilled across the road. The mules brayed and faltered, jerking the wagon from side to side.

"Whoa, whoa!" the driver of the wagon shouted. "Cornwall, what in thunder do you think you're doing?"

"Give me the boy or I'll shoot again!" Cornwall hollered back.

"He's my son."

"You stole him!"

"He's mine by rights." The wagon rolled to a halt directly beneath the oak tree where Rosie perched. "I aim to take him to my homestead, and neither you nor anybody else is going to stop me, hear?"

"What do you want him for—slave labor?"

"You forgetting I'm a Union man, Cornwall? We don't trade in human flesh like you Rebs."

"And we don't go stealing children out from under the noses of the grandparents who took care of them since the day they were born."

"My *wife* took care of Chipper—"

"Wife?" the man exploded. He edged his horse forward, once again leveling his shotgun at Hunter. "You claiming my sister would marry some good-for-nothing farmhand?"

Rosie gripped the oak branch. The two men were barely three feet beneath her, and she could almost feel the heat of their hatred. This was terrible. The little boy the men were arguing about was hunkered down in the wagon, terrified. He couldn't have been more than five or six years old, and as he peered over the wooden seat his big blue eyes filled with tears.

Rosie didn't know which of the men was in the right, but she wasn't about to let this Jack Cornwall fellow shoot someone. She spotted a stout stick caught in a fork of the tree. Maybe she could use it to distract the men, she thought as she shinnied toward the slender end of her branch.

"Your sister married me, whether you believe it or not," Seth Hunter snarled. "I'm this boy's father, and I mean to take him with me."

"I didn't track your worthless hide all the way to Kansas City to let you just ride off to the prairie with my nephew. No sir, Chipper's going south with me. My pappy's not about to let you work his grandson to the bone on your sorry excuse for a farm."

"I told you I don't plan on working him. In fact, I'm headed for this orphanage right now to hire me a hand."

"Hire you a hand," Jack scoffed. He spat a long stream of

brown tobacco juice onto the dirt road. "What're you aiming to pay him with—grasshoppers? That's all you're going to be growing on your homestead, Hunter. Grasshoppers, potato bugs, and boll weevils."

"I've got a house and a barn, Jack. That's more than a lot of folks can say, including you. And any young'un would gladly trade that orphanage for a home."

I would, Rosie thought. She was beginning to side with Seth Hunter, even if he had stolen the little boy. The other man was big, rawboned, and mean-tempered. For all she knew he planned to shoot Seth dead with his shotgun. And right in front of the child!

The branch she was straddling bobbed a little from her weight as she inched along it toward the stick. Truth to tell, it was the boy who stirred her heart the most. Neither man had even bothered to ask the child what he wanted to do. And where on earth was the poor little fellow's mother?

"A house and a barn," Jack said, his voice dripping with disdain. "What you've got is dust, wind, and prairie fires. That's no place to bring up a boy. Now let me have him peaceful-like, and I won't be obliged to blow your Yankee head off."

"You're not taking my son." Seth stood up on the wagon. His shoulders were square and solid inside his homespun chambray shirt, and his arms were roped with hard muscle and thick veins. Badly in want of cutting, his hair hung heavy and black. His thick neck was as brown as a nut. With such a for-midable stature, Rosie thought, he should have the face of the bare-knuckle fighters she had seen on posters.

He didn't. His blue eyes set off a straight nose, a pair of flat, masculine lips, and a notched chin. It was a striking face. A handsome face. Unarmed, Hunter faced Jack. "I already lost Mary, and I'm not—"

"You never had Mary!"

"She was my wife."

"Mary denied you till the day she died."

"Liar!" Seth stepped over the wagon seat and started across the bed. "If your pappy hadn't tried to kill me—"

"You ran off to join the army! We never saw hide nor hair of you for more than five years till you came sneaking back and stole Chipper."

"I wrote Mary—"

"She burned every letter."

"Mary loved me, and none of your lies will make me doubt it. We'd have been happy together if your pappy would have left us alone. He ran me off with a shotgun. I was too young and scared back then to stand up to him, but I'll be switched if I let him do it again. Or you, either."

"I'll do more than that, Hunter." Jack steadied the gun. "Now give me the boy."

"Over my dead body."

"You asked for it."

He pulled back on the hammer to set the gun at half cock. Rosie held her breath. No. He wouldn't really do it. Would he? She reached out and grabbed onto the stick.

"Give me the boy," Jack repeated.

"If you shoot me, they'll hang you for murder."

"Hang me? Ha! You ever hear of Charlie Quantrell, Jesse James, Bob Ford? They're heroes to me. I've joined up with a bunch down south to avenge wrongs done in the name of Yankee justice. Nobody messes with us, Hunter. And nobody hangs us for murder. Besides, I'm just protecting my kin." He pulled the hammer all the way back.

Seth stood his ground. "People are watching every move

you make, Jack," he said. "They know who you are. Don't do this."

"Chipper, come here, boy."

"Stay down, Chipper."

"Hunter, you Yankee dog. I'll get you if it's the last thing I do."

Jack lifted the shotgun's stock to his shoulder. As his finger tensed on the trigger, Rosie gritted her teeth and swung her club like a pendulum. It smashed into the side of Jack Cornwall's head and knocked him sideways. The shotgun went off with a deafening roar. Like a hundred angry hornets, pellets sprayed into the street.

At the end of the limb, Rosie swayed down, lurched up, and swung down again. Acrid, sulfurous-smelling smoke seared her nostrils. As screams filled the air, she heard the branch she was clinging to crack. She lost her balance, tumbled through the smoke, and landed smack-dab on Seth Hunter. The impact knocked them both to the wagon bed, and her head cracked against the wooden bench seat. A pair of startled blue eyes was the last thing she saw.

WELCOME TO

HEARTQUEST

HEART
QUEST.

Visit

www.heartquest.com

and get the inside scoop.

You'll find first chapters,

newsletters, contests,

author interviews, and more!

Must-Reads!

THE PERFECT MATCH
*Her life was under control,
until he set her heart on fire.*

HEART QUEST

OVER A MILLION BOOKS SOLD!

LIKE A RIVER GLORIOUS
*Rachel was an unwilling partner
in deception. Only a miracle
would set her free.*

MEASURES OF GRACE
*Corrine begins a new life—
unaware she is being pursued.*

Visit **www.heartquest.com** today!

BOOKS BY BEST-SELLING
AUTHOR CATHERINE PALMER

NEARLY
1 MILLION
CAREER
SALES!

HEART
QUEST.

Sweet Violet (coming spring 2005) . . . . ISBN 1-4143-0071-9
Cowboy Christmas . . . . ISBN 0-8423-8120-1
Wild Heather. . . . . ISBN 0-8423-1928-X
English Ivy . . . . ISBN 0-8423-1927-1
Sunrise Song . . . . ISBN 0-8423-7230-X
Love's Proof . . . . ISBN 0-8423-7032-3
Hide & Seek . . . . ISBN 0-8423-1165-3
Finders Keepers . . . . ISBN 0-8423-1164-5
A Touch of Betrayal . . . . ISBN 0-8423-5777-7
A Whisper of Danger. . . . . ISBN 0-8423-3886-1
A Kiss of Adventure . . . . ISBN 0-8423-3884-5
Prairie Storm. . . . . ISBN 0-8423-7058-7
Prairie Fire. . . . . ISBN 0-8423-7057-9
Prairie Rose . . . . ISBN 0-8423-7056-0

Prairie Christmas . . . . ISBN 0-8423-3562-5
A Victorian Christmas Keepsake . . . . ISBN 0-8423-3569-2
A Victorian Christmas Cottage . . . . ISBN 0-8423-1905-0
A Victorian Christmas Quilt . . . . ISBN 0-8423-7773-5
A Victorian Christmas Tea . . . . ISBN 0-8423-7775-1

TYNDALE
FICTION

Fatal Harvest . . . . ISBN 0-8423-7548-1
A Dangerous Silence . . . . ISBN 0-8423-3617-6
The Happy Room
    Hardcover . . . . ISBN 0-8423-5421-2
    Softcover . . . . ISBN 0-8423-5422-0
A Victorian Rose . . . . ISBN 0-8423-1957-6
The Loved One . . . . ISBN 0-8423-7214-8